"Yes, we made p‹...›
entire future be‹...›
eyes turned glass‹...›

She continued. "But t‹...›‹...›‹...› were apart, the more apparent it became that we were over. My family took precedence, Derrick. Decisions were made that moved you and me farther and farther from each other. This is my reality now."

He couldn't deny that truth. "So Prescott is the guy for you?"

She nodded. "He's been there. Since we met and later when Mom got sick. He's a good man."

"You love him?"

"You've met him. How could I not?"

"That's not an answer."

She pressed her lips together. He remembered that stubborn expression.

"Derrick, it's been a long time. We can't be in each other's lives," she said, but had hesitated for a fraction of a second.

A shaft of hope lit through Derrick. "Not even if you're the love I never stopped looking for?"

Dear Reader,

Do you love to travel? I do. Nothing is more exciting than hitting the open road on a new adventure. And when an interesting locale pops up on a television show, I love to say to my husband, "I've been there." There are so many outstanding places to set a story, so picking the right location for a book is important.

Years ago I was out west with some friends and we drove through Nevada. I was really impressed with the Lake Tahoe area. The mountains were so beautiful. The water so clear and blue. I love being in the woods, and let me say, there were so many gorgeous rustic areas, so many tall trees and lots of wildlife, I fell in love. So when I needed a special place for Hannah, my latest heroine, to live, the lake and surrounding region immediately jumped into my mind.

Research is a big part of planning a book, and when I get to "visit" new places to discover interesting tidbits to incorporate in a story, it makes writing so much fun.

I hope you enjoy Hannah and Derrick's story, and the return of the Matthews brothers.

Happy reading!

Tara

HEARTWARMING

Always the One

USA TODAY Bestselling Author

Tara Randel

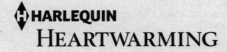

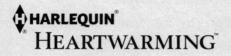

ISBN-13: 978-1-335-88957-7

Always the One

Copyright © 2020 by Tara Spicer

Recycling programs for this product may not exist in your area.

This edition published by arrangement with Harlequin Books S.A.

For questions and comments about the quality of this book, please contact us at CustomerService@Harlequin.com.

Harlequin Enterprises ULC
22 Adelaide St. West, 40th Floor
Toronto, Ontario M5H 4E3, Canada
www.Harlequin.com

Printed in U.S.A.

Tara Randel is an award-winning *USA TODAY* bestselling author. Family values, a bit of mystery, and, of course, love and romance are her favorite themes, because she believes love is the greatest gift of all. Tara lives on the west coast of Florida, where gorgeous sunsets and beautiful weather inspire the creation of heartwarming stories. This is her tenth book for Harlequin Heartwarming. Visit Tara at tararandel.com. Like her on Facebook at Tara Randel Books.

Books by Tara Randel

Harlequin Heartwarming

Meet Me at the Altar

Trusting Her Heart
His Honor, Her Family
The Lawman's Secret Vow

The Business of Weddings

His One and Only Bride
The Wedding March
The Bridal Bouquet
Honeysuckle Bride
Magnolia Bride
Orange Blossom Brides

Visit the Author Profile page
at Harlequin.com for more titles.

To my precious daughter, Kathryn. I love you.

CHAPTER ONE

"I DON'T LIKE the looks of this," Derrick Matthews said to his three brothers as they huddled around the beach bonfire, waiting for their mother's news. He hunched deeper into the fleece jacket worn over a T-shirt and jeans as a brisk wind whipped over the water. As the sun sank into the horizon, a damp chill settled in. The stacked logs snapped and crackled, pieces of ash rising in the air before being swept away.

"She's been cagey, even more than usual," Dante replied as he eyed the crowd. "Which is saying a lot."

"You don't think…" Dylan trailed off at the nods sent in his direction.

"Oh, yeah," Derrick confirmed. "They're going to make it official."

He and his brothers stared into the burning flames. Their mother was going to marry a man with a sketchy past and if they valued their relationship with her, there wasn't a thing they could do about it.

"It's not like we didn't expect this," Deke reasoned.

Derrick leaned back in the beach chair, his gaze traveling to his mother, Jasmine, who was currently surrounded by a circle of friends. "Still, this is Mom we're talking about."

He couldn't deny she looked happy. Happier than he'd ever seen her in the years since their father had died. Shouldn't that count for something?

As the conversation faded, Deke and Dante, his two youngest brothers, rose and wandered over to their girlfriends. Derrick watched, the envy he'd tried to ignore all weekend making a repeat appearance. He was happy for his brothers, too, wasn't he?

"You okay with Mom doing this?" he asked Dylan, the second brother in the Matthews line. All the brothers were dark-haired, with varied shades of blue eyes, concerned about the woman who had raised them.

"Not particularly, but it's what she wants."

"And you're tired of arguing with her?" Derrick asked, amused by his brother's failed attempt to rein in their mother.

"She's stubborn," Dylan muttered.

"I tried to talk to her, but she ended up lecturing me, so I gave up."

"She lectured you?"

"What can I say? I was deep into a case and she caught me off guard."

"Like she manages to do with all of us," Dylan said.

"You know you could investigate. We threatened Stanhope we'd do it."

Dylan looked at Derrick like he'd lost his mind. "Not if I prize my future."

Derrick chuckled. "Exactly."

"So I'll let it go. For tonight."

The Cypress Pointe crowd had gathered for the special occasion, which was all the insight their mother would allow. Neighbors, townsfolk, kids and teens swarmed the beach located not far from the city park. The sand ran up to the grassy area, which then led to sidewalks, picnic benches and a large gazebo used for town, or private, events. Everyone brought a dish to share. There were drinks galore, plenty of riveting conversation and the occasional firecracker set off farther up the beach. It reminded Derrick of his youth, even if he hadn't grown up in this particular Florida location, but the antics were still the same.

"So when's your big day?" Derrick asked, referring to Dylan's upcoming wedding.

"This summer."

"You're going to brave the Florida heat?"

"It's what Kady wants."

Right. Dylan's fiancée. The first of the brothers to make it to the altar.

Dylan and Kady had met during a DEA investigation in this sleepy little tourist town. Since then, Jasmine Matthews had moved to Cypress Pointe to be near one of her sons because the rest were scattered. What they hadn't expected was for her to fall for a man and remarry.

Derrick and his brothers were law enforcement, following in their police commissioner father's footsteps, or had been, anyway. Dylan had met Kady during an undercover stint in town, but was still on the job. Former criminal forensics, Deke had gone off to the Georgia mountains to get a line on the man in their mother's life and had fallen in love with Grace. He now worked as an outdoor guide for her family's adventure vacation business. And Dante, the youngest, had left his position as a detective with a local PD. His girlfriend, Eloise, had been promoted to sergeant, but Dante had decided to open a specialty mechanic shop to work on classic cars, located on the other coast of Florida.

They were happy with their decisions, in love and bugging the socks off him.

"Good luck with that," Derrick grumbled.

"Don't need luck. Just two words that'll make me happy."

I do. Yeah, he got it.

"You're still my best man?"

"Wouldn't miss it." Even though he'd like to. He didn't need a reminder of the love he'd once had and lost, but he wouldn't tell Dylan no. They were close, all the brothers were, and Derrick would do his part, even if it about killed him.

He must have frowned because Dylan said, "It's been a long time."

Like he'd ever forget. "Feels like a hundred years."

"Think it's time to move on?"

He barked out a harsh laugh. "Move on to what?"

"Happiness."

Derrick didn't hide his annoyance. "Happiness is overrated."

"Says the guy who won't give any nice woman he dates a chance."

Okay, that was true. He'd been accused of being a serial dater albeit it wasn't the case. He purposely let his brothers believe he was out enjoying the wild, single life when he was still hung up on Hannah. It was better for them to think he couldn't commit, instead of witnessing their pity if they knew otherwise.

"I don't need your opinion on how to live my life."

Dylan raised a dark eyebrow. "Aren't you the first one to stick your nose in our business? You made sure to give me unsolicited advice when Kady and I started dating. And if I remember correctly, you managed to butt into Deke's and Dante's love lives, as well."

"I'm the oldest brother. It's my job to put in my two cents."

"Even when it's unsolicited?"

Derrick lifted a shoulder. "Blame it on the cop in me."

"More like you want to be in control."

"Can't help myself. I've got Mom's genes."

Dylan snorted. "On that we can agree."

Derrick dug the toes of his boots into the sifting sand. Said in a quiet voice, "I was the first one to fall in love. The first one to talk about getting married. Now look at me. I work too much, don't ever commit, as you endlessly remind me, and have to put a smile on my face to make our mother happy."

"Don't beat yourself up. You tried to find her."

"A lot of good that did."

"You can't blame yourself."

Derrick shot him a sharp look. "Really? Who else?"

Dylan wisely kept his mouth shut.

"She's out there, Dyl. Somewhere, she's out there."

Hannah Rawlings had been his first love. His only love. The one who got away.

He glanced at his brother. "I was sure I had a good lead two years ago."

Dylan sighed. "You've searched for years. Never made any headway. Let *her* go. Give yourself a chance to grieve and then start embracing life. Get serious with a woman."

It wasn't like the idea had never occurred to Derrick. There had been a woman once, but in the end, the memory of Hannah had overshadowed the budding relationship. Still, he'd ignored the idea of moving on. Until now.

Recently he'd been rethinking his goals. Wondered what they'd look like without Hannah at the forefront. There was more to life and he was missing out by searching for a woman who didn't want to be found.

"For once I'm inclined to go along with that."

Astonishment flashed across Dylan's face but was quickly gone. "Wise choice."

Was it? He closed his eyes. Shouts of laughter and conversation surrounded him. He'd come to Cypress Pointe this weekend at Jasmine's summons—yes, he still jumped when his mother called—as did all his siblings. But this time was different. His mother was about to announce her engagement to a man he and his brothers had suspected of harboring a secret past. Turned out they'd been right, he had a shady history, mistakes he'd made after losing his wife and his way, errors he was currently atoning for by paying back the families he'd swindled more than a decade ago. Nevertheless, there could be more to him than they'd uncovered and even though Dylan still talked about investigating, Derrick had convinced him to drop it. The kicker? Derrick kinda liked James Stanhope. He too was intimately acquainted with regrets of the past. Sometimes it was okay to let it go.

Could he do that with Hannah?

A woman's bubbly laughter floated his way and memories bombarded him.

Bicycling to the beach under a blazing summer sun. Hannah's riotous auburn curls shining, her hazel eyes filled with teasing merriment. They'd exchanged class rings junior year and she'd been excited to wear the necklace that held his ring around her neck. Every year they'd celebrated their birthdays on the same day. He'd always said she was the best birthday present he'd ever received.

They'd started hanging out when they were eight or nine, became an item at thirteen and planned to run off and get married the day after their eighteenth birthdays. Except when he showed up that special morning to whisk her away, she was gone. Her entire family vanishing into thin air.

If Hannah could, or wanted to, wouldn't she have contacted him by now?

That was the part that tripped Derrick up, because bottom line, the real reason he'd never found her might be because she didn't want to be found by him.

"What's changed?" Dylan asked, drawing Derrick back to the conversation.

"I guess seeing my brothers have fulfilling lives. Even Mom. After years of being a widow, she found love again." He turned to his brother. "I want that."

"Then go for it."

Easier said than done. He'd only ever loved one woman in his thirty-five years on earth. Didn't know if he had it in him to try with another.

As if given a silent cue, the crowd started moving toward the gingerbread-decorated gazebo outlined in twinkling lights located just off the beach. Derrick and Dylan got up and followed the others. His mother and James stood in the center of the structure, his arm around her waist, his mother smiling into James's eyes.

Yep. Didn't have to be a crack FBI special agent to realize it was time for the big announcement.

Rather than hang around his brothers and their girlfriends, he lingered in the back of the crowd, staying in the shadows. The wind whipped through again. It was a cold January evening, even for Florida standards. They'd gotten together to usher in the new year, but when their mother asked them to stay a few extra days, they knew Jasmine Matthews was up to something.

"Thank you for coming tonight, all our family and friends." Jasmine's eyes glowed with a barely contained joy. As Derrick glanced at the couples around him, he noticed a similar theme.

The envy kicked up again.

"As you know, James and I were lucky to find each other. And we've been even more fortunate to have your support."

A snort escaped Derrick.

When he and his brothers had confronted James last autumn, they'd gotten two big surprises. One, James admitted his past as a con artist but confessed he'd been on the straight and narrow for a very long time. His mother ordered Derrick and his brothers to back off and they had. He kept waiting for one of his brothers to come up with a plan to break up the couple, but so far nothing had come to pass. At least nothing they were telling him since he'd landed on Team James.

And second, they were going to gain a sister. James' daughter Serena had become good friends with his mother. Which was a plus because that helped keep Jasmine from worrying about his private life. So if Mom and James got married, there would be one more sibling in the family. And even Serena had found her great love with Logan Masterson, the PI hired to dig up information on Stanhope.

It was like the universe was conspiring against him.

Weird, the thought of having a sister after a lifetime of brothers. But again, his mother was ecstatic and Serena was pretty okay, so he'd show up at his mother's wedding and smile, even though he and his brothers would never shake their suspicions of the man she intended to marry.

"I'm sure it won't come as a news flash that we're getting hitched," she told the crowd.

Cheers and claps echoed in the night.

"So, mark your calendars for the second weekend in February." She grinned. "The sooner the better."

Voices rose in celebration. His mother's gaze caught his and with a small lift of her chin, she motioned him over. He skirted the outer rim of the crowd to find his brothers already behind the gazebo with their mother.

"I have a request," she said as the four circled her. Derrick could have sworn he heard Dante groan.

She looked each of the grown men in the eyes. "I love you boys too much to decide who will give me away at my wedding. So I'll leave the decision up to you."

"Are you sure?" Derrick asked.

She cupped his cheek with her warm hand. "I'm sure."

After winking at him, she strolled away.

Reaching into the front pocket of his jeans, Derrick withdrew a worn coin. He ran his thumb over the warm metal, the raised edges smooth after years of being handled.

"Okay, guys. What do you say we decide who gives Mom away in the Matthews' family tradition?"

Dante rolled his eyes. "I hate this tradition."

"Poor loser?" Derrick asked.

"No, so far I've been fortunate, but the anticipation is agony."

Dylan slapped Derrick on the back. "What do you say we let those two go first."

"Works for me."

"Heads," Dante called.

Deke shrugged.

With a flip of his thumb, the coin sailed into the air then landed in Derrick's palm. He looked at it for a long time, stretching out the suspense, a grin curving his lips.

"Oh, for the love of…" Dante griped.

"No worries, little bro. Heads."

Dante blew out a breath and turned on his heel.

"Escaping so soon?" Deke called after him.

"I'm going back to Eloise where it's safe."

Deke turned back to the bearer of the coin. "Heads."

"You sure?" Derrick asked.

"Let's keep the good luck rolling."

Once again, Derrick made a show of letting the coin twist in the air. The wind picked it up, but after it came down, he winked at his brother. "Safe."

"Good," Deke replied, then narrowed his eyes. "By the way, I'm onto you."

Derrick's hand flew to his chest, and he projected an air of innocence. "Me?"

Shaking his head, Deke walked away but not before Derrick glimpsed a small smile.

"That just leaves us," Derrick said to Dylan.

"Why bother? The coin is double-sided."

"How do you know? You've never seen it."

Dylan sent him a *really?* glance. "My point, exactly. You wield that coin to do your bidding."

"Harsh."

"The truth."

"Then let me buck the system and call tails," Derrick said.

"Magnanimous of you."

With a chuckle, Derrick sent the coin into the air. It hovered. Dropped. Derrick eyed the metal and said, "Guess I had to lose some time."

"Let me see," Dylan said, reaching for the coin. Derrick snatched his hand away.

"Nope. Doesn't work that way."

"So you really lost?"

"You doubt me?"

"You've been known to cheat."

Once again, Derrick went for hurt. "I'm wounded."

Dylan crossed his arms over his chest. "Yet you haven't confessed."

Derrick shrugged.

"Fine. You win." Dylan took a few steps back, then turned to leave. A couple of minutes later Jasmine reappeared.

"How did it turn out?"

"We decided I'd have the honor of walking you down the aisle." He puffed out his chest. "I am the oldest, after all."

"And this decision didn't have anything to do with you manipulating the coin toss?"

His eyes went wide. "How…"

"You boys think you're a step ahead of me." She rolled her eyes. "That will be the day."

Barking out a laugh, Derrick hugged the woman who had loved him since birth, the woman he'd be pleased to give away in marriage.

She pulled back, her eyes bright as she searched his face. "You're okay with this?"

"I wouldn't want to be anywhere else," he said.

"With the upcoming weddings and happily-ever-afters, I don't want you to feel left out."

His chest squeezed tight. He knew his mother was referring to Hannah. "I'm okay, Mom."

She tilted her head. "Really?"

"Yes," he lied.

While she continued to read him, he led her in the direction of the beach. "Yes, I've always been in love with her. And yes, I'll continue to love her. But by her silence, Hannah's made it clear she doesn't feel the same way. I've tried to find her. Failed." He ran a shaky hand over his closely cropped hair. "Maybe Dylan is right. It's time to move on."

A bright sheen brightened his mother's eyes in the bonfire light. "I know how much this hurts."

It did. Every day. But it didn't change reality. He swallowed hard. Forced himself to believe the words he was about to say. "I'm ready. Probably should have been years ago."

"You never gave up hope."

"Sometimes hope isn't enough."

At those words, his mother tightly hugged him. Then she stepped back and wiped her cheeks. "I'm happy about your decision. And that you'll be here for the wedding."

"I have vacation time coming. And believe it or not, I'm happy you found James." He lifted his chin in the direction of her fiancé. "Go enjoy your night."

"You promise you'll be okay?"

"Promise."

She frowned. "I worry about you. You talk a good game…"

"Go."

At his directive, she made her way back to James, the smile from earlier returning to her lips.

He glanced around the crowd, catching glimpses of his brothers and their girlfriends. He was the odd man out here. He'd head back to DC early, get some paperwork done and take off on his unwelcome vacation. It was going to be a long six weeks, but what choice did he have? Sit around his apartment and mope? The idea of a solo trip didn't appeal, but he realized that maybe he was better off alone in the long run. In life.

On that sobering thought, Derrick made his way to the water's edge to escape the pervading good cheer. The surf rolled in at a steady pace as he approached. The scent of burning wood and wet sand should have relaxed him, but as he stared out over the dark horizon, his mind traveled elsewhere.

Usually he kept himself so busy at work that he didn't have time to dwell on the past. The pace in DC was hectic, and in his position as a special agent with the Federal Bureau of Investigation, he took every case he could. But coming here to Florida brought back memories he'd tried to block over the years. Even as they faded to black-and-white.

He and Hannah had come up with the idea to get married while they were at the beach, shortly after high school graduation. Hannah had been talking about college and how she didn't want them to be separated and before he knew it, they'd hatched a plan. It had been a night much like this, filled with promise and joy, but they'd been alone instead of in a crowd like the folks gathered here to celebrate with his mother. Seemed like it had always been him and Hannah against the world. He'd liked it that way. Didn't need anyone else and neither did she.

Excitement had gleamed in her eyes. She'd

thrown herself into his arms for a kiss that sealed the deal. Two months until their birthdays and then they'd make things official.

Until fate decided otherwise.

He let out a sigh as he heard someone approach. He looked over his shoulder and spotted Dylan walking his way.

"You going to be able to make it back in time for Mom's wedding?" his brother asked.

"Looks like I'll have to now."

"Because you cheated."

He canted his head. "Like that's a shocker."

Dylan chuckled. "You can get time off?"

"Turns out I've accrued a month and a half worth of vacation time my superior is hounding me to take. He hates paperwork and wants me to lighten his load by going, in his words, anywhere."

"Have you made plans?"

"I was thinking about hitting the road." Dante had restored and modified a classic '67 Challenger for Derrick. The same car that was a piece of junk when he'd arrived in Hannah's driveway the day he'd discovered her gone…

He'd jumped out of the car. Run up the brick path to the front door and rung the bell. Could barely keep still from the excitement coursing through him. After a few minutes of silence, he'd pressed the button again. And again. He'd moved to the large picture window and cupped his hands around his eyes to peer into the dark recesses of the house before stepping from the porch to walk around the house. No one out back. Stumped, he noticed the next-door neighbor watering her flowers.

"Hey, Mrs. Gaines. Have you seen Hannah around?"

The older woman frowned. "Heard noises last night. Couldn't sleep, so I looked out the window to see who was making the ruckus. The family got in the car and took off."

That couldn't be right. "In the middle of the night?"

"There were some official-looking men telling them to hurry. Hannah and her mother were crying but they were pushed in the car and left."

Gone? Just like that?

"But…"

The neighbor shrugged. "Can't tell you any more than that."

Derrick jerked when his brother spoke.

"I asked where you're headed."

He shook off the memories, including how his actions, and his father's, in retrospect probably set events in motion. Maybe if it had been a normal breakup—still not a great scenario— he would have had closure. But his nature, to find answers, kept him hooked.

"No destination in mind. Just get in the car and drive."

"Need a wingman? For part of the trip?"

"Nah. I'm good." He gazed over the water. "You're right, Dylan. It's time to let go. Maybe on this trip I can finally get rid of baggage from the past."

Dylan clamped his shoulder. "It's a good idea."

Derrick thought so, even if his heart cracked a little bit deeper.

MONDAY MORNING HE was back in his office, finishing the last of his stack of paperwork. His superior, Ron Collins, popped into Derrick's office.

"I thought you were leaving today."

"I am. Just wanted to clear my desk before taking off."

"You do have plans, right?" Ron asked, hope in his eyes.

Derrick laughed. "Yes. I'll be gone until next month. My mother is getting married in February and after that, I'm all yours again."

"Look, I know I sound like a broken record, but it was either remind you about your accrued vacation time or you lose it."

"It's fine. I needed the push."

Ron nodded at the computer screen. "You tied up the museum case?"

"Yep." He rifled through the papers on his desk to find the printed report. "Here you go."

"Nice job."

"Thanks."

"And Derrick?"

"Yes, sir?"

"Enjoy your time off."

Derrick allowed a small smile. "Will do."

Once he'd finished the last report, he gathered his mail from the corner of his desk. He tossed a few envelopes aside until he came upon a bulky 3 x 5 package. His name was scrawled across the front in a flowery script. Definitely not official. The return address came from Nevada. He didn't recall knowing anyone from there. Curious, he ripped the package open and peered inside. No paper. He tipped it upside down and out tumbled a small red gem, about the size to fit an expensive women's ring. When the late morning sunlight from his office window reflected off the gem, his breath caught in his throat.

He took a pen from the holder and pushed the cut stone closer. Leaned down to inspect it better. A flash of memory jolted him and he sat back in the chair—multiple stones scattered on Hannah's father's desk. Hannah asking him not to tell anyone what he saw.

Could this be a signal from Hannah?

He grabbed the envelope and scanned the return address again. Dark Clay, Nevada.

He swiveled in his chair and typed the name into the computer. Found the location about twenty miles outside Carson City near Lake Tahoe.

His heart started pumping wildly. Finally. After all these years. A connection. Was this Hannah's way of contacting him? And why now?

Did it matter?

No.

He picked up his phone and booked the next available flight to Reno-Tahoe International.

SOMEONE WAS WATCHING Hannah Rawlings. Or, Anna Rawley, as she was currently known. She was sure of it.

She'd been on the run long enough to recognize when the little hairs on the back of her neck were warning her, not acting up because of the biting wind. She walked around the playground of Ponderosa Day School, avoiding patches of ice as she pulled her wool coat more snugly around her. It had rained just after the morning bell and since then the temperature had dipped close to freezing. The sun barely peeked out from the cloud cover. Shivering, she watched her students, but her eyes flitted around the schoolyard. Nothing out of the ordinary for a Tuesday. But still, she couldn't shake the strange feeling.

"Miss Rawley, Tommy threw snow at me."

She glanced down to find William staring up at her. She controlled her exasperation. What was it with boys, always tussling and one-upping each other? She crouched down to his level, her heart squeezing at his mournful expression.

Teaching ten-year-old children required a patience level and skill she never thought she'd need.

"What happened?"

"You know the pile of snow in the corner? Chuck was kicking it with his boots and then Tommy scooped it up and made snowballs."

"I thought you boys were playing a game?"

He nodded, his blue eyes solemn behind glasses. "We were. It was my turn with the ball, but Tommy took it from me and then started throwing snow at me."

As usual, Tommy made his own rules.

"I'll talk to him."

William's face lit up. "You're the best." He turned and ran back to a group of boys.

"Hardly," she muttered under her breath. Not when she wondered every day why she was getting dressed to go to school and teach a class full of rambunctious fourth graders. Not exactly her grand plan, but then, nothing had turned out the way she'd dreamed.

But once she arrived, the kids reminded her why she loved being around them. Their optimism and energy filled her with a sense of hope she hung on to daily.

Rising, she stuffed her gloved hands in her coat pockets and watched the boys work out their problems just before the bell rang. The students hurried to line up. Taking one last look around the schoolyard, Hannah searched for the source of her uneasiness. No adults hung around the fence. The cars in the parking lot belonged to teachers or support staff. Even the cars along the street were a normal part of the landscape.

Okay, so she was overreacting. Wouldn't be the first time.

The next couple of hours dragged on as Hannah finished her day. The black slacks and white sweater she'd dressed in that morning did little to keep her warm. Despite the heated classroom, she couldn't seem to stop shivering. She was exhausted by the time the kids had been released and she was free to leave. As she took her keys in her right hand, she remembered her earlier prickliness and clutched the pocket-size container of pepper spray attached to the ring. With the other hand she gripped her leather tote bag, ready to head home to check on her mother and then relax with a strong cup of tea. She made her goodbyes to her colleagues and walked to the parking lot.

A frigid late-afternoon wind whistled around her. Pine trees swayed, the needles rustling, cones dropping to the icy ground with a thud. Clouds hadn't left the sky since she'd been outside earlier. Patches of crusty snow lingered along the curb from the storm a few days earlier. She shrugged deeper into her coat, wishing she'd remembered a hat. In the five years she'd lived here, she'd never gotten used to winter in Nevada.

Her car came into view. Hannah scanned the lot, but nothing seemed out of the ordinary. Silly, really. No one had bothered her in a long time. Still, the years of drills were seared into her muscle memory, most of them unnecessary. Heaving out a laugh, she reined in her imagination.

In her haste to cross the lot, her boots slid on an ice patch but she righted herself before wiping out. Carefully navigating her steps, she finally made it to her car. Relieved, she pressed the button to unlock the door. Her hand had just settled on the silver handle when she heard rapid footsteps on the asphalt behind her. She tensed. Continued to open the door.

Almost there.

She tossed the tote inside just as she heard, "Hannah."

Shock enveloped her. No one had called her that name in over fifteen years.

A presence drew up beside her. Panicked now, she turned, lifted the canister in her hand and aimed at the deepest blue eyes she'd ever seen…a color she'd never forgotten.

CHAPTER TWO

DERRICK RECOILED AS Hannah's hand rose, a small pepper spray canister in her grasp. She wasn't really going to… Flinging his hands in the air, he ducked, then slipped on the ice, his feet skidding out from under him, arms flailing as he dropped with a loud whoosh.

Thankfully the fall kept him from the full force of the spray, but the dose that did reach his eyes made him cringe. He sucked in a sharp breath at the combination of burning eyes and skin on fire. His right hip took the brunt of contact with the solid ground, but he managed to roll and scramble upright again. Through the stinging tears, he saw Hannah, eyes wide, mouth open.

"Derrick?" she whispered.

He rapidly blinked his stinging eyes, flushing the pepper spray as best he could, and tried to ignore the jolt of pain radiating through his body.

His vision may be blurry, but he saw enough to know Hannah was still as achingly beautiful as he remembered. Her usually curly auburn hair was pulled back into a tight knot, her hazel eyes still as luminous as ever as they stared back at him. In disbelief, if he had to gauge her reaction. Her skin was like ivory, but he couldn't miss the dark circles under her eyes. She was tall. Willowy.

He couldn't stop the racing of his heart as he stood mere inches from her.

"Oh my gosh. I thought…" She stepped closer. "Are you okay?"

"I will be once I can see again."

"I was sure someone was watching me."

"Guilty as charged," he mumbled.

She reached into her car and returned with tissues. Stuffed them in his hand. "If I had known…"

Derrick gently dabbed at his eyes. "How could you?"

"True, but I…" She leaned over, peering into his face. "It doesn't look too bad."

It wasn't. He'd been sprayed full-on in training and knew he'd survive this attack. Still, the burning sensation was not receding.

"I scared you. It was my fault."

"Should we go inside so you can flush the spray out?"

He blinked again, his vision clearing. "I'll be fine."

She looked doubtful, but instead asked, "Derrick. It's really you?"

"In the flesh." He balled up the tissue and stuck it in his pocket.

Her eyebrows angled together, the shock of seeing him finally hitting home. "How…how did you find me?"

"I got your street address from the package you sent. No one answered at your house, but a neighbor walking his dog told me where you work when I mentioned that I was an old friend."

She reared back. "That's impossible."

"You sent the gem so I'd find you."

"Derrick, I never sent you anything." She paused, clearly confused.

"Then who?"

"I don't know." She reached out to grab the open car door. "Right now, I'm needed at home."

He placed his hand on her arm to stop her. She sucked in a breath and jerked away. "I'm not sure what's going on," he told her, "but I'm not leaving until I do."

"Fine. We can have this conversation at my place."

"I'll follow you."

She nodded, then ducked into her sedan. He strode back to his rental car, thankful the limited amount of pepper spray hadn't incapacitated him enough to keep him from driving. Firing up the engine, he saw Hannah pull onto the street. He eased out of his spot, baffled and a lot disappointed.

No excited pronouncements of *You found me. I've missed you for so long. Finally, we can be together. I never stopped loving you.*

Instead he got, *I never sent you anything.*

Then how did that explain the stone delivered to his office? Her return address on the envelope? She was truly shocked to see him. Not surprising since it had been seventeen years since they'd known each other. Still, what had he expected? Angelic music from above and scattered rose petals leading a path to his one true love? That she'd run into his arms as if no time had passed at all? Not happening, apparently, but he'd hoped she'd at least be as excited as he was by the reunion.

The nagging feeling that she hadn't wanted him to find her struck again. Why? What had she been doing all these years? Despite her reluctance to speak with him, he wasn't going anywhere until he had answers.

Ten minutes later they pulled up to a ranch-style house in a neighborhood that had seen better days. The faded tan paint needed a touch-up. The grass, if you could call the brown stuff peeking out from under patches of snow, that could use the expertise of a good gardener. Of course, it was winter and grass tended to be dormant, but somehow Derrick suspected the neglected appearance was more about a lack of time and priorities than the season.

A long leg exited the car and soon Hannah was purposefully striding up the path to the front door. He parked behind her and made tracks to follow before she shut him out. A wave of heat smacked him as he stepped inside the house, igniting his burning skin again.

At first glance, the living room was cozy. An overstuffed couch and matching armchair took up most of the space, along with a large-screen television and a few end tables. Hannah was busy taking off her coat, not meeting his gaze. He shrugged out of his jacket. Waited.

"The bathroom is down the hall. First door on the right."

"Thanks." He hurried to the sink, rinsing the lingering pepper spray from his face. The skin around his glassy eyes was red, but splashing the water removed any residual effects. He dried his face with a towel and went back to the living room.

Hannah had the bay window curtain pulled back and was staring outside. When she heard him, she twirled around.

"Better?"

He nodded.

Crossing the room, she brushed by him to look down the dim hallway, the scent of vanilla enveloping him as she passed. Finding nothing out of the ordinary, she turned and repeated in a quiet tone, "How did you find me?"

"The red stone, Hannah. You sent it to me."

She shook her head. "I didn't send you anything. I don't even know where you live."

"It was sent to my workplace."

She held out her hands and lifted her shoulders. "I don't know that, either. I know nothing about your life."

Ouch.

"It was one of the four gemstones your father had in his possession."

She closed her eyes and ran a hand over her face. "The collection that ruined our lives." She lowered her hand. Stared hard at him. "Because of you."

"I never got a chance to talk to you." He took a step toward her. "You were gone."

A harsh laugh escaped her lips. "You have no idea what you did."

"Then tell me."

"What, you show up here out of the blue years after my family had to give up everything and assume I'm going to chat you up like we're long-lost friends?"

"We're more than that."

"We were. Not any longer."

The sharp words aimed at his heart did their damage.

She waved a hand in his direction. "It doesn't matter what happened. The bottom line is, you can't be here."

"Why not?"

"You don't know?"

"No. Why do you think I'm standing here asking questions?"

She began to pace the length of the living room. "You have no idea why we left?"

"As far as everyone was concerned, your family just disappeared in the night. No one knew why."

She stopped. "Even your father?"

Old wounds tore open at the mention of his dad. "If he did, he never said."

"And you didn't ask him before making this trip to find me?"

The lingering guilt and pain swamped him. "He died, Hannah."

She stopped, her face softening. "I'm sorry."

He nodded, swallowing around the obstruction in his throat. "I've been trying, without luck, to find you for years."

"There's a reason you had no luck."

"Which is?"

"I didn't want you to find me."

The blunt force of the truth smacked him square in the chest. He'd been correct. She didn't want him. Still, despite the searing pain, the part of him that couldn't let go had to ask, "But why? What happened?"

She opened her mouth and he waited for his questions to be answered when a weak voice came from the hallway.

"Hannah, I hear someone with you. Is Jonathan there?"

Something dark rose at the mention of another man's name, but Derrick controlled his emotions. He didn't know anything about this Hannah and could not jump to conclusions. Not when he was finally in the same room with her.

Hannah sent him a now-you-did-it look and hurried to the entrance of the hallway. A woman joined her, her hair gray and her face lined as she shuffled into the room wearing a housecoat and slippers.

"Mom, you should have stayed in bed."

"And miss the commotion?"

When Derrick realized this was Hannah's mother, his jaw dropped. This woman was obviously ill and looked way older than Derrick thought she should be, a far cry from the feisty, petite dynamo who had opened up her house, especially her kitchen, to him when he was a kid.

He stepped forward. "Hi, Mrs. Rawlings. It's Derrick Matthews."

The older woman stilled. Squinted her eyes. Then a warm smile curved her lips. "My goodness. It is you."

Hannah steered her mother to the armchair. "Sit, Mom."

Once Mrs. Rawlings was seated, she gazed at Derrick for a long moment. "I never thought I'd see you again. You or anyone from our old life." She grinned and pointed a shaky finger at him. "You always were full of surprises."

"If anything, finding you and Hannah has been the major surprise."

Mrs. Rawlings glanced at her daughter as Hannah wrapped a knitted afghan over her mother's knees.

"Have you eaten today, Mom?"

A grimace crossed her mother's face. "No."

"Let me get you some tea and toast."

"Please."

Always one with gracious manners, Hannah asked Derrick, "Can I get you anything?"

Yes, he wanted to shout. *The truth.*

"I'm good."

Hannah hesitated as if she didn't want to leave them alone, then hustled to the kitchen.

After a tense moment, Mrs. Rawlings said, "I'm sure you're startled by my appearance."

He nodded.

"Cancer. Had my last treatment yesterday."

He swallowed hard.

She offered a small grin. "But Hannah takes good care of me."

"Where is Mr. Rawlings?"

The older woman blinked. "Gone."

"I'm so sorry. I didn't know."

"Oh, not dead," she rushed to say. "Just gone."

"I don't understand."

"I believe it would be best if Hannah explained."

A shrill whistle sounded from the other room. Seconds later Hannah returned with a steaming cup for her mother. She took it with shaky hands.

"Your mother was just telling me your father left."

Hannah's brow pinched. She shot her mother a glance, then faced him. "We…separated years ago."

Separated? What did that mean?

"Go ahead," Mrs. Rawlings instructed.

Hannah sank down on one end of the couch. He took the other, breathing easier now that the burning sensation on his skin had subsided.

"We were trying to stay under the radar

when some things happened." Hannah brushed her black pants. "Dad thought it would be safer for us if he left."

"For where?"

"I don't know. It's been ten years and we haven't heard from him."

Okay, this entire catch-up session was getting muddier instead of clearer. "I'm stumped here."

"You might as well tell him the whole story," Mrs. Rawlings said. "He did come all this way."

Hannah blew out a breath. "We had to leave Florida. For our safety."

"From whom?"

"My father did business with some shady guys. They wanted him to make a transaction with them and he said no. Let's just say they weren't pleased."

"They threatened him?"

"Yes. And then we went away."

Unease shivered down his spine. Her father had owned the town jewelry shop. How could he have gotten into dangerous business? "What kind of help?"

A ding came from the kitchen. Hannah jumped up. "Let me get my mother's toast."

He rose, an uncomfortable sensation settling over him. "What kind of help, Hannah?"

He didn't miss the anger radiating from her as she spat, "Witness protection," and raced into the other room.

HANNAH RAN A trembling hand over her forehead. Derrick was standing in her living room. Her living room, for Pete's sake! She had absolutely no idea how to process this.

No matter how many times she might have dreamt it, she never thought she'd see him again. Yet he stood in the doorway, confusion shadowing his handsome face. He was dressed in a navy cable-knit sweater that brought out the blue in his eyes, worn jeans encasing lean legs, and boots, looking as gorgeous as the last time she'd seen him. More so. He'd aged well, the youthful face now matured into that of a man, with hard angles and wrinkles around his eyes. And the red skin that looked like he'd been sunburned, courtesy of her knee-jerk reaction.

Acrid black smoke drifted from the toaster oven. With a yelp, she pulled open the door and waved her hand to disperse the cloud. The slice was charred and inedible. Pinching it between her fingers, she flung it into the sink then pulled another slice from the bag to start over.

Once the bread was toasting, she rested her palms on the counter.

"Witness protection?" came Derrick's deep voice at her shoulder.

With a start she swung around and placed a hand over her tumbling stomach.

"Yes."

He ran his fingers through his short, dark hair. "This has got to be some story."

"It is."

He rested his hip against the counter. Crossed his arms over his broad chest. At such a short distance, she could smell his spicy cologne. Good grief. He'd been back in her life for less than an hour and here she was all over the map. She straightened her shoulders and ignored his grim expression.

"I never would have guessed," he said.

"That was the point."

A heavy silence settled over the room.

"So, who are you now?"

Tears burned behind her eyes but she blinked them away. "Anna Rawley. My mom is Sophie."

"A close variation of Sofia."

"Yes. I haven't been Hannah for a long time, Derrick." Nor was she the person she used to be. That girl was gone, replaced by Anna who took care of every problem that came their way.

"You've lived here this entire time?"

"No. This is just the latest place."

He went silent. She gazed out the window

over the sink. The sky was still a dank steel gray, not a ray of sun to be found. She shivered, brushing her hands up and down her arms.

"So this gem," she said with hope in her voice. "Is it possible my father sent it to you?"

"Does he know where you live?"

She turned back to him. "No, but he could have found out."

"The stamp indicated the envelope came from Carson City. Do you think he's there?"

"I honestly don't know."

"But why would he send anything to me if you were in hiding?"

Unable to answer, she massaged her throbbing temples with shaking fingers.

"Hannah, the stone was identical to the ones I saw on your father's desk before you left."

She shot him a sharp glance. "He claimed that because of the confusion the night we left, he lost track of those four gems. But then, he said and did a lot of things I found out later weren't legit."

"I don't have any knowledge about that."

The toaster dinged again. With quick hands, she removed the toast to a small plate and spread butter over the top. "The government insisted they didn't take the stones either." She glanced his way. "Who sent it to you?"

"I swear I'm as in the dark as you are."

She believed him. One thing she remembered about Derrick—he was always up-front. If he didn't know, that was the truth.

"Let me see it."

"It's in a safe place."

Convenient. She pressed her lips together, then said, "Let me get this to my mother. I'll be right back."

He nodded, his eyes distant as if he were lost in thought. She went back to the living room. The pang of fear that attacked her whenever her mother was so still tweaked her heart. With relief Hannah realized her mother had only dozed off. At least she'd put the teacup on the table next to her chair first. "Mom," Hannah said softly.

Her mother roused. "Did I fall asleep again?"

"Yes. It's okay." Hannah set the plate on the table. The treatments had wiped her mother out. Her last infusion had been the day before so now they would hope for the best.

"Just rest."

Her mother's lids fluttered closed again. Hannah tucked the afghan around her slight form. She was the one person in the world who meant everything to Hannah, other than Derrick had been once upon a time.

"Your mom told me she has cancer," Derrick said as Hannah walked back into the kitchen.

Drained by the worry over her mother and Derrick unexpectedly showing up, she pulled out a wooden chair and sat. "Lung. When the doctor made the diagnosis, he surgically removed the tumor and started her right away on radiation and chemo. Now we wait for the results."

"I'm sorry, Hannah."

She pressed her trembling lips together. Nodded.

"Are you the only one taking care of her?"

She would have laughed out loud if she wasn't so close to tears. Yes, she was her mother's caregiver. Her father had made sure of it. "I'm afraid so. Carol, our next-door neighbor, has been wonderful, checking in when I work or taking Mom to the doctor if I can't make an appointment."

"I wish I had known."

"So you could do what? Derrick, why are you here?"

"I've been searching for you since the night you left."

She found that hard to believe. "Why? You had to know."

"How can you ask me that? Especially after what we meant to each other."

She refused to answer.

"I had no idea the depth of trouble your family was in. And even when I pressed my father, he never gave me any details."

Her voice trembled. "That was a long time ago. Things are different. I'm not the same girl I was back then."

"I get that, but it doesn't change how I feel."

"It should."

He moved closer. "I want to help you and your mom any way I can."

"Help?" Her voice rose again and broke off with a croak. "You're why we're here in the first place."

"You alluded to that but I'm not making the connection."

"Those gems? The ones I asked you not to tell anyone about? They were my father's downfall." She fisted her hands on her thighs. "Because you told your father."

"But not to get your dad in trouble. I was concerned when I heard your father on the phone begging someone to leave his business alone. I just asked my dad some questions."

"And as police commissioner, he called the proper authorities."

His expression didn't change but his eyes wavered.

"You knew," she said.

"Suspected. But I didn't want to believe it was related to your leaving."

"We ran in the middle of the night, Derrick. Only had time to pack our barest belongings. Lived in a motel somewhere for weeks until my father went to court. Then we were given new identities. Started over in Illinois before moving multiple times since." The weight of the years pressed on her. "Now my mother is sick. How does that seem right or fair?"

He reached for her hand, paused for a long, drawn-out moment, and pulled back. Disappointment swept over her. After years apart, did she still want Derrick to comfort her?

His astute gaze roamed her face. "Why did you shoot me with pepper spray?"

"I had this feeling I was being watched. The one thing they don't tell you when you become part of WITSEC is that you're always looking over your shoulder. You never feel completely comfortable or let your guard down." She shook her head. "I tend to be a bit suspicious anyway and my overreaction this afternoon proves it."

"Has something happened to make you jumpy?"

"Not recently. Like I said, I'm overly attuned

to my surroundings. I was right in being concerned, but since it was you, not some bad guys, I made a mistake."

"Somehow I don't think that happens often."

She briefly met his gaze and looked away. "So now what?"

"If you're still concerned about your safety, I can help. I have contacts through my job."

"Which is?"

"I'm an FBI special agent."

She closed her eyes and groaned. "I don't want any more help from government agencies."

"Then how about from an old boyfriend?"

It would be so easy to fall into his arms. Let him carry the burdens she'd been laboring with for so long. Go back to the days when the biggest decision she had to make was what color lip gloss to use or which jeans to wear. As much as she might want the reprieve, it wasn't possible. This was her reality now. Not glamorous or flashy, but she had a good job. A few friends she trusted. Her mother would get well. She had to.

Squaring her shoulders, she met Derrick's gaze. Recognized that look. The one that said "I'll take care of everything for you." Yeah, well where was he when she'd needed him? When she'd been scared to death the night the

US Marshals took them from the only home she'd ever known? When her father left, thinking his absence was the best solution for all of them? When she'd had to change her mother's name and her own and find yet another job in a new city? Or when she'd cried alone at night after her mother's diagnosis?

Did he think he could just show up out of the blue and things would go back to the way they were? After he'd changed the entire trajectory of her life because he'd posed questions when she'd asked for his silence? Yes, they'd been children back then. Their dreams had been just that, dreams. But she'd needed him when the world was falling down around her, when things were off-kilter and scary, and he was nowhere to be found. She'd learned to forget the past, then carve out an existence without the heaviness of memories weighing her down. So why did he think she needed him now? She'd taken care of her mother alone. Put her dreams aside to make a stable life for both of them. And now, with her mother's diagnosis, they couldn't leave Dark Clay until they knew for sure the cancer was gone.

So no, he didn't get a free pass to barge into her life, with his list of questions and offer to make things right.

She met his gaze dead-on and said the words sure to keep him at bay. "I don't think my boyfriend would appreciate your assistance."

CHAPTER THREE

"BOYFRIEND?"

"You didn't think my life stopped because you were no longer in it, did you?" Hannah asked, the heat of her words scorching her tongue.

"Well, no. I…"

For once he was speechless. Good, because she couldn't deal with the torrent of emotions racing through her right now.

"Jonathan?"

She blinked. "How…"

"Your mother mentioned him when she first came into the living room."

Right. So much had transpired since they got to her house, she didn't remember her mother mentioning her boyfriend's name.

"He owns an art gallery in Carson City."

"So you're still interested in paintings?"

"It's not like I have the time to indulge my interest, but yes."

"I always thought you'd work in a museum."

"Obviously that would have been in another life."

Annoyance crossed his face. "Yes, we've established you're mad at me."

She pinched the bridge of her nose. "You seriously caught me off guard. And now we're sitting around like long-lost friends bringing each other up to date when I never expected to see you again. It's surreal."

"I get that you're off-balance. I've been the same way since the package arrived."

She folded her arms on the table and rested her forehead on top, at a total loss for words. Was this really happening? And why did she keep noticing those wide shoulders of his and that lopsided smile that still left her a bit breathless. Surely she should have gotten over her first love…right? Especially when he'd blown up her life once already.

"I guess I thought small talk might ease the shock."

She lifted her head. "At this point, I'm numb."

"Sounds like you have a lot on your plate."

Her hackles rose at his statement. "I can handle it."

"Didn't say you couldn't. It's just an observation."

Those pesky tears she kept blinking back

made an untimely appearance. She shook them off. "What do you want, Derrick?"

"To make sure you and your mom are okay."

"Tall order."

"Good thing I'm a tall guy."

Biting back a grin, she rose. Wasn't it just like Derrick to make jokes in a tense situation? He'd always had a quick sense of humor. It had been one of the qualities that drew her to him the most. Some things never changed...including her feelings? Impossible.

"I've been taking care of us for years, Derrick, without anyone's help."

"Point taken. But I have time off. If you'd—"

"We've been perfectly fine, and will be, without you."

"Hannah," came a strained voice from the living room, cutting through the tension simmering between them.

"I need to check on Mom."

"I'm not going anywhere."

With a resigned sigh, she went to the other room only to return to the kitchen with her mother's teacup. "Mom dozed off and when she woke up her tea had gone cold. The day after chemo she sleeps a lot." Hannah dumped the tepid remains and refilled the cup with steaming water from the kettle. She glanced at the clock, hoping Derrick would leave soon so she could rest. After everything that had gone on today, she needed time to organize her thoughts and suppress her wayward emotions for a man she'd vowed to forget. "I suppose I should get dinner started," she said mostly to herself, trying to hide the exhaustion that never seemed to go away. She shook off her fatigue, not wanting Derrick to feel sorry for her.

She returned the cup to her mother who seemed more awake now. "I'll fix you something else to eat."

"I'm not hungry."

"Mom…"

"I'm also not twelve. If I don't want to eat, I won't."

"You need to keep up your strength."

"Tomorrow. I'll feel better then."

Hannah blinked back hot tears. She knew not to push. Tomorrow would be here soon enough. She bent down to kiss her mother's cheek. "I love you, Mom."

"Back at ya," her mother teased with their little catchphrase, and what Hannah thought might be a cocky grin.

"I'm cooking anyway."

Her mother rolled her eyes. "Help us all."

A laugh escaped Hannah, sounding hoarse and rusty to her own ears. She turned to go back to the kitchen but stopped short in the entryway. Surprisingly, Derrick was at the stove.

"What're you doing?"

He glanced over his shoulder. "You said you wanted to get dinner started."

"Me. Not you."

He grinned. "First come, first serve."

"You sound juvenile."

"And you look beat. Sit down and let me worry about the meal."

She had to admit, letting someone else cook tonight was fine with her. She sank onto the chair.

"What smells so good?"

"I found leftover chicken in the fridge, pasta and sauce in the pantry."

Despite the crazy day, her stomach growled. "You cook as well as solve crimes?"

He stirred the sauce, then turned to face her. "I live alone. It's either learn to cook or order a lot of takeout."

He lived alone? Why did that tidbit fascinate her, even when it shouldn't? It wasn't like she was dying to know what he'd been doing in the years they'd been apart. Okay, she was lying to herself, but there was no way she was going to broadcast her curiosity.

She rose to gather plates and glasses from the cupboard and set the table for three, even though she was sure her mother would decline. "Sit, please," he insisted again, then placed a small portion of plain chicken and noodles on a plate to carry to the other room. "Should I add sauce?" he asked. At her head shake, he left, returning empty-handed. She raised a brow.

"Mom took it?"

"I'm very persuasive."

How well she remembered. When they were kids, he'd managed to talk her into one adventure after another. She was a stickler for doing things the right way, but he'd been able to coax her to the dark side a time or two. Well, not dark, exactly, but definitely gray in her world.

Like prom night. He'd picked her up in his run-down car, promising an evening she'd never forget. She'd laughed, excited about the final high school dance. They'd stayed for an hour before Derrick rushed her back to the car and they drove to the ocean. It was there, sitting on a blanket in the sand under a full moon, that he gave her a promise ring he'd saved up to buy with money from his part-time job at the pizza place. The tiny chip of a diamond had glittered in the moonlight. It could have been as big as a carat for all she cared, but the fact that he'd picked it out touched her heart.

Even though it was years ago, she'd occasionally dreamed about her time with Derrick and woken with a sense of loss she found difficult to shake.

Derrick dished out the amazing-smelling concoction. She picked up her fork and twirled the sauce-covered pasta before taking a taste. "If you get her to eat even a tiny bit, that's more than I can do."

"It's been tough?"

"Lately. Once she gets her strength back I have no doubt she'll run circles around me." She took a bite and nearly groaned out loud. "This is amazing."

"And it's from a jar. Imagine if I made it from scratch."

She couldn't. If she had her way, he wouldn't be around that long.

"What happened to your dad, if you don't mind my asking?"

He pushed aside his fork and she thought she saw him grimace. "He wasn't feeling good one morning. Got up and went to work, but during the day he keeled over. It was an aneurism."

Hannah's voice was quiet when she said, "I don't think you're ever prepared whether the end happens suddenly or if an illness is drawn out."

"How long has your mom been sick?"

"Feels like forever, but it's actually been a few months. She started coughing one day and it persisted. I talked her into seeing a doctor and, long story short, they found a spot on her lungs. After the surgery and subsequent treatment, we're hoping for positive results."

He covered her hand with his. The warmth radiated up her arm and straight to her heart. Okay, there was still a tangible connection to Derrick that hadn't seemed to lessen, but no way would she trust him. Look what had happened because of that misguided belief.

Slowly easing her hand from his, she took another bite. A frown marred his forehead but he didn't press the issue.

"So," he said instead. "You're a teacher."

"Elementary. Fourth grade. Ponderosa Day School is private, so it helps to keep my visibility low."

"I never would have pegged you as the teacher type."

"Why not? I tutored you in art history."

"Which I sat through because I wanted to be with you, not learn about old paintings."

"I can't work in a museum. Too high profile."

"Because someone might recognize you?"

She tamped down the old resentment. "We were discouraged from any kind of job that might put us in a spotlight. Teaching, even if it should be given more attention, is never highly publicized."

"It's a noble profession."

"I do enjoy the children. Ten-year-olds are quite imaginative." She pushed the pasta around on the plate. "You?"

"I work with the Art Crime Team out of DC." She blinked.

"Hey, those lessons paid off," he said.

Envy swept over her, swift and hard. He got to be around artwork? Her dream job? Well, not the crime aspect, but being part of that world. Touching masterpieces. Showcasing new artists. Being in the glamorous world of high-end art. He got to have that job while she'd ended up on the run.

He must have mistaken her silence with the end of the topic—more like she was incredulous at his career choice—and switched the conversation back to her.

"So you're okay with your job?" he asked.

Was she? It was hardly her dream career, but it was all she knew. "Content."

A pause. Then, "And you're serious about this guy you're seeing?"

"I don't think that's an appropriate question."

"Why not? I'm trying to catch up."

"Yes. We're serious." She ran her thumb over her left ring finger. Derrick saw the motion and froze.

"You're not wearing a ring," he said.

"It's on my dresser."

He laid down his fork and sat back in the chair. A wounded look flashed in his eyes before disappearing.

"I have every right to date, be engaged if I want."

"I'm not saying you can't, I just…"

"Thought I'd pine over you forever?" She rose, took her plate and tossed the remains in the garbage. "You have a lot of nerve—"

The doorbell stopped her midtirade. She placed her dish in the sink and hurried to the door. Lynny Dunlop, her best friend and co-worker who lived down the street, stood on the other side, a bright smile on her face.

"Your mother called. Said she and I should have a movie night." She held up a DVD. "She told me you had an old friend in town and needed to catch up, so I'm here to keep her company."

Hannah suppressed a groan. It was obvious her mother wanted to give her and Derrick some time alone.

"Come on in." As she shut the door, Hannah shot her mom a chagrined look. Her mother simply smiled.

"Brought *Mama Mia!*" Lynny said as she shrugged out of her heavy coat.

"Perfect," Sofia said as Hannah spoke at the same time.

"Which isn't necessary," Hannah added. "He's not staying."

"He?" Lynny asked, full-blown interest lighting up her elfin features.

It figured that would be the one word her friend would pick up on. Derrick chose that moment to stroll into the living room.

"And this must be him," Lynny said, shooting Hannah a raised eyebrow.

Yes. Derrick was ridiculously handsome. Anyone with eyes could see that.

Derrick walked over and held out his hand. "Derrick."

"Lynny. Hannah's BFF."

Hannah bit the inside of her cheek.

"Who was helping me to the bedroom," Sofia interrupted as she tried to rise from the chair. Lynny hurried over to assist.

"We'll leave you two alone," Lynny said, winking at Hannah as the women disappeared down the hallway.

Hannah loved Lynny, really she did. They'd met a few days after Hannah and her mother had moved into the neighborhood. She was also instrumental in getting Hannah a position at Ponderosa Day School. Between Lynny's sunny disposition and habit of getting her own way, she'd been responsible for prodding Hannah out of the house more times than Hannah could count. It was on one of their impromptu outings that Hannah had met Jonathan and was now engaged.

She glanced down at her ringless finger. Could this day get any more weird? Derrick had to leave before she lost her head and said things that she would regret. Like admitting she had lingering feelings for him. Which she shouldn't because she had a fiancé. A man who *had* been there for her when she needed him. Who hadn't betrayed her, despite the fact that she'd been up-front when she'd told him she couldn't reveal her past. A man who was steady and dependable. Who didn't show up and demand answers.

Yes, Derrick ought to go.

"Look, Derrick, I think you should leave now." She walked to the couch where he'd dropped his jacket. "Mom and I are fine. You can take off now that your curiosity's appeased."

"It's more than that and you know it."

"That's all it can be." She handed him his jacket and crossed to open the front door. The freezing night air sent shivers over her skin, the cold waking her up to reality. She jutted her chin, hoping it made her look tougher than she felt. "You don't deserve to be in our lives after what you did."

"Correction, after what *your father* did. And I only just found you."

"I don't want you here." Yeah, it was a lie, but his standing here was a reminder of what she'd lost. What they'd lost. No amount of hoping was ever going to change what had transpired in their past.

He didn't move.

She opened the door wider, not taking no for an answer.

"Fine," he said, fisting the jacket in his hands. "But until I find out who sent that stone, until I get answers, I'll be around." He brushed by her and marched into the frigid night. His words sent tremors over her that had nothing to do with the weather.

SIX DAYS LATER, Derrick stood outside the front entrance of Ponderosa Day School, dressed in an official security guard shirt, jeans and boots, watching students file into the tan building after being dropped off in the car zone. He'd gotten more than one curious look. Most of the kids were expecting to see an older man, Glen Harvey, on duty, but today and until he solved the gem situation, they'd get Derrick.

After talking with Hannah on the first night

he arrived, Derrick was legitimately concerned about her. Not only because of her mother's health issues, which she was handling admirably, but also because of the fact that at some point her father had taken off. That in itself raised red flags. He needed to find out if they were still under WITSEC protection since Hannah gave so little information. After settling into a hotel room, he had checked into the school where she worked, looking for a way to stay close. He discovered that the private school hired guards from a local security firm. Armed with the name of the company, Derrick applied for a position with the security company the next morning.

Using an alias, he'd created for the occasional undercover FBI op, Derrick Fields was vetted through a background and fingerprint check, then hired. When he showed up for his first day of work, he went through an orientation and then came the conversation about where he would be assigned. He made sure to point out that he thought working at schools was a high priority and had noticed that Ponderosa Day School was in the middle of a security upgrade. Relying on his innate power of persuasion, he asked to be sent there to assist the lone guard during the system upgrade. Thankfully, the owner agreed.

Now Derrick was on duty, bright and early on a clear and crisp Monday morning, good to go.

Until Hannah found him here. Then he expected fireworks.

He nodded at a group of girls. A buzz sounded and then a click as the door opened. Their laughter faded when the heavy door closed behind them. It was another freezing day, even with the sun shining. He rubbed his hands together and blew on them as a young boy strolled right up to him.

"Where's Glen?"

"In his office."

"You taking over?"

"No, just helping out."

"You got training?"

Derrick fought back a grin. "Extensive."

The boy nodded as if satisfied.

"I got my eyes on you," the kid said, leveling Derrick with a serious gaze.

"Then I hope to live up to your expectations…?"

"Tommy. I run this place."

"Do you? Then I'll see you after school for a report."

The boy's eyes went wide. "Really?"

"Those of us who watch out for this place should compare notes."

A bell rang. Tommy shifted his backpack. "I'll be there."

The boy hurried inside and Derrick allowed himself a small smile. As more children entered, he found he approved of the remote lock system. Those outside the building had to press a button to be allowed inside. A camera installed high in the corner at an angle facing the entrance offered the office staff a view of whoever wanted to gain admittance. Since this was a smaller school, the principal had informed him that the staff knew the parents or those permitted to come into the school on a child's behalf. In the aftermath of school tragedies, Derrick was glad this administration implemented serious security.

Shaking off the cold, he scanned the parking lot. Fewer students were arriving now that the last bell was about to ring before classes. A gray sedan pulled into a slot and Hannah emerged from the car, wearing the same coat as yesterday. She zigzagged through the cars as she hurried up the sidewalk to the main door. She stopped abruptly when she saw him.

"Good morning, Miss Rawley."

"What are you doing here?"

"Working."

"You have a job."

"Yep. Security officer at Ponderosa Day School."

"No," she glanced around and stage-whispered, "with the FBI."

"I told you I wasn't leaving until I get the entire truth out of you." He held out his hand to shake. "Derrick Fields. Additional help until the new security system here is in full working order."

She barely contained an eye roll.

He wanted to laugh but couldn't. Apparently, she'd forgotten how tenacious he could be. There were holes in her story, which he was desperate to fill in. And her father leaving? Why would he do that? From what Derrick could remember, he'd doted on his wife and daughter. There was more she hadn't revealed and he was the guy to get to the bottom of things.

And then there was the boyfriend issue. Or fiancé? He glanced down to find a bright, shiny diamond on Hannah's ring finger. His heart lurched. Yeah, he hadn't quite decided how to react to that piece of news.

"You're unbelievable," she muttered through clenched teeth.

"So I've been told."

She blew out a breath. "Derrick, you can't

stay here." She looked down at her finger. "It's complicated."

"You keep telling me that, but, put simply, I want to help."

She met his gaze, heat flashing in her eyes. "No one asked you."

He shrugged. "Never stopped me from inserting myself anyway."

"Fine. Suit yourself."

As she passed by, he fell into step beside her. "Hannah, you have the look of a woman who has too much on her plate. Even though you think I'm where I don't belong or I'm a huge inconvenience, please let me hang around for a while to assure myself you're okay. Is that too much to ask?"

They stood in the bright sunlight, eyes locked. Yesterday when his vision had been blurry, he'd missed the smattering of freckles scattered over her nose and cheeks. Standing this close reminded him of the times they would disagree and have a silent standoff until one of them conceded. The bell rang again and she blinked.

"I need to get to my students," she said, sweeping past him to enter the building.

Since she didn't argue with his decision to be here, he took that as approval. He remained at his post for five more minutes. When no additional students showed up, he went inside. The warmth of the building made his fingers tingle. He'd never been a fan of the colder weather, even though he lived in DC, preferring tropical climates instead.

He turned the corner to head to the main office. He'd already gone over the layout of the school and where Hannah's classroom was located. After hanging his jacket in the small room that served as the security office, he checked the schedule on the desk. Time to patrol the halls.

Just before he left the room, his cell phone rang. He smiled when he glimpsed his mother's name on caller ID.

"Hi, Mom."

"Derrick. So glad I caught you. I wasn't sure if you'd answer the phone since you're on vacation."

"For you, always."

"Here's the thing," she said getting right to the point. "I'm busy planning the wedding. It's only weeks away and I've decided I want your opinion as I go along."

"Mine?"

"Not just yours. Your brothers', too."

"Why?"

"This is such a big deal. I never imagined I'd

ever get remarried. I thought your father and I would grow old together."

His throat went tight at the sorrow in his mother's voice.

"But here we are. And since things with James got off to a rocky start, I'd feel so much better if I could chat with you from time to time about my ideas."

How could he say no? This was an unexpected gesture he realized he couldn't turn down. "Sure. Contact me any time you want."

He heard her sigh of relief. "Thank you. I know you're off on some grand adventure, so I promise not to bother you too often."

"I mean it, Mom, any time."

"You're a wonderful son. I wish you could find a woman to love."

"Mom," he warned.

"I know, I know, stay out of your love life. But still, a mother worries."

"Focus that energy on your wedding. It'll be better spent planning the details."

"You're right." She drew in a breath. "Okay, panic over. Now, how is your trip?"

"You know, same old."

"That doesn't tell me a thing."

"Nothing to tell." Yet. He hoped that would change in the near future.

"Where—oh, James just walked in the door. I should run."

"Bye, Mom."

He hung up, thinking that despite the moment of sadness in her voice, his mother sounded good. Must be the excitement of the upcoming nuptials. He chuckled at the thought of his mother wanting his input. His steps echoed off the concrete walls as he walked down the deserted hallway lined with lockers. The familiar smell of paste, chalk and rubber erasers, mixed with the stringent odor of cleaning supplies, had him recalling his school years.

He'd had a great childhood. Parents who had loved him, brothers who were his friends. His father had made sure to engage in an activity with each of his boys, making them feel connected in a special way. He and his dad had bonded over woodworking, his father teaching him how to use specialized tools to create mini works of art out of chunks of wood. The skill also came in handy when he had to make repairs around the house.

It wasn't until Hannah that he understood the meaning of romantic love. And the pain of losing that love. Hannah's leaving had not only torn his heart apart, it had put a huge strain on his relationship with his father.

When Derrick had confronted him after

finding the Rawlings family gone, his father had remained silent. Derrick railed, asking if he had taken the information Derrick had confided in him and used it against the Rawlingses. His father had justified his actions by saying he was looking out for the best interests of the family. That he was a police officer sworn to uphold the law. Even though he never revealed what happened, they'd argued and a wide chasm had formed between them, lasting right up until the day his father suddenly died. Derrick had never repaired the relationship and it had haunted him ever since. He didn't want that for himself and Hannah.

He shook off the bitter memories as he stopped at the door to Hannah's classroom. Peeked in through the window. Chalk held by slim fingers, she was writing on the board, teaching a math equation, it looked like. She wore a slim-fitting green dress and tall black boots. The fluorescent lights shone down on her beautiful hair, pulled back again, only today a few reckless curls escaped confinement. He could just make out the lilt of her voice through the barrier between them.

The walls were covered with various posters, the desks lined up in straight rows. He noticed two types of students: those studiously writing down the information Hannah presented, and the others, talking to their neighbor or gazing out the window. One industrious student hurled spitballs at the girls seated in the desks in front of him. Like every teacher in the world who had eyes in the back of their head, Hannah turned a stern look on the children, bringing the group back to order.

He wished she'd called him the night she left. Did she even try? The Marshals wouldn't have allowed it, but he and Hannah had such a close relationship—or at least he thought they did. Couldn't she have found a way? It still hurt that she hadn't let him know what was going on. Surely she could have snuck around the authorities? He would have if their positions had been reversed.

Realizing these were questions to be posed at a different time, he continued his rounds. By the time the lunch buzzer sounded, he was ready for some action.

The large cafeteria was bustling with activity, noise echoing off the high ceilings. The hot lunch aroma had his stomach growling, but he stood in the designated spot to observe as the kids found their places at the tables. He might be here to get the truth out of Hannah, but that didn't mean he wouldn't take this job seriously.

As the kids got busy eating, Derrick noticed a motion out of the corner of his eye. The young boy from earlier, Tommy, stood by his table and wildly waved his arms. Curious, Derrick headed his way.

"Is there a problem?"

"The guys don't believe I'm working with you."

Derrick swallowed a chuckle. "Well, technically, you're a student."

"So am I working with you or not?"

"In a limited capacity."

"What does that mean?" asked a smaller boy with glasses and a serious expression.

"It means I do the work, but I will listen to Tommy's report at the end of the day."

Tommy puffed his chest out, fist-bumping the boys around him. The serious boy motioned Derrick to come closer. Leaning over, the boy whispered in his ear, "Tommy is mean."

"Really?"

"He thinks he's the boss of everyone."

Derrick sent Tommy a narrow-eyed glance. The kid suddenly looked unsure of himself.

"Can you make him stop?"

"I can certainly try."

This earned him a big grin and a serious case of hero worship. He wanted to show these kids how to get along without taking advantage of their places in the power structure. He'd hated that hierarchy when he was in school and imagined it hadn't changed much.

The lunch hour ended and Derrick spent the afternoon doing various security tasks: patroling the campus, going over the surveillance equipment with Glen, monitoring some of the student activities. With only a half hour left of classes, Derrick headed to his position outside the front door to watch over the lineup of cars for student pickup. He hadn't gotten far when he heard a ruckus come from the direction of Hannah's room. He took off on a brisk run and skidded in front of the door. The voices were louder now, more alarmed. He pushed the door open to step into bedlam.

Girls were running about, checking inside desks and cubbies. Boys scurried around the perimeter of the room, rummaging through bookshelves. Hannah was calling them to order, without much success. Tommy stood before a cage, the door wide-open, a grimace on his face.

Hannah finally noticed Derrick and came over.

"What's going on?" he asked, his tone sharp, his reflexes ready to take control of the situation.

"Sally is missing."

His instincts to protect a child kicked in. "Can you give me a description?"

"She's stout and short legged, with short brown hair, a bit fuzzy, wearing a pink ribbon."

He gaped at Hannah as she described her student.

"Sally's our class guinea pig and she's escaped her cage."

CHAPTER FOUR

HANNAH LEFT HIS SIDE, her brow puckered in concern, and hurried to the young boy, who looked close to tears.

"I was cleaning the cage. It had *you know* and she got loose," Tommy explained.

She placed a hand on his shoulder and squeezed. "Sally can't have gotten far."

Skirting the kids running around the room, Derrick came to her side. "What can I do?"

She shot him an amused glance. "You're the federal agent. I'm sure you'll come up with something."

Was she purposely goading him? That satisfied smile sure said so. How he'd missed her sassy attitude. And her eyes, sparkling like she was keeping a secret only the two of them were privy to. He couldn't tear his gaze from her. Until she pointed to the students. Right. Back to work.

Hands on hips, he surveyed the room and came up...empty. He'd stared down criminals, avoided gunshots and been in a high-speed car chase. But this? Children, escaped animals and a beautiful teacher were not covered in the usual job description. He needed to get it together and figure out a way to be useful.

Before he could come up with a plan, Hannah clapped her hands. "Class, quiet down. You'll only scare Sally."

The volume level dropped. Hannah barked out orders like a seasoned drill sergeant. Impressed, Derrick walked the perimeter of the room, his eyes peeled for movement. He'd just started another circuit when he heard a young voice cry out, "Found her!"

A small girl cradled the guinea pig in her arms as she carried her back to the cage. She elbowed Tommy out of the way and placed the animal safely inside. "That's how you take care of Sally," the girl informed him with a huff.

Tommy opened his mouth but quickly shut it. Wise move.

Hannah clapped her hands again. "Okay, class. Let's get ready for dismissal."

Derrick needed to get outside to keep an eye on the students as they left the building and make sure they successfully got to their rides, but something held him back. His gaze landed on Tommy. Dejected, and probably embarrassed, he shoved his hands in his pockets and stood near the cage. He looked about as unsure as anyone could look. No sign of the bossy kid now. Taking pity on the boy, Derrick joined him.

"So, cleaning up Sally's *you know*, huh? That's a thing?"

"It's gross," Tommy cringed. "We take turns. Sally is our class project."

"I see. And has she gotten loose before?"

Tommy looked down and shuffled his feet. "Yeah."

"On your day?"

A long sigh. "Yeah."

"You sure she got away all by herself?"

Tommy's head shot up and guilt glittered in his eyes.

Derrick crossed his arms over his chest and spread his feet out in an authoritative stance. "Tell me the truth."

"I hafta take care of my dog every day at home. Dad says it's my job. I don't wanna pick up *you know* twice a day."

Derrick hid a smile. "Is Sally getting loose your way to get out of pet duty?"

Tommy shrugged. His unrepentant look reminded Derrick of his youngest brother. Growing up, Dante had charmed his way out of unwanted tasks without the slightest compunction.

Derrick leaned over. "You must be someone people feel they can trust if you have two animals to care for. That's a good quality to have—especially in law enforcement."

Interest gleamed in Tommy's eyes. "Really? Do you think I could be an officer when I grow up?"

"First, you have to take your job seriously. You need to be fair, respect everyone and keep your eyes open. What good would I be if I was standing guard outside the school but focused my attention on playing a video game on my phone? Anyone could get past me." He shook his head. "Don't be afraid of responsibility. Take pride in it, even if you make mistakes."

"So you've never messed up?"

"Didn't say that. But I've learned from my errors." His gaze darted to Hannah for a second before moving back to the boy. "Just do better next time."

"I can. I promise." With that, Tommy trotted off, his good mood restored.

Derrick strode across the room. "I need to take my post out front."

Hannah reached out and laid a hand on his arm. Heat shot over his skin and it was all he could do not to swoop her into his embrace.

She met his gaze and he read the gratitude there. "I don't know what you said to Tommy, but thanks. He's a little rough around the edges sometimes and I have to work with him."

"He seems like a good kid. Misguided, and a little overly enthusiastic, but at this age, they're not very sure of themselves."

As if she suddenly realized her hand still rested on his arm, she removed it. He immediately missed her warmth, a link to the easygoing relationship they'd once shared before misunderstandings and disappearances got in the way. "You were always confident."

"Nah. I had you fooled."

Her brow wrinkled. "I doubt that."

"Oh, you think you know me so well?"

Her smile faded. "I used to."

And just like that, the emptiness from the years apart burrowed deeper. Even standing this close to Hannah, he couldn't tamp down the pain that had been his companion since she'd left without a word.

"In fairness to Tommy," she said, never once catching on to his sadness, "the latch hasn't been working properly. I've been meaning to get it fixed…"

He pushed away his despair. Hannah and her family had had it worse than him all these years. After she left, his family had rallied around him, he went to college and worked his way into a good career. Unlike her, Derrick hadn't been forced to leave everything he knew and loved, unsure of the future. "You've had a lot on your mind."

"Yes. I worry about Mom."

"You should cut yourself some slack."

Anger flared in her eyes. "Look, you can't just blow in to town and understand what I'm going through."

"I'm not…" He ran a hand over the back of his neck. *Smooth, Matthews*. "I was only making an observation."

"Which I don't need to hear."

"You're right. I'm sorry."

During their conversation, the students had gotten boisterous again. Hannah blinked as if just realizing they were standing in a classroom full of fidgety children ready to go home.

"I need to settle the class down."

He nodded. "I'll see you later?"

If she heard his question she didn't respond, instead focusing on her students, leaving him to wonder if she wanted to shut him out for good. The same question he'd asked for years—had she kept her location a secret on purpose?—was still relevant, even though he'd finally found her and learned what had caused her departure without a word. A tight knot of hurt lodged in his throat. Just because he was standing in the same building as her didn't mean Hannah wanted the reunion he'd envisioned.

"Way to go," he muttered as he strode through the halls and out the main door into the frigid afternoon air under the cover of a gloomy sky.

Forty minutes later he was back at Hannah's classroom door. Lynny, the woman he'd met at Hannah's house was leaning against the desk, her hands gesturing as she talked. There was an ease in the posture of the two women that spoke of the friendship between them. While Hannah was tall and slender, Lynny was about a head shorter with more of a gymnast's body, her merry blue eyes, bright blond ringlets and sunny smile showcasing her sweet nature.

Hannah's back was to him so he couldn't gauge her mood. He needed to apologize, because Hannah was right. He had no right to tell her what to do.

He hesitated, something he wasn't used to. Then Lynny's gaze met his and her eyes went bright.

"So," she said, still addressing Hannah but loud enough for Derrick to hear. "This out-of-towner. You two know each other how?"

"We dated in high school."

"Nice that he showed up when you could use a pair of extra hands around the house."

Hannah waved her off, unaware Derrick was behind her. "I'm taking care of everything just fine."

Lynny's smile was wry. "I seem to remember the back door sticking every time you attempt to open it. You can't make it budge without working out at the gym first."

"Like I've ever worked out." Hannah chuckled. "I'll get to it."

"How about fixing the garage door opener? The water softener?"

"I don't care if my water's soft," Hannah said as she rounded the desk, collecting a stack of papers. "And I park in the driveway."

"Well, you won't bother your landlord."

"Because I can take care of it myself."

"Stubborn."

"Capable."

Hannah noticed him at last and froze.

Busted.

He slowly moved into the room. "Safe to come in?"

With a sigh, Hannah tidied the papers. "Yes. Sometimes things get a little crazy around here. Sorry I lost my temper."

Lynny's eyes went wide. "You? Lose your temper? You're the poster child for calm and collected."

"I wouldn't go that far."

"Anna, since I've known you, you've handled your mother's health crisis and maintenance of the house, all the while teaching full-time, and you've never once lost control."

Hannah sent a guilty glance his way when Lynny used her "new" name. "I can't let my mother down."

"But you expect to do everything?" Derrick asked, venturing farther into the classroom.

"Not everything. I ask Jonathan to help."

Lynny snorted.

"What?" Hannah asked, her eyebrows rising in surprise.

"I can't remember a time when he's helped you. He's always got," she finger quoted the air, "'important things' going on at the gallery."

"He's busy." Hannah shrugged. "Besides, Mr. Bartholomew lends a helping hand when he can."

"He is a sweetie," Lynny agreed, then noticed Derrick's blank look. "He's the neighborhood handyman."

Derrick would have him vetted as soon as he could. He'd already had a friend check into Lynny and there were no red flags. So sue him, he was concerned about Hannah's welfare and would do whatever it took to keep her and her mother safe.

"And now you have me," he said, puffing out

his chest. "I've been known to pick up a hammer from time to time."

"You were handy," Hannah said, her lips curving in a smile that made his heart gallop. "But from what I remember, you escaped unless the work had to do with a building project."

He shot her his most charming grin. "Allowed for more time with you."

Hannah rolled her eyes.

"Just give me a list and I'll drop by this weekend with a tool chest."

"Don't you have fed—I mean, security things to do?"

"Nope. I'm free."

Lynny nudged Hannah with her elbow. "If you don't take him up on his offer, I will."

"I can't impose," Hannah told him.

"Impose away."

"Who's being imposed on and for what?" came a decidedly male voice from behind him. Hannah's eyes went wide, Lynny emitted a strangled laugh and Derrick turned to face a debonair stranger, wondering if he was about to meet Hannah's boyfriend.

Tall, dark blond hair with brown eyes and impeccably dressed, he came across as sophisticated. Urbane. The kind of guy who fit into the art world that Hannah loved. No wonder she was drawn to him.

Hannah hurried over. "Jonathan. I thought you were coming by the house?"

"My meeting ended early." He sized up Derrick. "And this is?"

"Um, this is an old friend of mine. Derrick um…"

"Fields." Derrick shot his hand out.

Jonathan took it, sizing him up. "Jonathan Prescott. Owner of the Prescott Gallery in Carson City."

"Anna mentioned you."

"Of course, she did," Prescott said, pulling Hannah into a hug. "We're engaged."

Derrick's gaze went to Hannah's ring finger and the sparkling diamond, then back to her red face. "Yes. I've heard."

Jonathan smiled at Hannah. "And we have a dinner date tonight." His gaze left hers and met Derrick's. "To discuss wedding plans."

Hannah's eyes shot wide-open. Why had she reacted with discomfort to her fiancé's words? Another question to add to his growing list.

"Well, this is fun," Lynny said, "but I need to get going."

"Always a pleasure," Prescott replied, even though Derrick got the distinct impression he meant otherwise.

Lynny perused the three of them with amusement and then she was gone.

"I'll leave you to it." Derrick thumbed in the direction of the guinea pig cage. "I'll find some tools and fix the latch so there aren't any more escapes."

"Thanks, Derrick."

"And I'll have to stop by the gallery sometime," Derrick told Prescott. "Check out the artwork."

Prescott didn't mask his surprise. "You know art?"

It was all Derrick could do not to look at Hannah. "Quite extensively."

Prescott opened his mouth—probably to ask how a school guard knew about art—but before he could say anything, Derrick nodded to them both and left the room. He walked away, controlling every urge he had to tell Prescott to take a hike. That Hannah was with him. Except she wasn't and he had to remember that.

He'd been trained to size up people pretty accurately, and what he came away with from the encounter was that Prescott was genuinely fond of Hannah. What did Derrick expect? Hannah might have been given a raw deal and had to grow up faster than she'd wanted, but the woman she'd become was anything but naive. Hannah would never date Prescott unless he was good to her. And since Derrick had been out of the picture for such a long time, Prescott had taken his place. Quite a bitter pill to swallow.

Once inside the security room to retrieve his jacket, Derrick reached into his pants pocket. Removed the red gemstone he kept in his possession at all times and worked it between his fingers. Was it really possible this was one of the four missing stones? As he watched the facets of the stone shine under the overhead light, he vowed to stay in town until he came up with a reasonable answer as to who had sent him the stone. Figure out why he hadn't been able to let the case, or his feelings for Hannah, go. He gripped the stone in his fist, determined to solve all these mysteries.

ONCE THE ROOM was empty, Hannah pulled out of Jonathan's embrace and returned to her desk to create some space between them. Why was she so flustered? This situation was out of the normal, yes, but so were the past seventeen years. And this was Jonathan. The man who'd treated her like she was someone special ever since they'd met two years ago. The man who stayed by her side through her mother's cancer scare. Well, maybe not physically by her side, he did have a business to run, but any time she called, he listened. He brought Hannah her favorite treats when she didn't have the energy to cook, especially the cinnamon cookies she craved from a bakery near the art gallery or the savory vegetable soup from a trendy bistro she visited whenever she was in town. He made sure to make her mother feel special by bringing her flowers when she was at her lowest. But best of all, he supported her decisions without questioning her abilities. Jonathan. Her fiancé.

But he's not Derrick.

She groaned at the inner voice taunting her. She was awful. A terrible girlfriend. And really ticked by the doubts creeping into her heart.

At Jonathan's voice she snapped out of her reverie. "I'm sorry?"

"I said if your mom is up to it, we should go to Luigi's for dinner."

"She'd like that." Hannah eyed her desk. "I have a few more things to do and then we can leave."

"No rush," Jonathan said, kindness in his eyes. "I didn't mean to come across so strong, but it was a surprise to find you'd reconnected with an old friend. Especially since you insist you can't have anything to do with your past." He stopped a beat. "Did you neglect to tell me about him because you two were more than friends at one time?"

Her jaw dropped. "Why on earth would you think that?"

Jonathan's gaze locked on hers. "I couldn't miss the way he looked at you."

Her stomach twisted. She'd never wanted to keep Derrick a secret from her fiancé, but she was still coming to terms with his sudden re-entry in her life. "I meant to tell you. But I was focused on Mom's last treatment and you've been so busy with the upcoming show, I never got a chance."

"You must have known for a while. It looks like he's working here."

"First day."

"Huh."

"I was just as surprised as you are," she hurried to say, trying to keep her frazzled emotions in check.

His mouth thinned. In disapproval?

"Okay, meeting Derrick like this was…awkward," she allowed.

With a chuckle Jonathan walked over and placed a kiss on her cheek. "Indeed."

Pushing thoughts of Derrick out of her head—well, trying anyway—she returned the kiss. "So, we're making plans tonight?"

"Don't you think we should start?"

"I suppose. We haven't set a date."

"Which we need to rectify."

Hannah stuffed papers she needed to grade

into the tote and gathered up odds and ends while Jonathan strolled around the classroom.

"Why do I have the feeling you've been working on the details without me?" she teased.

"Two reasons. We need to pick a venue. I think the gallery would be perfect, but then, I'm biased."

Hannah agreed. The gallery was elegant and would actually be a wonderful place to exchange vows.

He turned to face her. "And because as much as I'm concerned about your mother, I haven't been on the emotional rollercoaster of seeing her go through the treatments. I understand that you've had your focus on her—I wouldn't expect anything less." He held up a hand to stave her next words. "It's okay, Anna. Now that she's finished the treatments, we have to get serious about making arrangements."

"Sure." She took a breath as Jonathan continued walking around the room. "Thank you for understanding. You're right, the past few months have been a challenge. You seem to handle stress better than me."

He glanced over his shoulder. "I have perspective."

She was glad someone did.

He continued to amble, stopping from time to time to admire the artwork displayed on the walls. "I see my tutelage has improved your students' command of drawing."

Hannah wasn't sure most of her fourth graders cared about mastering drawing skills; they were just happy when they got a break from math and spelling. "I appreciate you sharing your passion. I hope some of the kids are inspired to create art."

He turned to walk back to the desk and winked. "Sure, they will."

She grinned. Jonathan thought everyone in his orbit shared the same exhilaration for art as he did. Granted, she wasn't immersed in that field as much as she'd one day dreamed she would be, but attending new artists' showings at Jonathan's gallery kept her tethered to creative endeavors to some degree.

Her gaze fell on her open day planner. "I told you I'm taking the class to Styles Museum of Arts and Crafts next week. You should come."

"As much as I'd like to, you know I've been busy. Discovering two talented artists mere weeks from each other has taken over my schedule."

"Well, if you get a break, we'd love to have you."

He stopped on the other side of the desk as she shrugged into her coat. "You are coming to the showing Wednesday night?" he asked.

"I wouldn't miss it."

Last fall, Hannah had stopped into a coffee shop around the corner from the gallery and been drawn into conversation with Layla, a barista working there. They began talking about painting and Layla confessed she was a struggling artist. She'd pulled out her phone to show Hannah some of her creations and Hannah knew right then and there that Layla was gifted with exceptional talent. Once she convinced Jonathan to take a look and he viewed Layla's canvases, he was as smitten with her talent as much as Hannah. It had taken months of preparation, but now Jonathan was ready to reveal his newest discovery—as he referred to Layla, even though Hannah had talked to her first—to the public. Layla's watercolors were otherworldly, much like the waif of a girl herself. Hannah couldn't wait to watch her career take off.

"I'd come pick you up but I'll be at the gallery, preparing for the event."

"I figured as much. Lynny and I will be there as soon as we can get away. I don't expect much of a holdup after Mom's follow-up scan, but I want to be there to support you."

The excitement in his eyes dimmed for a flash, then went back to normal. She wasn't sure if he was unhappy about the possibility of her running late or bringing Lynny along. "Of course. Your mother comes first."

"Thanks."

"Michelle will be there to help me greet guests."

At the mention of Jonathan's assistant, Hannah went cold. There was something…predatory about that woman.

"And if you want to invite your other friend…"

He wanted her to bring Derrick? No way. She was having a hard enough time dealing with his reappearance as it was. She wasn't about to let him get more ingrained in her routine. Especially at her fiancé's new showcase.

"No, it'll just be Lynny and me."

Again, the slight show of displeasure.

"Is there a problem with her coming?"

"No, I just get the feeling she doesn't approve of us."

Hannah never got that vibe. "You couldn't be more wrong."

He shrugged. "Still, I don't mind more people attending."

Back to Derrick? "Really, Jonathan, I'm not sure Derrick tagging along would be a good idea."

"Why? You're only old friends, correct?"

How to answer that question? It wasn't that Hannah had kept the truth from Jonathan, she just hadn't told him anything about her previous life. She'd explained that her father had gotten into legal trouble. That they were broke and unsure of the future. That she and her mother had decided they should build a new life, away from the problems that had torn their family apart. Jonathan had understood. Hadn't pushed for more when she put brakes on the conversation. He definitely didn't suspect that her name was an alias or that she'd once been engaged to another man. He'd been fine with what she'd confided, until now. Because of Derrick suddenly showing up?

He skirted the desk and stood before her. "Anna, you are my love and I trust you completely. I only want you to be happy."

Tears prickled the backs of her eyes. This wonderful man deserved better than she'd given him. Should she lay it on the line? Tell him the truth? Or would he run from her as fast as he could?

"I do love you, Jonathan."

She smothered a cringe. Even she could hear the *but* in her tone.

"That's all I ask."

He leaned down to kiss her when a chirpy voice broke the spell.

"Look at you two lovebirds."

Jonathan tensed and moved away. "As usual your timing is impeccable."

Hannah playfully tapped his arm.

"Hey, what can I say?" Lynny replied without rancor. "I'm talented like that."

Jonathan returned his attention to Hannah. "Sweetheart, I'll meet you at your house."

"I'm right behind you," Hannah answered, her eyes glued to the stately bearing of his shoulders as he left the room.

"Really, could he be any more stuffy?" Lynny asked.

Hannah chuckled. "You're just jealous."

Her friend let out a gusty sigh. "Guilty." She pulled herself from her pity party and said, "So, what are you going to do?"

"About what?"

Lynny sent her a *don't even* glare.

"Plan a wedding."

"Good try. I meant about your old flame and your fiancé."

"Why do I have to do anything?"

"Please don't tell me you're that naive."

Hannah sent her a blank look.

"C'mon. Surely you know Derrick wants to win you back."

Hannah ignored the increase in her pulse. Those words shouldn't give her as much pleasure as they did. "How did you come to that conclusion?"

"Because I have eyes. And I'm observant. From the first second I met Derrick I knew he still wants a relationship with you. And Jonathan? He pretty much drew an imaginary line in the sand. You, my friend, have a dilemma."

Her stomach flopped at the thought.

"I didn't ask Derrick to come here."

"No, but he's here and if I'm any judge of character, he's not going away."

"Lynny, I am getting married."

"Are you? You've been engaged what, six months? No engagement party. No mention to our coworkers." Lynny grabbed her left hand and held it up. "And you rarely wear his ring to school."

"I don't like wearing it here. Between the chalk dust and the glue and chasing after animals, I don't want to ruin it."

"It's platinum. A nuclear explosion couldn't destroy it."

"Still, I…"

"Have an answer for everything."

Hannah slumped, growing warm under her heavy coat. "If you'd asked me a few days ago if I was excited about planning a wedding, I would have said yes."

Crossing her arms over her chest, Lynny stared her down.

"I would have," she protested. "But I will admit, Derrick showing up out of the blue has created a little…hiccup."

"Hiccup?" Lynny burst out laughing.

"Okay, honest truth. I'm a little unnerved by the situation."

"Spoken like a woman with two guys after her. If only I was so lucky."

"I don't think I'd call this luck."

Lynny dropped her arms, then gave Hannah a big hug. "It'll work out."

Would it? Jonathan wanted to set a wedding date. Derrick looked at her with the same fire in his eyes she remembered from when they were teens. "How on earth am I going to plan a wedding to Jonathan when Derrick is hanging around and throwing me off-balance?"

Lynny pulled back. "Thankfully you have me and your mom to stand by you. I believe deep down, you'll know the right thing to do."

She pictured Derrick's beloved face. Heard Jonathan's velvety voice telling her he wanted her to be happy.

Why all of this now?

She grabbed her scarf to wrap around her

neck before venturing out into the icy air, wishing she could truly say she was happy instead of majorly confused.

CHAPTER FIVE

EVENING SHADOWS GREW LONG and distorted Wednesday evening as Hannah steered her car onto the wet highway leading to Carson City. A love song played on the radio, which Hannah pointedly tuned out. She didn't need reminders of what was. She and Derrick had had their chance. Now she was with Jonathan. She was content, convincing herself that Derrick showing up out of the blue hadn't thrown her off-balance.

As she clicked on the headlights, Lynny asked, "How did the scan go today?"

"We won't know until the doctor's appointment next week." Hannah smiled despite the ache that had set up permanent residence in her chest. She'd be relieved when they learned the outcome of the last scan and returned to their new normal. "You should have seen Mom. Every day since the treatments have ended she's been picking up strength. You would have thought she was there for a party instead of a test this afternoon."

"That's your mom." Lynny shivered and rubbed her hands together. The temperature still hovered around thirty degrees outside. "She doesn't mind missing the opening-night exhibit?"

Hannah reached over to adjust the heat. "This is really just a preparty, invite only. The official public viewing starts Friday night."

"I'm excited. You've gone on and on about the artist's work."

"Layla is talented. I wouldn't be surprised if she makes a big splash in the art world."

Her friend twisted in the passenger seat to face Hannah. "Why do I hear a hint of envy in your voice?"

Hannah shrugged. "I've always been interested in art. I guess I thought I'd work in that field. Find raw talent like Jonathan does." She chuckled. "Not become a teacher."

Lynny's smile faded. After all, she'd gotten Hannah the job at Ponderosa Day School. "You don't like teaching?"

Hannah wrestled with her answer for a drawn-out moment. Listed the pro and cons in her mind. "I do. I love the expressions on the children's faces when they understand a new concept or discover a special book or can locate a country we're discussing on the map." A thought occurred to her. "In a way, seeing the excitement on my students' faces when they learn something new is like watching the public discover a new artist. Both bring a deep satisfaction."

"Is that why you were attracted to Jonathan? Because of the gallery?"

"I suppose. At first."

She thought back to their first meeting. Just before school went back into session after summer break two years ago, Hannah had taken a rare day to herself and ventured to Carson City. She'd shopped, treated herself to a fabulous lunch and just meandered downtown, gazing in store windows. When she happened upon the Prescott Gallery, it didn't take much of a push for her to venture inside. She'd never forget the echo of her heels on the marble floor as she moved about the quiet room, admiring the exhibits staged in a way to entice the viewer. Colorful paintings, landscapes mixed in with still life and abstract, were mounted on the stark white walls. Pottery and sculptures crafted by local artisans were strategically set out on pedestals or long tables, meant to catch the eye. The sound of a voice in the back room was muffled, until Jonathan emerged to greet Hannah, a potential customer. Certainly not a love interest.

He'd been solicitous, friendly and so knowledgeable as they chatted that Hannah couldn't squelch the disappointment at not being a part of this world. But soon, Jonathan invited her to different events, informed her when a new artist showed work at his gallery and before she knew it, they were dating. He was smart, handsome and fun to be with, coming into her life when she'd finally decided she wanted more than a friend.

"I'll be honest, Lynny, I never thought Jonathan would take an interest in me. Not that I'm complaining."

"I don't know why you do that."

Hannah took her gaze from the road for a split second to catch Lynny's expression. "Do what?"

"Act like you aren't special. Like it's a big surprise that someone like Jonathan would fall in love with you. You are engaged."

"I didn't realize…" Hannah bit her lip. True, she and Jonathan had gone over details for the ceremony and reception at dinner the other night. He'd been excited to take the lead, but also very interested in her suggestions. "I just never thought I'd fall in love again. It sort of surprised me."

"Derrick had that much of a hold on you?"

He had. For many years. Despite the anger.

"Think back to your first love. Tell me what you remember."

"Laughing," Lynny answered, her voice light. "I met Sam in college. We clicked and our time together was like a brightly burning light."

"What happened?"

"The light dimmed."

Hannah caught Lynny's shrug out of the corner of her eye. "It wasn't a bad breakup or a horrible situation that drew us apart. It was gradual and sad. But I have wonderful memories."

"It's not the same for Derrick and me." She blew out a breath. "Because of something Derrick did, my family paid the price. So there was no closure. No goodbyes. No way to make things right. I'm just not sure I can forgive him."

"Seems like he's trying to make amends."

Could he ever do enough to make up for the upheaval he caused her family? She'd lost her dreams, her dad and her future, because he hadn't kept his promise. "I think it's too late."

"Because you have Jonathan now?"

"And a good life here. I love my students, my mother will get well and I have wonderful friends, especially you." Maybe things hadn't turned out so horrible after all. Unexpected, for sure, but not horrible. "What more could I ask for?"

Even though Derrick was law enforcement, she wasn't nervous around him like she had been with the Marshals. It wasn't as if she'd done anything wrong. She hadn't taken the gemstones, and if Derrick insisted on investigating where the one he'd received had come from, no way would she stop him. In fact, if Derrick found who had sent him the stone, then maybe it would lead him to find the other gems and she could go back to being Hannah. A wonderful thought, but he didn't have much to go on, so for the foreseeable future, she would remain Anna.

An upbeat song, with a lively drumbeat and a cool brass section, came over the airwaves. Hannah turned up the dial and they both sang along. Once the tune finished, Lynny adjusted the volume. They were close to the city now, ten minutes from the gallery.

"I have to ask you something," Lynny said, her tone tentative.

"By the sound of your voice I'm guessing I might not like it."

"No, it's nothing bad." She glanced out the window and back again. "Are you one-hundred-percent certain about marrying Jonathan?"

"Of course."

"I only ask because Derrick showing up was unexpected and, well, I feel like you'll never be truly committed to Jonathan if you don't get that closure you talked about."

Could Lynny be onto something? She wanted to marry Jonathan, but perhaps she needed a little time to move on from Derrick and the past. Not that she wanted to be with Derrick; that ship had sailed, right? Right? Good grief, why was she even thinking this way?

"I get what you're saying and you're not off base. I do need that closure in order to move on with my future." She eased down the ramp and picked up speed on the main thoroughfare leading to the gallery. Interior lights came on in businesses along the route as the night sky settled into deep tones of purple and navy. A cherry glow emanated from the streetlamps dotting the way to her destination. "Maybe it's a good thing Derrick came to town. Now we can say what needs to be said and I can marry Jonathan without any regrets."

Hannah found a parking spot in the public lot. She gathered her purse and slipped on gloves before exiting the warm confines of the car to brave the frigid night air. Avoiding icy patches, she and Lynny speed walked the block to the gallery.

"That was perceptive of you," Hannah told

her friend. "About getting closure before marrying Jonathan."

"I just call 'em like I see 'em."

"Yeah? And how are things progressing with Mr. Garver, the cute gym teacher at Ponderosa?"

The corners of Lynny's lips angled down. "Roger and I are still in the friend zone."

"So there's still a chance?"

"I suppose."

Hannah threw her arm around Lynny's slumped shoulders. "Just give it time."

"You think?"

"I call 'em like I see 'em?"

That got a laugh out of Lynny. "You're a good friend."

"Back at ya."

A lively group of people had just entered the gallery before they walked up. Hannah grabbed the door to hold it open for Lynny before following her inside. As they stepped just beyond the door, Hannah unwound her scarf and shrugged out of her heavy coat, stuffing her gloves in the pockets. She'd just draped it over her arm when a cultured voice greeted her.

"Anna. You made it."

She grinned when Jonathan came her way. He wore a dark suit that made him more handsome than usual. "I said I'd be here." She went on tiptoes to kiss his cheek. "And I must say,

I've only just walked in, but the gallery looks beautiful."

"I wouldn't have been able to get this done without Michelle."

At her name, a slim woman in a tight black dress, her dark hair pulled back into a chignon and her makeup flawlessly applied, joined them.

"You're too sweet, Jonathan." Michelle's eyes grew frosty and her voice cold when she greeted Hannah. "So glad you made it."

Hannah smiled back despite the cool reception. "I wouldn't miss this."

As Michelle viewed Hannah's outfit, a shimmery silver dress with tall black boots, she wrinkled her nose. Hannah, insecure whenever she was with this very fashion-forward woman, tucked a few stray hairs into the knot at the back of her neck. She'd added dangly black earrings and a chunky black necklace to her ensemble, but suddenly she felt like she was wearing a paper bag.

"I hope I look all right," she said in a low voice for only Jonathan's ears. Years of hiding out and downplaying her appearance to avoid her past made her a bit apprehensive about her clothing choices.

"You'll be fine," he said with a flick of his wrist. "Tonight the art is all anyone will notice."

Hannah tried not to let his words sting, but

she understood what he meant. This wasn't a fashion show. People were here to discover a new artist. She blew out a breath, glad he hadn't said she was totally off base. After being at the hospital this afternoon and then rushing home to change for tonight's event, she'd thought she'd done a decent job choosing her outfit.

Jonathan took Hannah's coat then handed it off to Michelle, who frowned at the exchange. He took Hannah's hand and placed it in the crook of his elbow. "A tour, sweetheart?"

"I can't wait."

Lynny waved them off.

Just as Hannah had expected, Layla's watercolors were magical. There were eight canvases in all, professionally matted and framed. Each was strategically placed, allowing plenty of room for admirers to gather and critique the piece. Three small works were grouped together to create a focal point. Subdued lighting dimmed the gallery, except for bright spotlights positioned to illuminate each canvas. The colors reached out and grabbed Hannah as she scrutinized them, touching a place in her soul she only felt when surrounded by undeniable talent.

"Where is our gifted artist?" Hannah asked after they'd stopped by two of the pieces.

"Hiding in the back, I'm afraid. She's nervous." He pulled up the cuff of his jacket to view his Rolex. "I'm going to introduce her in a few minutes. If you don't mind, I should give Layla a pep talk."

"Of course. Go on. I'm going to keep admiring her work."

He brushed his lips over her cheek in a distracted motion, hurrying off in a trail of his expensive cologne. She waited until he'd disappeared into the crowd before moving on to the next piece. Hannah studied the breathtaking snippets of the mountain town Layla had captured with her keen eye. The colors were bright, the brushstrokes whimsical and the lighting airy. The theme seemed to be friendship, whether the artist captured two friends in a scene or an entire group of people, there was no disguising the joy of being surrounded by others.

Hannah swallowed hard, taken aback by the canvases. Was it because she understood the importance of belonging when she hadn't for so many years? Being in WITSEC had isolated her, first out of fear, then later out of practicality. As her family moved from one place to another, it hurt too much to make friends and then leave them. And when her father left? That had been the cruelest blow of all. Loneliness had been a constant companion until she and her mother came to Nevada and put down roots. Things had turned around then.

She reached the end of the circuit, studying the grouping. As she moved closer to get a better look at one piece in particular, she noticed a couple on bicycles racing off from the group of friends. A memory flashed in her mind, reminding her of the times she and Derrick would leave their friends to ride their bikes to the beach. Truth be told, they'd had more fun when it was just the two of them, heading off on one adventure or another.

A nostalgic smile curved her lips. They'd had the best times. But that was so long ago, before events had thrown them a curveball.

"There you are," Lynny said as she came up beside Hannah.

Blinking back the memories and the sting in her eyes, Hannah managed a smile.

"Look who I found," her friend said, stepping aside as another person joined them.

Hannah's heart froze as Derrick approached, dressed in a charcoal suit and wild-patterned tie, his distinctive blue eyes alight with his lips curved in a secret smile. Her breath caught in her throat and she shivered all the way down to her toes. How unfair that he was the most handsome man in the room.

Even more handsome than Jonathan? an inner voice taunted.

Yes.

Oh boy, she was in trouble.

DERRICK HAD STOPPED SHORT when he'd first spotted Hannah in the gallery. In this lighting, she was beautiful. Better than any daydream he'd had in the years he'd searched for her. He still couldn't believe he'd found her, but the obstacles to their relationship, whatever they turned out to be, were far from resolved. He needed to remember that.

As Lynny wandered off, he slowed as he reached her. "You look gorgeous."

"Thanks," she said as she smoothed her dress, an uncertain frown marring her forehead.

"Please tell me you haven't gotten more than one compliment tonight."

A pretty blush covered her cheeks. "You're the first."

"I find that hard to believe."

She held out her hands palms up, as if to say, *It's the truth.*

"Then I'm glad I told you."

Her smile dimmed. "Derrick, what are you doing here?"

He tried not to let her reaction bother him. He had hoped this would be a pleasant surprise.

"Jonathan invited me the other day when he left the school."

"Oh. He didn't tell me."

Trouble in paradise? No way was he getting that lucky.

"I guess he forgot since he's been busy getting tonight's exhibit together." He gestured to the paintings. "The artist is quite talented."

"She is." Hannah glanced over her shoulder. "Um, have you seen Jonathan?"

"He's been talking to potential clients."

She nodded, biting her lower lip.

"So," he asked, "are you familiar with the artist?"

"Yes. I actually met her first."

Now it was his turn to be surprised. "You discovered her?"

"In a way. I met Layla in a coffee shop where she works and after chatting a while, she mentioned her artwork. When she pulled out her phone and showed me a few pictures, I knew people needed to see her watercolors."

"I'm impressed."

"Because in your job you see wonderful works of art all the time?"

He heard the frustration there and understood. The art world had been her dream. "Not always. Most of the time I'm investigating, not taking in gallery shows."

She tilted her head. "But you do frequent galleries, right?"

"Again, in an investigative capacity."

"Have you worked on any cases I might have heard of?"

He mentioned the case of a priceless painting going missing from a museum in New York City.

"Wow," she gasped. "I remember following that story on the news. Did you ever find it?"

"About a year later. The thief got tired of waiting for his payday and we staged a sting when he tried to sell it."

Her eyes went dreamy. "You must find your job so interesting."

"I do, but most of the time it's a job. Long hours asking questions, following leads and doing paperwork. Hardly as glamorous as you'd imagine."

"Still, I'd—"

"Sweetheart, there you are." Prescott swooped in and handed her a glass of wine before circling his arm around Hannah's waist. It was all Derrick could do not to snap the stem of the glass he was holding.

"Fields. You made it." Prescott held out his hand and Derrick shook.

"Thanks for the invite." Derrick nodded at the group assembled. "Good turnout for a Wednesday night."

"Better than we'd hoped." Prescott grinned. "I have quite a knack for finding talent."

Derrick's gaze moved to Hannah's but she quickly glanced away. Yeah, her boyfriend not mentioning her part in the discovery had to hurt.

"Congratulations."

Prescott smiled, then turned his attention to Hannah. "Have you told Lynny our plans?"

"A bit," Hannah replied, her face turning red again.

"Wedding plans?" Derrick asked, because really, why else would Prescott mention it except to rub his nose in it.

"Yes. We're thinking of exchanging vows here at the gallery."

Derrick's eyebrows rose. "Here? I'm surprised."

The gallery owner looked annoyed. "Why is that?"

"I remember Hannah wanted an outdoor wedding."

Prescott jerked his gaze to Hannah. "Why didn't you say anything?"

She shrugged. "I love the gallery."

Hmm, Derrick thought. *A lot unsaid there.*

"You discussed wedding plans with your friend?"

"It was a long time ago," she explained, sending Derrick a *keep quiet* look. "Just high school friends talking."

Prescott looked dubious. "You must have been very good friends."

Hannah continued to appear uncomfortable at the direction of the conversation. Derrick decided to cut her some slack. "Yeah, we were at the time. But now it looks like she's found happiness."

Prescott sent him a pointed message. "Indeed. And I intend to keep it that way for many years to come."

"Yes, you do," she said, patting her fiancé's chest. Derrick wanted to reach for her hand, but instead kept his muscles in check so he wouldn't do anything foolish.

A striking woman approached and spoke quietly into Prescott's ear. He nodded and removed his arm from Hannah. "If you'll both excuse me, a potential buyer needs my attention."

Hannah waved her hand. "Go."

"Yeah," Derrick added. "I'm sure we can keep each other company."

Prescott scowled and an annoyed light flashed in the other woman's eyes. Interesting.

A few moments of awkwardness passed before Derrick said, "Since you know the artist, why not give me a tour of her work."

"Sure." Hannah held out her arm and led him to the nearest canvas. Her vanilla scent ignited his senses. He wanted more than anything to draw her close, to rediscover the romance that had once mesmerized them like magic. "Her technique with lighting is quite moving."

Derrick agreed, appreciating Hannah's insight. There was a boldness in the strokes and paint colors that captured his attention. "She's taken command of the scene she created."

"Which is surprising in a way. She's quiet, reserved even and very modest, but she obviously lets her big personality loose when she's painting."

It was agony not to take Hannah's hand as they continued to discuss the other pieces before ending up on the far side of the gallery, away from the crowd. Folks lingered around the refreshment table after having viewed the work, and chatted, leaving Hannah and him relatively alone.

"Derrick, how long is this going to go on?"

He knew what she meant. Why was he hanging around when she'd clearly moved on? She was getting married soon. At least, that was the plan.

"I told you, Hannah—"

Her eyes went wide.

"Anna," he amended. "I need answers about who sent the gemstone and why."

"And you can't do that in DC?"

"Not when whoever delivered it brought me here. There must be a reason."

He saw that she wanted to argue, but what could she say?

"Aren't you the least bit curious as to what's going on?" he asked. "Why send me this information now?"

She tucked a stray curl that lingered on her cheek back into her hairdo. He wanted to reach over and touch her hair, let his fingers linger on her soft skin as he brushed the curl away, but knew Hannah wouldn't appreciate the gesture. Not here, in her boyfriend's gallery.

"I'll admit, the timing is odd. I mean, I've been gone for ages. Why would someone think you'd want to find me now?"

"Are you kidding?"

She tilted her head. "You weren't serious when you said you never stopped looking for me, were you?"

He moved closer, his gaze locked on hers. "Dead serious. But my dedication only led to one disappointment after another."

"I just…there was no one else in your life?"

He wasn't about to admit there'd been a time when he'd almost moved on. "You're hard to forget." He turned to look across the room at Prescott holding court. "But I guess you had it easy getting over me."

"That's not fair. I honestly never thought we'd cross paths again." Her fingers trembled when she set her glass on a nearby table. "And that was fine, since I was angry with you. But as time passed, I realized there was no way you could find me with a new name. How on earth would you have access to WITSEC? You couldn't."

"So you never imagined me sweeping in to save the day?"

"If I did, it was wishful wishing."

"I never stopped missing you. Wanting you. Hoping things had turned out differently." He fisted his hand in frustration. "I thought you stayed away because you didn't want to see me."

She opened her mouth, then closed it. It looked as if she was debating her words. "Yes, we made promises. Had our entire future before us." Her eyes turned glassy in the bright light. "But the longer we were apart, the more apparent it became that we were over. My family took precedence, Derrick. Decisions were made that moved you and me farther and farther from each other. This is my reality now."

He couldn't deny that truth. "So Prescott is the guy for you?"

She nodded. "He's been there. Ever since we met and later when Mom got sick. He's a good man."

"You love him?"

"You've met him. How could I not?"

"That's not an answer."

She pressed her lips together. He remembered that stubborn expression.

"Derrick, it's been too long. We can't be in each other's lives now," she continued. "We must accept that."

"Have you ever known me to give up on something?"

"I'm not a *something*."

"You're the love I never stopped looking for."

Teardrops sparkled on her lashes. "This isn't fair."

"Sometimes we get a raw deal. It's how we handle the tough circumstances that makes all the difference. That leads to a positive outcome."

"Which is finding out who sent the gemstone and why?"

"For starters."

"Then I guess that means you're here for the foreseeable future?"

He shot her his cockiest grin. "You always were smart."

CHAPTER SIX

AFTER A SLEEPLESS NIGHT replaying her conversation with Derrick at the gallery, Hannah woke up groggy and out of sorts. The day didn't get any better. It was like her students sensed her weakness and played off it. By four o'clock she didn't think Thursday would ever end. And to make matters worse, tonight was the winter session parent-teacher night.

Tidying a pile of papers on her desk, she blew out a sigh.

Derrick wasn't going away any time soon. He'd told her that he was going to keep investigating the circumstances surrounding the gemstone. It made sense. Probing for answers was his job. His nature. But for Hannah, a myriad of questions hounded her the more she thought about it. How did he expect to find out where the stone came from? Did he have leads he hadn't told her about? Could his digging into the past create danger in the present? And the big question, was he going to keep her informed of his progress? Or go behind her back to handle the situation like he had before?

Here lies the rub. On the one hand, she wanted him to keep his distance. She was engaged to Jonathan. But on the other, she was as curious as he was to find out why someone had sent the gemstone now, after years of hiding it. What made the timing so special?

This entire scenario would make a great suspense movie if she wasn't actually living it. At that thought, a shiver racked her body. She grabbed the bulky sweater from the back of her chair to throw on over her denim shirtdress. Thankfully her feet were warm inside her knee-high boots. As she told her mother regularly, winter was not for the feeble of heart, especially with the vast amount of snow that had blanketed the area this winter.

Her cell phone dinged. Pushing aside her wayward thoughts, she checked the incoming text. Jonathan, making sure she'd be at the official exhibit tomorrow night.

Hannah stared at the screen, uncertain. She wanted to support Layla, but before she'd left the gallery last night, she'd gotten the feeling that Jonathan wasn't happy with her. She didn't get a chance to ask why, but she sensed it had to do with Derrick. She hadn't invited him to the opening, Jonathan had, so why be ticked at her? Okay, maybe she'd spent a little longer than was appropriate talking to him, but in all fairness, Jonathan had been working and left her on her own a lot. What was she supposed to do, wait quietly until he was finished with his clients? She knew how important the show was, both for the gallery and the artist. There was no way she would have interfered with their special night, which meant keeping to the sidelines. Just so happened Derrick had decided to hang out there with her.

Which brought her back to the reasons why she couldn't sleep last night. Yes, Derrick was ridiculously handsome and still as fun as she remembered. But there was such a huge history between them, not all good. She was honest enough with herself to admit she'd missed him, but her mind had moved on. Had her heart? And if she still had deep, lingering feelings for Derrick, shouldn't she figure that out now? Jonathan deserved to know the truth.

If she had the answers. Which she didn't. All she was certain of was that Derrick was the past and Jonathan was the future.

So yeah, she had to decide if she would attend Layla's public gallery show. With a firm shake of her head, she set the phone down on the desk surface. She'd deal with this later. Now she had parents to get ready for.

On the blackboard, Hannah noted what the students were currently learning in their grade-level curriculum. Next, she gathered the packets she'd made specifically for tonight, containing copies of the children's work to go over with their parents. She surveyed the room, happy with the results. Most of the parents were wonderful to work with, so she wasn't expecting any conflict. Okay, make that much conflict. There was always that one person who wasn't happy with anything she did.

She heard Lynny's voice out in the hallway just before her friend swooped into the room with a large takeout bag.

"Up for Chinese?"

"As long as I don't have to cook, anything is fine."

Lynny took out the containers and placed them on two of the front desks. The zesty scent of chicken and vegetables had Hannah's stomach growling. Both of them took a seat and dug in. Hannah realized she was famished.

"Did you eat anything today?" Lynny asked as she watched Hannah wolf down her food.

"I had a quick lunch that wasn't very filling. These meetings stress me out."

"I hear you. The kids were especially excited today. By midafternoon I just let them have free time so they could burn off their energy."

"Same here. At least we didn't lose Sally today. After the last escape attempt, Tommy has been hyperdiligent in making sure she doesn't leave her cage."

"I thought Derrick fixed the cage?"

She swallowed after taking a bite. "He did. Even got Tommy to help him."

Lynny laughed. "Derrick's like a father duck with little ducklings following him around. Only in his case, they're ten-year-olds. It's so cute."

Too cute, as far as Hannah was concerned. She appreciated his help, a little too much. When he'd volunteered to lend a hand in her classroom, coming across so sincere, she couldn't send him away.

"What's that frown about?" Lynny asked.

Hannah rested her fork in the food container. "When he and I were kids, Derrick had a way of getting me to go along with his schemes. In my mind I'd be ready to say no and the next thing I knew, I was off getting into mischief with him." Nostalgia made her smile. "Seems that hasn't changed."

Lynny chuckled. "He does have a way with people. Yesterday he got the principal to sign off on new traffic cones to make the car line easier, then went to the store to pick them up. I heard he's been staying after school to watch basketball practice, encouraging the boys to up their game."

"He's always been competitive. Probably because he has three brothers. I can remember them going at it over sports or cars or girls."

"When is he starting on the to-do list at your house?"

"He mentioned stopping by on Saturday."

"Think he'd mind if I nabbed him for a while? My kitchen faucet is acting weird and Mr. Bartholomew went out of town to visit his grandkids."

Hannah shrugged, purposely keeping a calm demeanor. It wouldn't bode well to let Lynny stir the pot just to get a rise out of her. "Fine by me. I'm not his priority."

Her friend sent her a sly glance. "You don't mind if I offer to make him dinner?"

Yeah. Pot stirrer.

Hannah swallowed her irritation. "What about Roger?"

"What about him? No calls. No invites to school functions. I swear the other day he ran down the hall in the opposite direction when he saw me."

Hannah lowered her carton. "What did you do to the man?"

Lynny's expression turned sheepish. "Suggested that maybe we quit the dancing around and go out on a date."

Hannah nearly choked on her vegetables. She coughed, then said, "That was direct?"

"I wasn't asking him to marry me, it's just a date. He was taking too long." Lynny set down her carton, her expression earnest. "We have a vibe, Anna. I know he feels it, too. And things were going okay until the principal asked us to work together on a school project. I said yes right away." She paused. Stared into the air and grimaced. "Maybe I was too zealous with my answer. Anyway, Roger agreed, but I think maybe I scared him off."

"I don't know about that. He's pretty confident." Hannah pointed her fork at her friend. "School project aside, maybe he wanted to ease into asking you."

"It's possible. I do tend to jump into situations before thinking."

"Like the time you took me to the lake, rented a sailboat, then proceeded to take out your phone and Google how to sail?"

Lynny grinned. "Exactly like that. You know, we're opposites. You research everything to the nth degree before you start something. Well, everything except art, but you're more cautious than I am." She picked up her carton and poked her fork around her noodles. "I guess that's why you and Jonathan suit each other."

Surprised by Lynny's remark, Hannah asked, "You think Jonathan is cautious? He takes risks on artists all the time."

"For his job. But whenever you mention doing something new, he resists. Like when you wanted to go hiking. You found the best trails, bought the best boots and the day before you were supposed to go, he canceled."

"He had a client meeting."

"Which he could have scheduled for another day. It was a big step for you to arrange an outing. I think that was the first time you finally seemed settled enough here to go out and explore. When you and your mom first moved here, you hesitated to go anywhere. You asked me over for dinner or to watch a movie. I have to admit, I thought someone was after you and you were hiding out."

Hannah bit the inside of her cheek.

"But then you got comfortable and started doing things. I hated that Jonathan let you down. You were so excited."

"I don't know what you're complaining about. Because he canceled you got to go hiking with me."

"No offense, but if it were me, I would have wanted to go with my boyfriend."

Hannah couldn't argue her point. She had wanted to spend the day with Jonathan, but respected the fact that he had a business to run. If it had only been that one time, Lynny wouldn't have commented on it, but he'd canceled last minute on several occasions.

"He's not an outdoorsy kind of guy."

Lynny shook her carton and fished for the last of her food. "Did he ever make up for bailing on you?"

"Yes. He took me to an art lecture at the university."

Lynny rolled her eyes. "A lecture? How romantic."

"It was. I enjoyed the speaker. We had fun."

"Then I guess it really does work for you two."

"Why would you even doubt it?"

"I don't know. You've seemed a little more…" Lynny waved her fork in the air as she searched for the right word. "Animated since Derrick's been around."

Hannah felt her shoulders go stiff. "If I have it has nothing to do with him."

"Are you sure?"

"I am," she said a little too strongly.

"Because he seems to like hanging out in your classroom."

"That only happened three times and he was talking to the kids about sports."

"Three times, huh?"

She sent her friend her best teacher frown. "I'm not keeping count."

Lynny rose and gathered up the empty containers. "No, but I bet he is."

"Would you stop. Derrick and I are just old friends."

"Whatever you say."

Hannah tossed her crumpled napkin into the bag. "I'm not having this conversation with you."

Lynny smirked and hightailed it from the room.

Still, her friend's words hung in the air.

Oh, who was Hannah kidding? She liked seeing Derrick interact with the students. He had a natural ease about him and the children picked up on it. They teased and laughed, yet he still commanded their respect. Hannah knew much of what Derrick taught the kids was a direct result of his own upbringing. Mr. Matthews had made sure his sons were polite, respectful and compassionate to others. Hannah had liked that about the Matthews family.

But since he'd walked back into her life, Hannah also noticed an alertness about Derrick. He was sizing up any situation he found himself in, even the classroom. Did he expect bad guys to come barging in during school hours? She attributed his intensity to his law enforcement roots. She had to admit, after all she and her family had been through, his attentiveness was extremely attractive. He made her feel safe, even if he was just stopping by to say hello. It was a feeling she hadn't experienced in a very long time.

Then there was Jonathan. Well versed in art, but not a bit snobby when it came to that world. He laughed a lot and Hannah had missed that after the years of tension when her family moved around. He was kind and supportive about her profession, but his stiff approach when he spoke to her class was the opposite of the effortlessness Derrick radiated. Jonathan didn't connect. Came off a bit stuffy. Hannah had reasoned it was because he was so passionate about his calling that he forgot to bring the topic down to the kids' level. Still, he was happy to come to the school anytime she asked.

And why was she even comparing the two men? They both had their strengths and weaknesses. She was marrying Jonathan, so she shouldn't be entertaining these thoughts. It was Lynny's fault, she decided. Then expelled images of both men from her head and focused on the meeting to come.

Before long, parents started to arrive. They milled about the classroom, studying art projects taped to the wall, reading compositions tacked to the corkboard, or reviewing the class pet's daily routine. Hannah went over the class schedule, along with expectations for the students and what they could look forward to for the remainder of the school year. Everything went well until Tommy's father stopped by her desk as the group was leaving.

"Tommy's doing okay?" He brushed a hand through his unruly hair, the corners of his mouth angling downward. "Not getting into trouble?"

"Not since the last time we talked, Mr. Parker."

"I've told him to behave. He doesn't seem to listen."

"Tommy is very spirited. Smart and funny, too. If I had one suggestion, it would be that you both go over his homework before he hands it in."

"I work long hours and can't go over his work every night," the man bristled. "Besides, that's your job."

"You're correct, but working together will keep you informed about what he's learning."

"Again, your job. Just let me know if he's acting up and I'll talk to him."

"I will, Mr. Parker. Thank you for coming in tonight."

Before the man left, Derrick walked into the room. He greeted Mr. Parker and watched as the parent hurried from the room.

"What'd you do to that guy? Grade him on his parenting skills?"

She sighed. "If I did, he probably wouldn't like the score." She glanced at Derrick, taking in his windblown hair and red cheeks. He smelled like fresh air and a hint of spice. "That was Tommy's father."

"Oh, yeah? I would have liked to talk to him."

Her trouble antennae went up. "About?"

"Just guy stuff." He rubbed his hands together. "It's cold outside."

"The weather here is so much different than Florida."

He unzipped his jacket. "I don't get down there much anymore."

"Because of work?"

"Mostly. Mom, Dylan and Dante are still there. Deke lives in Georgia."

"How is your family?" She was ashamed of herself for not asking after them before now.

"Good. Two engagements and two serious relationships. I expect wedding bells will ring a bunch of times this year."

"Really? Which brother?"

"Dylan."

"And?"

He grimaced. "My mom."

"Oh." She looked him over, trying to decipher his reaction. Derrick and his father had had a solid relationship while he was growing up. "That's got to be hard."

He shrugged. "She's happy."

"Good to hear."

"So, do these questions about my family mean you're interested in what's going on in my life?"

"I'm merely being polite."

He leaned in and winked. "You sure?"

DERRICK LOVED CATCHING Hannah off guard. She sputtered. Her cheeks went pink and she looked alive.

"So, Tommy's dad," he said, giving her a break from the walk down memory lane and her telltale reaction to his presence.

"Why do you do that?"

He wrinkled his brow. "Do what?"

"Throw an innuendo at me and then change the subject?"

"Because it's fun?"

His cell phone rang and he held up a finger to pause their conversation. She huffed and marched to the first row of desks to collect the folders on each one.

"Mom, is everything okay?"

"That depends on your definition of okay."

"What's going on?"

Her voice wavered. "We've hit our first snag."

Derrick glanced at Hannah. Clearly, she was curious about his conversation but continued picking up folders.

"James wants to be married at the courthouse and I want the ceremony at the church."

"Why can't you both come to common ground?"

"Because of his past he doesn't think we should say our vows in the church, but I told him it's the perfect place for redemption and new beginnings."

"Mom, this is way above my pay grade."

Hannah chuckled.

"Don't you agree with me?"

"Not necessarily. I can see James's point, but it sounds like you have your heart set on the location."

"I suppose I could give in. It is James's wedding, too."

Derrick rubbed his thumb over his forehead. *Note to self. If ever in this situation, elope.*

"Just talk to him. I'm sure you'll work it out."

"I suppose…" his mother's voice trailed off.

"Or stand your ground. Pick one."

"You think I should force the issue?"

He pressed his fingers against his temple. "No. Mom, he's your fiancé. Talk to him."

"I'm never this unsure of myself, but the wedding preparations are giving me fits."

"You're a strong woman. You and James will find the perfect place to get married."

"We will. Thank you, Derrick."

"Sure. Listen, I need to run."

"What happened to your directive to contact you anytime?"

"How about with a question I can actually answer."

His mother laughed. "Touché."

He ended the call, sending a sheepish look Hannah's way. "Wedding drama."

"I gathered." She finished one row and started back up another. "I liked your family. Especially your mother."

"She is one of a kind."

"So it would be normal for me to ask about them."

"Okay. Any other questions?"

"Yes. Are you happy your mother is remarrying?"

"Jeez. Go right for the jugular why don't you."

"It's a reasonable question."

It was. He just didn't want to discuss it.

"You always used to do that," she said. "Deflect when you didn't want to deal with an issue."

"Is it working?"

She sent him a frown reserved for teachers when faced with unruly children. "Just because years have gone by doesn't mean I never think about the people I left behind, including your mom."

"Sorry. I shouldn't have given you a hard time."

She hugged the folders to her chest. A wistful expression crossed her lovely face. "It's so complicated. Through the years, I've wondered about everyone. Your brothers. My friends in high school. Our neighbors."

"Mrs. Gaines still lives in the house next to yours."

Her face lit up with her smile. "How do you know this?"

"I'm an investigator, remember?"

"Which means you won't say how you obtain your information."

"Now you're getting it."

She shook her head. "Mrs. Gaines must be quite old now."

"Last time I checked, her son and his family had moved in with her."

"She loved that house. I remember helping

her plant flowers in her garden when I was young. Impatiens. She had them in varying shades of pink. As a reward for helping her, she'd give me a plant or two for our yard." Her smile dimmed. "What about my old house?"

"A new family moved in."

"My father mentioned something about the sale of the house, but I just never thought…"

He reached over to touch her arm. "They've taken good care of it."

She sent him a steely-eyed glance. "I thought you said your mother moved away from our hometown."

"She did, but I still have contacts there."

Hannah stepped sideways to remove his fingers from her arm and resumed her task. He missed her warmth and her familiar scent.

"Is the man your mother is marrying like your dad? I remember he was quiet but very reassuring."

Derrick glanced at the floor. Swallowed against the knot in his throat. "Yeah, Dad had this presence about him. Everyone felt at ease when he was around." He looked up and caught her gaze. "That's why I went to him when I was concerned about your father. I knew he'd take care of the situation, just like he had hundreds of times before, and you'd be safe. Guess

I miscalculated. I never thought there might be another outcome."

Hannah made her way up the last aisle. "Being mad at you is water under the bridge now, but I can see why you confided in him. You two were close."

"Not so much at the end."

She reached him and leaned her hip against a desk. "What do you mean?"

"Even though he never admitted to me that he called the feds, I knew he'd played some part in your leaving. I was so torn up when I found out you were gone. I blamed him. Said some rotten things. We never fixed our relationship before he died."

Now it was her turn to touch him in comfort. Her fingers barely formed a dent in his heavy jacket, but the fact that she'd willingly initiated the gesture made his heart soar.

"I'm sorry, Derrick. That must have been hard."

"Probably no harder than your father leaving you and your mom."

"That was different." She removed her hand. "And a topic for another day."

"Right. I should probably take my final walk through of the building and make sure everyone is out before locking up."

Her eyes still glimmered with compassion.

Not wanting to be the subject of her pity, he left the room and quickly checked the building. Only the principal remained and she was buttoning up her coat and leaving as Derrick said good-night. The hallway echoed with Hannah's footsteps as she headed his way, ready to go home for the night.

"All clear?" she asked.

"Yep. Just you and me."

She shook her head and started for the door. "And we're leaving. I'd hoped to be home earlier in case Mom needs anything."

"You just got finished with a room full of parents. I'm sure your mom contacted a friend if she had any problems, but why don't you check in."

"I spoke to her before the meeting." She sent him a chagrined look. "She's finally getting her strength back but doesn't appreciate me going all mama bear on her."

"You know you can't take care of everyone and everything twenty-four/seven."

She looked at him as though he was dense. "But if I don't, who will?"

He opened his mouth with a retort, then realized she was serious. Did she really think she had to take care of everyone? Her somber expression answered his question. Was that what moving around and then later, taking care of her ill mother, had done to her? Made her feel responsible beyond her years?

When she didn't blink or change her expression, he shook off his concern and said what she needed to hear. "Then let's get you home."

He opened the heavy door, surprised when she hung back while he locked the main entrance. The temperature had dipped low into the thirties again. The damp air made him shiver under his jacket. Hannah wrapped her scarf closer to her neck while he tugged on his hat.

"Careful," he said, taking hold of her arm as they walked to the parking lot. The frigid conditions made moving across the slick asphalt treacherous.

"You don't have to stay with me," she said, her boots sliding on the ice patches.

"You honestly think I'm going to let you walk to your car by yourself?"

"No, I'm just saying you don't have to. I've been getting myself to and from places by myself for a long time now."

He hid a grin. "Yes, you're independent. I get it."

In the moonlight he saw her smile. "Thanks for noticing."

"I'm not surprised. You knew what you wanted even when we were kids."

"Until my choices were taken away from me." She gripped her tote bag closer to her side. "It took me what seemed like forever to regain my confidence. To take some sort of control of my life."

He softened his voice. "Hannah, it looks like you're doing fine to me."

She paused for a moment, then nodded. "I am."

They hurried across the deserted lot as the wind began to gust. He didn't want to be out in the cold any longer than necessary.

"So, you never answered my question," Hannah said. "Is your mother's fiancé much like your father?"

She wanted to discuss family now? With a sigh, he hunched into his jacket. "Polar opposite."

"In what way?"

"He was a con man before he went legit."

Hannah stopped so suddenly he slid before halting. She faced him, her expression incredulous. "Did you say con man? Like in a guy who swindles people?"

"That would be him."

"Wow. I'm—I don't know what I am."

"Yeah, that was pretty much the reaction when my brothers and I found out." He slowed as they reached her sedan. "The wedding is in February."

"So soon?" Hannah reached into her coat pocket and removed the key fob.

"She didn't want to wait long."

As she concentrated on unlocking the car door, Derrick couldn't take his gaze from her. The moonlight illuminated her creamy skin. Her hair lifted in the breeze, curls taking shape in the humid night air. She looked over and her eyes met his. Taking a chance, he removed his glove before he reached over to run a finger down her satiny-soft cheek. "I can understand her motivation."

"Derrick," she said, but didn't move.

As he leaned in slowly, he heard her breath catch. His lips brushed hers, tentatively at first, then with more confidence when she leaned into the embrace. The heat in the kiss shouldn't have surprised him, considering how long he'd waited for this moment. She sighed, then moved closer. He wrapped his arms around her waist, and pulled her close, knowing nothing could surpass this moment. Nothing was more important than Hannah in his arms once again.

When she made a sweet sound and tightened her arms around him, he wanted to shout for joy, but refused to remove his lips from hers. The cold night didn't matter. The late hour was a mere blip in the grand scheme of things. Hope swelled in his heart and he thought maybe, just maybe, fate had allowed them a second chance. He'd make up for the past, he swore as she moved her lips against his. Give her everything she'd ever wanted. Everything she'd ever deserved. He'd make things right and promise her forever if she'd accept his love. He'd even—

A car door slammed in the distance, making Hannah jump. She jerked back, her eyes wide as she grimaced. "We shouldn't have done that."

Not exactly the reaction or words he'd anticipated. "You can't tell me you haven't wondered if we still have the same spark."

"Wondering and testing it out are two different things."

"You kissed me back, Hannah."

"And it was a mistake. I'm with Jonathan." She pressed the control and the car lock disengaged with a click. "I need to get home."

"Hannah—"

"Please, don't make this more uncomfortable than it needs to be."

He stepped away as she opened the door.

"I thought I'd spend the rest of my life kissing you," he told her, his heart in his words.

Eyes level with his, she said, "Never again." Then slid in the car and pulled the door shut.

He watched her drive away, standing in the middle of the parking lot, freezing, wondering how he could have made things with Hannah any worse.

CHAPTER SEVEN

DERRICK OPENED AND CLOSED the back door off the kitchen for the third time. "It's warped, Hannah. I could shave off a section of the door-jamb to make it fit better, but I don't think it'll improve things. The cold air is going to seep through no matter what I do." He tried it again for good measure. "You need a new door."

Hannah ran a hand through her delightfully tousled hair. This morning when he showed up early on her doorstep, she'd answered wearing a sweatshirt, baggy flannel pajama bottoms and bunny slippers. Yep, bunny slippers. The whimsy made him smile, even as Hannah's scowl dared him to utter a word.

He was a smart man, so he kept his mouth shut.

"Give me a few minutes to get dressed and we'll go to the home-improvement store." She turned to leave the room, then spun around. "You can replace the door, right?"

"Yes, ma'am."

He decided to err on the side of caution by

answering in a light tone. Hannah had been giving him the stink eye ever since he walked in the house. If he had to guess, her mood came from the kiss they'd shared the night of the teacher-parent meeting. She'd been standoffish at school and this morning came across more than a bit antsy. She may have regretted his impulsive move, but he'd replayed it in his head a dozen times. Savored the feel of her soft lips against his, her sigh when she'd slipped her arms around his neck. Still, his best bet was to ignore the elephant in the room and pretend things were normal.

Tall order.

"Then we'll go to the store now," she announced. As if leaving the house and going to a place where they'd be surrounded by people would change the friction zipping between them.

Just as she turned to leave, her mother, dressed in a fuzzy robe, entered with a teacup in her hand. "Did I hear you say you were going to the store?"

"You need a new door, Mrs. Rawlings...er, Rawley."

The older woman grinned. "It's rather a bother keeping track of our identities. Why don't you call me Sophia when it's just us? It'll be easier."

"I will."

Sophia turned her attention to Hannah. "The store?"

"We need a new back door."

"That's the landlord's job."

Hannah's back went up. "I can take care of it."

"It's not your responsibility."

"It's just easier. This way I make sure it's what we want."

Sophia frowned and Derrick got the feeling this wasn't the first time they'd had this discussion.

Maybe he should mediate.

"I agree with your mom," he cut in. "You should let the landlord know first. He probably wants to be made aware of what's going on with his property."

Hannah sank her hands on her hips. "Are the two of you ganging up on me?"

Derrick held up his hands in surrender. What had happened to the even-keeled Hannah? Today she was wound tight. "Hey, I'll get a new door if that's what you want."

Sophia eyed her daughter and said, "Why don't we get out of the house. I'm sure it'll do us good."

When Hannah ran her hand through her delightfully disheveled hair again, Derrick's fingers itched to do the same. Her take-charge attitude reminded him of the girl she used to be. Stubborn and attractive at the same time.

"Sorry. I just always take care of things that need to be done around here."

Her mother walked over and placed her palm against Hannah's cheek. "But you don't have to. Mr. Rand appreciates the care you take of the house, but it's his duty as the owner."

"I know, but I can't help myself."

Hannah removed her mother's hand.

"How about this," Derrick offered. "Why don't we go to the store and you can pick out a style you like. Then call the landlord and ask him if I can go ahead and replace the door."

He read the hesitation in her eyes. He got that she wanted to feel in control. He imagined the years in witness protection had made her lose her autonomy, but it seemed like there was more buried there, more than Hannah would let him see.

"I suppose that'll work." She sent him a questioning glance. "You'll wait?"

He grinned. "I'm not going anywhere."

She rolled her eyes and left the kitchen.

Once she was gone, he heard a loud sigh behind him. He turned. Sophia rinsed her cup, placed it in the sink drainer and stared out the window.

"Hannah's not the same girl she used to be."

"I can see that."

She turned. Rested her back against the counter. "It was bad enough when Jerome left. When I got sick…" She stopped and pulled the lapels of her robe to cover her neck more snugly. "Sometimes it's too much."

"I'm sure you could get assistance if you asked."

"From whom?"

"The US Marshals."

She frowned. "They won't help us now."

"Why not?"

"We left the program. Years ago."

He tried to temper his surprise.

"I thought Hannah would have told you," she said.

"She's been pretty closemouthed—"

"Because of the time spent in hiding." Gesturing to the table, Sophia took a seat. Derrick followed.

"When did you get out of the program?" he asked.

"After two years. We were living in Illinois and Jerome swore he saw one of the men who had been threatening him before we left Florida. He told the deputy in charge of our case. They checked into it and said Jerome was mistaken."

"But your husband didn't believe him?"

"No. So we moved to Nebraska." She shivered and pulled her collar up to her ears. "Jerome swore he saw the man again. We moved a few more times and still Jerome insisted we weren't safe. The man he'd sent to jail had promised revenge and Jerome believed him. By this time, the idea of being watched had become an obsession with him." She let out a long, jagged sigh, conveying so much in the one sound. "We discussed it and agreed we should leave the protection program and separate. Jerome was convinced it was the only way to keep our family safe."

"You *both* made the decision?" Hannah asked from the doorway, her face pale. She'd changed into a sweater and jeans and had stopped in the process of brushing her hair.

"We did." Sophia rose, her eyes pleading. "Your father thought it best if we told you he'd made the decision."

"Like the decisions he made about the gemstones?"

"That was part of his business."

"A part that sent us from our home."

Sophia frowned. "I'd never seen him so scared, Hannah. Even more than when he testified." She held out an imploring hand. "He thought the Marshals weren't doing enough.

If we separated, at least you and I could go in a different direction. Throw the bad guys off the track."

"For all we know, he walked right into danger."

"No. He promised he'd do whatever he had to do to keep safe."

"But you don't know if he succeeded, do you?"

Sophia sank back into the chair. "No. I don't." Tears glimmered in her eyes. "And I go to bed every night praying he's safe."

With a strangled cry, Hannah hurried to her mother's side, kneeling beside her. "I'm sorry. I know that had to be hard for you."

Sophia ran a hand over her daughter's hair. "It's been hard for you, too."

For both women, Derrick surmised. In very different ways. Bottom line, they should know what had happened to their family. Maybe, if nothing else, he could find some answers for them.

"Your father never meant for those gem-stones to cause as much trouble as they did." Sophia looked up and met Derrick's gaze. "He bought them at an estate sale for a reasonable price. After the sale, two shady looking men came by the shop demanding he sell them. Jerome refused. Still, the men kept after him, hounding him to give up the stones. Jerome locked them away in the safe at our house hoping the men would go away."

That explained why Derrick saw them on the desk in the home office. "But they didn't."

Sophia shook her head.

"They never do," Derrick said quietly.

Sophia gripped Hannah's shoulder. "Your father was out of his element dealing with those men."

The room fell silent until Derrick said, "If you don't mind my asking, what did Mr. Rawlings need to testify about?"

Hannah rose from her position beside her mother and took a seat at the table. She wiped her eyes with her fingers and stared out the window.

"It came to light that the jewelry supplier Jerome had done business with for years was a fence for stolen goods. He wanted the four gemstones because they were worth a great deal. He tried to get Jerome to sell them to him for a fraction of their worth, but Jerome refused. My husband had no idea the type of man he'd been dealing with for years."

"Were the stones stolen property?"

"No, Jerome had purchased them legally. He had ideas to design his own jewelry to showcase the gems, but the supplier wanted them."

"Is that when the feds got involved?"

"Yes. Your father, Derrick, reached out to Jerome and since he was in so deep, he grabbed on to the offer like a lifeline. In the course of the investigation, we learned just how illegal some of the transactions Jerome had been involved with were. It was just the tip of what the supplier had been associated with. His network was deep and wide. Jerome was able to cut a deal by providing information to put away the supplier. With his testimony, the FBI could shut down a ring that had been operating for years."

"Which was good for the government," Hannah piped up, "but not for our family."

"There wasn't a day that went by that Jerome didn't regret dealing with the supplier, especially when the threats continued even after the trial."

"So that's why he thought he was being followed?"

"Yes. Most of the people involved in the theft ring were arrested, but not the men who had threatened him. Somehow they slipped through the cracks and Jerome was sure they had found out where we had relocated."

Derrick thought about the red stone in his pocket. It practically burned a hole in the fabric as they talked. "Mr. Rawlings never got the stones back."

Hannah leaned her elbows on the table. "Dad

didn't know what happened to them. He assumed the authorities confiscated them when we left and took them as evidence."

Derrick leaned back in his chair. Man, there were a lot of holes in this story. And a file he needed to access. To think, the mystery of what had happened to Hannah had been under his nose the entire time he'd worked for the Bureau.

He was about to ask more questions when the phone rang, breaking the tension in the room. Sophia jumped up and muttered that she'd get it. Hannah slowly rose to her feet, wiping tears from her cheeks. Derrick grabbed a tissue from the box on the counter and handed it to her.

"That was probably more than you wanted to know," she said, her voice wobbly.

"No, I asked your mother because I want answers. It's my fault you had to overhear the part about both your parents making the decision to split up your family." He watched her for a long moment. "You really didn't know?"

"No." She reached for another tissue. "I can't believe my mother kept that from me. We had talked about leaving and I thought we'd agreed together, but then, our family motto seems to be, Keep the Truth from Hannah."

"I doubt they'd look at it that way."

"Obviously." She blew her nose, most undainty-like. Derrick hid another grin. "I'm so tired of feeling guilty. But because I confided in you and you broke your promise to keep quiet, we'll never have a normal life."

Derrick didn't know what to say.

She balled up the tissues and threw them into the garbage bin. "You do have a way of seeing me at my worst."

He took a step toward her, longing to ease the suffering on her face but when she went stiff, he stopped in his tracks.

He swallowed. Tried to make his voice steady. "Are you going to be okay?"

She met his gaze. Honesty shimmered in the hazel depths. "I have no idea."

"You always were honest. That hasn't changed."

"Small favors, huh?"

He chuckled. "Why don't you finish getting ready and we'll go buy you a door."

"Thanks, Derrick."

"My pleasure."

When she walked out of the room, leaving behind a trail of her sweet perfume, he blew out a frustrated groan and pulled his cell phone from his pocket to speed-dial Dylan.

"Hey, bro," Dylan quipped, starting the conversation. "Mom says you're staying busy."

"Please tell me she's calling you for wedding advice, too."

"Yep. Deke and Dante, as well. She wants—and I quote—'all of us to be an integral part of my big day.'"

"She knows we're just going along with her because we love her. She deserves to do what she wants, but I have a feeling she won't let this go until we meet her at the altar."

"In the meantime, she wants our opinions."

Derrick rubbed his aching temple. Like he had time for wedding talk when he had to find out what happened to the gemstones and how to keep Hannah and her mother safe from a threat he wasn't even sure existed any longer.

"Moving on, how's your vacation?" Dylan asked.

"I'm not actually on vacation."

His brother laughed. "I thought your boss insisted."

"That's putting it nicely."

"Do I dare ask?"

"I'm in Nevada. Standing in Hannah's kitchen."

Silence greeted him from the other end.

"Come again?"

"I found her."

"What…how?" Dylan sputtered.

Derrick proceeded to bring his brother up to speed.

"That's some story."

"Especially since I have one of the stones in my possession. Makes me think whoever sent it has the others."

"Which doesn't sound reassuring."

"Dyl, I can't leave here. Not right now. This story is far from over."

"So what can I do?"

"Right now, I think it best if only you and I know what's going on. If Mom finds out, she'll insist on details and I can't give them yet."

"You're right. Deke and Dante won't like it—"

"But they'll understand."

"Agreed." Dylan paused. "So, what's it like? Seeing Hannah again after all these years."

"She's as beautiful as I remember. Both inside and out." He paused when his throat got tight. "And a survivor, Dyl. She was thrown a loop and has managed to do really well for herself and take care of her mother. She's amazing."

"So, you two? Any chance of reconciliation?"

"Not if her fiancé has anything to say about it."

Silence again, then, "Don't you hate it when there's competition?"

More than his brother could ever know. "I'm more concerned about why the stone turned up at this point and what that means for Hannah and her mother."

"Why don't I believe you?"

Okay, in fact, he wanted things to go back to the way they were, when he and Hannah once thought they were the only two people in the world so deeply in love. He couldn't fathom what would happen when he got to the bottom of this and Hannah went off into the sunset with Jonathan. He knew his heart would never survive. So he pushed the possibility way back into the far recesses of his mind and dealt with the facts at hand.

When Derrick didn't respond, Dylan blew out a long breath. "Okay, fine. Keep your secrets. Need anything else from me?"

"No. I'll handle the rest from my end."

"Which is?"

"Keeping Hannah and her mother safe until I figure out who sent the gemstone."

While hoping his heart didn't split in two before his time here was over.

THE BIG-BOX STORE echoed with voices as Hannah tried to focus on a new door. It was difficult when the itchy feeling on the back of her neck wouldn't go away. She tugged at the neckline of her sweater, but it made no difference.

"Hannah, I like the one with the window. What about you?" her mother asked.

Shaking herself from her musings, she focused on the two doors Derrick had pulled from the shelf and stood side by side on the aisle floor.

"No, it's too…open." She knew she sounded paranoid, but couldn't help it. "Anyone could look in on us."

"Fine. We'll take the solid door."

After following Derrick's advice to get in touch with the landlord, she'd gotten permission to replace the door. Actually, Mr. Rand was happy he didn't have to go to the bother of shopping and installing. He told Hannah he'd reimburse her when she submitted the receipt.

"Now that's decided, I'm going to look at area rugs. Be good."

"Back at ya," Hannah called after her.

With a wave her mother tootled off to another section of the store.

They returned one door back into inventory and placed the one they would purchase on a panel cart to wheel up to the cashier. "You okay?" Derrick asked.

She tried to smooth her expression. "Sure. Fine."

"Right." He came up beside her. "Try again."

She glanced at him out of the corner of her eye. "I forgot how perceptive you are."

"True." He sent her a tentative glance. "This isn't about me kissing you the other night, is it? Because I know I stepped over the line and I'm sorry."

"That's not a topic I'd like to discuss, thank-you-very-much." Although, she had given that amazing kiss a lot of thought. She just wasn't sure what to do about it.

"Then what is it?"

Before they left the aisle, she put her hand out to stop him, stuck her head into the main area and looked both ways. Satisfied that they were alone, she turned to him.

"I'm not overreacting."

He arched an eyebrow. "Never said you were."

She placed a hand on her chest to slow her pounding heart. "I have this feeling that some-one is watching me."

"Like the first day I showed up at school?"

"Just like it." She ran her damp palms over her jeans. "I get that we're in a busy store, but…"

"You said it's a reaction you've lived with since you went into WITSEC."

She nodded. "All the talk about the past this morning, I guess it affected me."

"Then your reaction shouldn't be dismissed. It's probably your subconscious telling you something isn't right."

She hadn't realized how tense she was until her shoulders relaxed at his words.

"You believe me?"

"Why wouldn't I?"

"I guess because of your line of work, I thought you might be more jaded."

"No. I've learned to listen to people, Hannah. Lots of times they know more than they think."

"So, I'm not imagining things?"

"I didn't say that, just that you should trust your intuition." He watched her for a second. "Did this happen before I showed up?"

"A couple times when we lived in Illinois and Nebraska."

Although Derrick's expression remained calm, he had been scanning the periphery of the store the entire time they spoke. Was he jittery too or was the action a consequence of his job?

She held her hands out. "I've never told anyone before this."

He met her gaze. "You didn't want to worry your mother."

"Yes. She's had enough on her plate."

"And you haven't?"

"I can take it, Derrick."

He reached over and lifted her chin with his finger. Her heart flip-flopped. She barely concealed the thrilling shivers at his touch. Would he kiss her again like he had in the school parking lot? She wanted him to, oh how she did. They were in a busy store and she really didn't care if he leaned over and brushed his lips over hers. She wasn't even worried about Jonathan. All she could think right now was that she wanted more. Did that make her a bad person?

Instead of kissing her again, Derrick warmed her with his steady gaze. She couldn't be disappointed when he made her feel like the most cherished woman in the world. "I know you can. You're the strongest woman I've ever met."

"Right."

"I'm telling you the truth. I'm stunned at what you've been through and how you've coped so well. You're remarkable."

His words were a balm for her bruised soul. For so long she'd been what others needed her to be: first, a dutiful daughter, then a caregiver for her mom, and finally, a happy fiancée. But it hadn't seemed real. Not until the day Derrick had shown up at her school and reminded her of the old Hannah. The Hannah who had once stood up for herself. The woman who'd had dreams of a very different future than how her reality looked now. One who used to reveal her emotions instead of boxing them away.

"Um…thanks."

"It's the truth."

She wasn't used to this much praise. Wasn't sure she liked it. Never felt like she'd deserved it. She'd only been doing what she could in the circumstances handed her; taking care of those she loved.

"What do you think?" she asked, wanting to move on from her current thoughts.

Derrick went serious. "Keep an eye on the people around us. Tell me if you notice anyone who gives you goose bumps."

A nervous giggle tickled her lips. "Is that a professional term?"

"No." He chuckled. "Just practical."

She smiled. Suddenly the weight on her shoulders lifted.

"I'm relieved not to have to keep my concerns bottled up inside."

"It's tough carrying everything solo." He pushed the cart and they moved on. "How much does Jonathan know?"

She cringed. "Not much. I told him I had a difficult past. He accepted that and said he'd wait until I wanted to tell him more."

"And when will that be? Just before you say *I do*?" he asked, heat in his tone.

She glared at him. "You were doing good up until this point."

"You need to think this through, Hannah. He deserves to know."

Guilt swamped her. Yes, she knew full well that Jonathan deserved the truth, but still had difficulty trusting anyone out of her small circle of confidants, which included only Derrick and her mother. She guessed that didn't say much for her confidence in her fiancé. Or her friendship with Lynny.

"We should find Mom."

Derrick looked up to read the aisle signs hanging from the ceiling.

"Rugs. Row eight."

As they walked in that direction, Derrick almost bumped into a shopper bolting from an aisle, his attention on his phone. Derrick pulled up short and the man stopped.

Hannah's jaw dropped. "Jonathan?"

He looked up, relief in his eyes. "Anna. There you are."

She blinked, making sure she wasn't seeing things. "What are you doing here?"

"Looking for you."

"How did you know I'd be here?"

He held up his phone. "I have you on Finding Friends."

"You put me on your app?"

"Well, yes. Remember when I sent you a request?" His tone indicated he didn't see a problem.

Preoccupied with her mother's health concerns, she'd forgotten. "Why didn't you just call me?"

"I have been, but you didn't answer. Especially after last night."

Last night. When he'd insisted that she attend the gallery showing and barely said two words to her all evening. He'd been busy taking care of business and conversing with his assistant Michelle, who couldn't resist making sure Hannah saw them together. She'd finally gone home when it became apparent his clients were his first priority, muted her phone and forgot to turn the volume back on.

"I know we didn't get a chance to talk much and I felt bad," Jonathan explained as he placed his phone in his jacket pocket.

Her irritation melted a bit.

Jonathan finally noticed Derrick. His eyebrows angled together. "Fields."

"Prescott."

"I didn't realize you were shopping with my fiancée."

Hannah had to keep from rolling her eyes at the uptight tone in Jonathan's voice.

"Just doing a little home-improvement job."

"I see." Jonathan glanced at her. "Why didn't you ask me to help with the project?"

"You're always so busy. I didn't want to bother you." That, and Hannah was pretty sure he didn't have the necessary skills. "Could you fix a door?"

"Well, no. I'd hire someone."

"I know my way around tools and uh, doors," Derrick explained.

At Jonathan's uncharacteristically unsure expression, Hannah found herself a little less miffed at his high-handed behavior the night before. He stepped closer to her and placed his arm around her waist. "Thank you for looking out for Anna."

"Hey," Derrick said, his gaze locked on hers. "What are old friends for?" Then he nodded and walked away with the cart.

"Did I do something wrong?" Jonathan muttered.

Hannah mustered up a smile. "I just didn't expect to see you here."

Was it Jonathan who had given her the feeling she was being watched? Made sense, since he was in the store searching for her. It also made her feel foolish for voicing her fears to Derrick, even though he believed her.

"You never mentioned that you needed anything repaired at your house."

Hannah swore she heard hurt in his tone.

"I'm used to handling these things."

"Now that we're getting married, I thought we'd gotten to a point where we talk about the things that make up our daily lives, including home improvement."

"You're right." She swallowed hard. "There are probably lots of things we should discuss."

His charming smile returned. "How about going for lunch and we'll get started on that resolution."

"I need to get Mom home and make sure Derrick gets the door installed."

"Dinner?"

"It's a date."

He held out his arm so she could place her hand in the crook of his elbow. They met up with the others and Hannah found herself dismayed when Derrick chatted up her mother and pretty much left her alone.

She understood. He was being respectful because she was engaged. And while she admired that, she wondered why she wanted to confide in him instead of Jonathan. Or why just being near Derrick made her heart race while Jonathan made her…content.

And here she thought her biggest dilemma today was being followed by an invisible menace when she was clearly torn between both men.

CHAPTER EIGHT

"I FEEL LIKE ice cream," Hannah's mother announced Monday afternoon when they'd bundled up and stepped out of the doctor's office into the extremely cold winter day.

"In this weather? It's not exactly an ice cream kind of day."

"Humor me."

"And to top it off, you've been sneezing on and off all afternoon."

Her mother waved off her concern. "Don't you remember when you were kids," she said, pulling a knit hat over her short gray hair, "and whenever we had a celebration we'd go get ice cream?"

A zap of pain and longing swept over Hannah. She could envision the happy times like they'd happened yesterday. "You'd make this grand announcement that we were going to Uncle Sonny's shop. Dad would make a huge production of searching for his car keys before you hustled me into the car."

"Those were special times." Her mother

tugged Hannah's coat sleeve. "And today is a good day, so we're going to celebrate."

It had been. The doctor's words had been positive. Still, talking about the past made the idea of celebrating bittersweet.

"Gosh, I haven't thought about Uncle Sonny in years," Hannah said as she dug for the car keys buried deep in her purse. At least not until Derrick showed up and reminded her of their old hometown. "I wonder if he ever found out what happened to us."

"No one knew why we left." Her mother sent her a wry glance. "But your father may have sent a mysterious letter to your uncle informing him we were okay."

"Even though it was against the rules?"

"Some rules you break for the people you love."

Like letting an old boyfriend into your life when you were currently engaged?

"Remember when Derrick started coming to the ice cream parlor with us?" Her mother laughed. "He was one of the family."

Hannah led them through the crowded medical center parking lot to her car.

"Every holiday, even if his own family had plans, he'd tag along," her mother continued. "Really, anytime you were there."

"Kind of like now."

"Not nearly as much as when you were kids."

It sure felt like it. Every time she turned around he was there, at school, at home. Was she complaining? "You always had a soft spot for him."

"How could I not? He loved you like crazy, even when you were both too young to understand the meaning of lasting love."

Oh, they'd understood, if taking a serious step like marriage was an indication.

Hannah inhaled a deep breath and blurted, "Before the Marshals showed up Derrick and I were going to elope."

Her mother jerked to a stop and had to brace herself with a hand on the car hood. "Come again?"

"We had it planned." Hannah unlocked the passenger door. "Once we both turned eighteen we were going to city hall."

Her mother placed a hand over her heart. "You never said a word."

She shrugged. "We didn't want you and Dad or his parents trying to talk us out of it."

"And you kept it a secret?"

"Yes. Between the Marshals showing up and our family fleeing in the night, it kind of put a damper on our plans."

Hannah got her mother settled in the car. She drove them to the little downtown area of Dark

Clay. The town boasted an excellent ice cream shop, with an adjoining coffee shop.

The silence stretched until her mother said, "I'm sorry, Hannah."

"It's in the past, Mom. We readjusted our dreams." Hannah took her eyes off the road to meet her mother's. "Everyone did. Even you."

"We all sacrificed," her mother replied, staring out the window. "Your father doesn't even know I had cancer."

They'd cut off communication in hopes it would keep them safe. Hannah wished she'd insisted her father get in touch with her once he found a new place for himself . Now…they'd always wonder.

On a sigh, Hannah continued down the road. The day hadn't warmed up much even though it was early afternoon. The temperature still hovered around thirty degrees, with a few weak rays of sun poking through the cloud cover. The roads were damp and piles of dirty snow sprinkled every curb. Hannah shivered, envious of those enjoying a temperate Florida winter.

"We won't stay long," Hannah said as she pulled up to the building. "I want to get you home."

"Stop worrying."

Sorry, Mom, that's my job.

Once she parked, Hannah went for coffee

while her mother ordered ice cream cones for both of them. The shop was decorated in shades of pink and purple and smelled exactly like Uncle Sonny's shop had, sweet and yummy.

"Mint chocolate chip?" Hannah asked as she set two steaming cups of freshly brewed coffee on the small bistro-style table and sat down.

"Only the best," her mother said after taking a long lick.

Chuckling, Hannah dug into her cone. "Mmm. This is good."

"That's the only flavor you'd ever order. Even Derrick couldn't get you to try any other."

"Why mess with perfection?"

They both focused on their treats. Once Hannah had had enough, she sipped her rich coffee and waited. Her mother hadn't said a word about the doctor's visit, but Hannah knew it was coming.

"The report wasn't exactly what I'd hoped for," her mother started. "The tumor is gone, but I'd expected Dr. Owens would have told me I'm in remission."

"The doctor was being realistic. After the surgery and treatment, he said it would take time for a definitive answer. You only just ended your treatment. Even though the tumor didn't show up in the scan, he was right not to tell you the cancer was gone."

As her mother enjoyed her sugary treat, Hannah could see that she looked so much better. In the two weeks since she'd completed the chemo, her skin bloomed with color and her eyes were bright. She had renewed energy, which encouraged Hannah the most. She didn't like that her mother might be getting a cold, but Sophia was so upbeat, and refused to stay at home, instead going out and about with her friend Carol. Hannah had hated seeing her seem so defeated during the treatment, so she hadn't created much of a fuss over her mother's busy activities.

"You didn't have to come, you know."

"And miss all this?" Hannah scoffed, her tone leaving no doubt that she would have rescheduled everything on her calendar that day to be with her mother. "No way. I actually got the gym teacher to cover my class since he had a free afternoon."

Roger had been more than happy to fill in for her. He'd actually suggested he and Lynny combine the classes in the gym for a special game time. Lynny had agreed immediately, practically pushing Hannah out the door, in case either she or Roger might change their mind.

"Did that young man ask her out on a date yet?"

"No. But she volunteered both of us to work

at the home basketball games. I think her philosophy is, if she's in his line of vision, he can't forget about her."

"She does go after what she wants." Her mother wiped her fingers with a napkin. "She certainly made it her mission to get you out of your comfort zone when we moved here."

"Have you ever tried saying no to her? It's next to impossible."

Her mother laughed. "I can't thank her enough for taking you under her wing."

Hannah wanted to grumble that she'd been fine all along, but who was she kidding? After they'd set up the house, she wasn't sure what she'd do for a job. Moving again had been another blow. All she wanted to do was stay in bed with the covers pulled over her head. Then Lynny knocked on the door, a plate of cookies in hand and so full of fun, she sort of took over, a reminder that Hannah had to get her act together.

When her mom got sick, Lynny had helped Hannah find a doctor and stayed by her side during the surgery. Now that things had settled down some, Lynny was determined to see Hannah out and about, regaining some balance in her life. But since Derrick had showed up, she wondered if the balance part was even possible.

Her mother sneezed, grabbing a napkin from the table to cover her nose.

"See. You're overdoing. Your immune system took a hit, Mom."

"So I'll go home and rest after we're finished here."

Somehow Hannah doubted that.

Her mother took another sip of her coffee. "He's been good for you since he showed up."

Hannah tilted her head. "What? Who's been good?"

"Derrick. Since he came to town you've been more like your old self."

She bristled at the idea. "I've always been the same old me."

Her mother didn't look convinced.

"Okay, maybe not, but I doubt it's to do with Derrick. Meeting Jonathan helped a great deal."

"You know I adore Jonathan. He's such a sweetheart, but he doesn't know you like Derrick does."

"Did, Mom."

"Fine. But I don't see Jonathan getting a rise out of you if you don't agree with him. Or a blush of color cross your cheeks when he gives you a compliment." She leaned across the table, a conspiratorial expression on her face. "You laugh a lot more since Derrick arrived, and I've seen you sending looks his way when you don't think anyone is looking. Never seen you do that with Jonathan."

Was she that obvious? Apparently. Mortified, she dropped her head into her hands.

"Some connections are hard to break," her mother said.

Hannah looked up. "I'm getting married."

"Yes. You are."

"To a man who isn't Derrick."

"True."

Hannah frowned. "Why do I hear a *but* in your tone?"

"No buts. You'll do what you think is right." She reached over and patted Hannah's hand. "You always have."

No pressure. She'd spent more than one sleepless night trying to decide what to do about the two men in her life. And despite the extra hours awake, she hadn't come up with any concrete answers. Derrick would be gone after he solved the mystery he'd come to investigate, right? He'd go back to his exciting FBI job, chasing after art thieves, while Hannah would remain in Dark Clay teaching fourth grade, a fulfilling job in many ways, just not the dream she'd wished for since she'd been on her first museum field trip. Oh, and she'd be getting married.

Her mother glanced at her watch. "What do

you say we run by the grocery store before heading home. The pantry is getting a little bare."

"As long as we pick up plenty of chicken noodle soup. I swear you're coming down with a cold."

"Soup it is."

Fine with her. She was pretty much done discussing Derrick.

An hour later she pulled into the driveway after they'd stopped at the grocery store. She popped the trunk, ready to haul the bags in when a figure rose from the porch steps. Her heart pounded until she saw who it was. Jonathan.

Disappointment washed over her.

He hurried over, presenting a large bouquet of flowers to her mother.

"Oh, Jonathan. These are lovely."

The beautiful spring flowers, bright yellow daffodils with white snowdrops sprinkled in the mix, were joyful, just like her mother's expression when she took the unexpected gift.

He sent Hannah a scowl. "I didn't hear anything from you about the appointment, so I drove over."

With her mind in the clouds, she hadn't noticed his car parked in the road. "I'm so sorry, Jonathan." She lugged a bag out of the trunk. "Tell him the good news, Mom."

"The scan was clear."

Jonathan's handsome face lit up. He hugged her mother. "That's fantastic."

Her mother pulled back. "I still have to have regular tests to make sure nothing reoccurs, but the doctor seemed pleased."

"You know, I think this deserves a celebration." He spread his arms wide. "What do you say we have dinner at a nice restaurant."

"We already—"

"That sounds wonderful," her mother cut in, shooting Hannah a glare. "Why don't I get these flowers in water."

As her mother hurried to the door, Jonathan came to help her with the groceries. "You must be relieved."

"You can't imagine. The waiting was excruciating."

He brushed a strand of hair from her cheek. "You both deserve good news. It's been a rough year."

It had. But she'd had Lynny, her fellow teachers and Jonathan to get her through the hard times.

"I'm sorry I didn't call. One minute we were in the office and then my mother talked me into getting ice cream."

"Now that I know Sophie had a good report, I can't be mad at you."

They walked up the sidewalk.

"I hope the flowers were okay. Michelle and I wanted to do something nice, no matter the outcome of the appointment today."

Hannah tried to tamp down her annoyance at the mention of his assistant's name, but really, did that woman always have to horn in? Still, they worked well together and Michelle had boosted the gallery's social media presence. Jonathan was a good man and deserved the best for his business.

"I know Mom appreciates it. It was a lovely gesture."

Smiling wide, Jonathan said, "So, dinner? Just the three of us?"

Her heart melted at his loving expression. Even though she worried about her mother's health, she couldn't deny them a night out. "Sounds wonderful."

"This will be good for your mom." He paused, caught her gaze. "And for you. I know how anxious you were to hear the results of the test."

"Honestly, it's the only thing I've been able to focus on."

"Then tonight we'll paint the town red."

She chuckled. "I don't know about that. It's a Monday night and I have that field trip tomorrow."

"Field trip?"

"I told you last week."

He sent her a frown.

"I'm taking the class to the Styles Museum of Arts and Crafts."

"Yes, you did mention it. How could I have forgotten? I enjoyed going to the museum when I was a kid." His shoulders straightened. "I would have been an excellent tour guide, if I do say so myself."

After his last foray in entertaining her students, she thought the kids might disagree, even though he meant well.

She placed a hand on his arm. "Listen, you're more than welcome to come."

"I'd take you up on that offer, but I have a meeting that can't be rescheduled. Bernard has finally decided to show his work at the gallery."

"Jonathan, that's wonderful. He's been on the fence for a while, but his creations of glass and metal couldn't find a better home."

"He is one of the finest sculptors around." He grinned at her. "I can't take all the credit. My two favorite ladies convinced him to show at the gallery. You're so positive about his work that you boosted his confidence. Michelle came up with a marketing campaign to showcase his art. Between both of you, he finally settled on the Prescott Gallery to show his newest collection."

"I'm happy for you."

"The gallery's success is on the horizon. We have to celebrate."

The ever-present guilt she experienced whenever she was with Jonathan grew. Yes, she'd been so concerned about her mother and the follow-up appointment with the doctor that she forgot to call him. But what bothered her even more was the fact that since Derrick had blown into town like a sudden summer storm, she couldn't deny the attraction that had revved up her heart.

"How about I join you on the next field trip?" he asked.

"Definitely."

He grinned at her, then leaned down to brush a kiss over her lips. Okay, it wasn't a three-alarm fire like the kiss she'd shared with Derrick, but it wasn't bad.

As he led her up the stairs and into the warm house, she wondered if she could live with his tepid kisses after they were married. Then immediately chastised herself for the thought.

As THE DOOR closed behind Prescott, Derrick's hands tightened on the steering wheel.

He'd missed Hannah at school because early

this morning he'd driven forty minutes south to the FBI resident agency to access the Rawlings case files, then speak to his boss. They'd discussed the situation and strategy, with his boss informing him he'd call a colleague in the Marshals' office and speak to the agent who'd been in charge of the case. When he got back and found Hannah gone, Lynny told him about Sophia's appointment and his curiosity took over. Was she okay?

After the students left for the day, he jumped in the rental car and drove over to learn the results. What he hadn't expected to find was the loving couple sharing a kiss on the front porch.

Firing up the engine, Derrick slowly drove through the neighborhood until he came to the main thoroughfare. Now what? He glanced at the box of specialty cookies he'd picked up at the bakery on the way over and frowned. Cookies? What was he thinking? Prescott had upped his game with flowers.

Derrick stomped on the gas pedal and headed south to his hotel. He didn't want to be cooped up in his room so he changed into running clothes and braved the elements to sweat the frustration out of his system.

Why had he been disappointed when Hannah failed to tell him about her mother's doctor visit? It wasn't like he was family. Shoot, he was just the guy who showed up on her door-step after having caused the disruption in her family to begin with. He didn't deserve to be part of the inner circle, not like her fiancé.

The more he considered his place—or lack of it—in Hannah's life, he pounded the ground and pumped his arms to move faster. Maybe if he forced himself to the brink of exhaustion, he wouldn't think about her.

Highly unlikely.

Still, he pushed himself as if he were running a sprint. His breath fogged and perspiration beaded his face. The damp air misted his hair. When he reached the small town park he slowed down to check his pulse. The sun would set in about an hour and it would be cold and damp and miserable outside.

Just like his mood.

He walked now, regulating his heart rate, when he noticed a few boys on the concrete court at the end of the park throwing a basketball at the hoop. A teenage girl sat on a park bench, busy scrolling through her phone. As he moved closer, he recognized one of the kids from Hannah's class. He opened the gate and headed inside the enclosure.

"Hey, Tommy."

The boy turned, dropping the ball as a smile

split his face. "Mr. Fields. What are you doing here?"

"Out for a run. You?"

"Practicing. Mr. Garver said I had a good chance of starting the next game."

Derrick held out his hand for a high five. "Good for you."

"I'm not the best on the team. When we don't have practice after school, I come here."

"I've watched you play. You aren't bad."

He'd been drawn to the gym the first day he'd started work at the school. The squeak of sneakers and shouts from the coach had fueled his curiosity, so he went to watch the intramural basketball team practice. The gymnasium with hoops at either end reminded Derrick of his school days, from the hard bleachers to the smell of socks and disinfectant. He'd ended up having a conversation with the coach and, since that day, stopped by to give Roger a hand with the team after seeing the children off with their parents.

Tommy wiggled around on tiptoes. "Really? You think I'm good?"

"Yes." Derrick glanced at his watch. "Where's your dad?"

"He'll be home soon." Tommy jutted his chin toward the girl on the bench. "Casey watches out for me and her brother when we practice."

Good to know. He wouldn't have liked the idea of Tommy out here on his own.

"You come after you do your homework, right?"

The kid looked at him like Derrick had spoken a foreign language. Puffing out his chest, most likely so his friends would hear him, Tommy said, "Nope. I go home, change and come to practice."

"That's dedication."

Tommy picked up the ball and threw it Derrick's way. "Mind practicing with me?"

"Not at all."

The other boys joined them and they spent fifteen minutes shooting, dribbling and stealing the ball. When Tommy's face grew tomato red, Derrick suggested they take a seat on an empty bench. The other players remained on the court.

"So, your folks don't mind you working out so hard?"

The boy frowned and averted his face. "Dad works late."

"And your mom?"

"She left."

Derrick's heart sank. "Sorry to hear that."

Tommy shrugged like it was no big deal, but Derrick saw the sorrow in the young boy's eyes.

"My dad died a few years ago. It's tough when someone leaves."

Tommy glanced at him. "Do you wish he'd come back?"

"Sure, even though I know it's impossible." If his father could come back, Derrick would have the chance to apologize for the ugly words he'd spewed at him after Hannah left. He so wanted to tell his father he loved him. Swallowing hard, he gazed over the park. "Your mom?"

"I don't know. Dad won't tell me what happened. At first I got a card from her every once in a while…"

"Now?"

"Nothing."

Derrick reached over and squeezed the boy's thin shoulder. "Sometimes life feels like we're stuck in a bad passing drill. It's when we make good throws that counts."

"I wish Dad was home more."

"I'm sure he does, too."

Tommy quickly turned away. "I don't know. Sometimes I think I'm a pain."

"Hey, don't ever think of yourself that way. Your dad's just trying to make a living and sometimes adults don't show their feelings in the best way."

Tommy shrugged again as if not convinced. Derrick now understood why the boy tried to control the other kids at school. Clearly he worried about his father's love for him.

Derrick remembered Hannah telling him about Tommy's father and asked, "Do you two have problems?"

Tommy frowned. "Like fighting and stuff?"

"Yeah."

"Nah. Dad's too tired."

"You do help out at home, right?"

Tommy's cheeks flushed red. "Well..."

Derrick chuckled. Watched as the other boys grappled over the ball. "I know, chores are the worst. When I was a kid my brothers and I tried to pawn off our jobs on each other."

"Did it work?"

"Not like we planned."

Tommy sighed. "Maybe if I had a brother I wouldn't miss my Dad so much."

"It's tough running a house alone. He'll appreciate your help."

Tommy seemed to consider that for a moment. "You live alone?"

"I do."

A car passed by, steam billowing from the tailpipe as the vehicle cautiously moved down the road.

"So..." Tommy said. "No girlfriend?"

"Not at the moment."

"Then I guess you're no help."

Derrick let out a strangled cough. "Excuse me?"

"There's this girl."

"There's always a girl."

"You like someone who doesn't like you back?"

The question of the ages. And sadly, his situation right now. Time to redirect. "C'mon, who doesn't like you?"

"Tawny Hughes."

"Isn't she the quiet girl from your class?"

One of the times he'd stopped by Hannah's classroom he'd noticed Tommy hovering by the girl's desk.

"Yeah. I never know what to say to her."

"No matter what age you are, it never gets easier."

Tommy held out his fist for a bump. "Women. Am I right?"

Derrick let out a gusty laugh. "You are right, little man."

"What about Miss Rawley? You hang around her classroom."

"We're old friends."

"You're way more fun than that boring guy who came to our class. That's her boyfriend." Tommy's face crunched into a grimace. "Sure you don't want to ask her out?"

That had been the plan until he realized Hannah was happy with Jonathan. If he'd expected her to tell the guy that Derrick was back and now she was complete, he'd been disappointed. Years ago, she'd done what anyone in her situation would do; she'd picked up the pieces and moved on. He was the one wishing things had turned out differently.

Tommy slid off the bench and they played again until the darkness grew and the air became so frosty it began to bite. Casey had had enough of the weather and told the boys to wrap it up. Tommy's friends said goodbye and hurried down the block.

"How about I walk you home?"

"You don't have to." Tommy collected his ball. "It's not far."

"Humor me."

Tommy shrugged and they walked a block to a small Craftsman-style house. The lights were on inside but there was no vehicle parked in the driveway.

"Will your dad be home soon?"

"Yeah. I should go and get stuff ready for him to make dinner."

"Hey, Tommy, why don't you help him cook tonight?"

"But SpongeBob is on TV," the ten-year-old whined.

"For tonight, keep the television off and work with your dad. It'll be fun."

Tommy didn't look convinced.

"I used to spend a lot of time with my father. Best years of my life."

"Really?" He tilted his head like he was giving Derrick's idea some thought. "Okay."

"I expect a full report at school tomorrow."

"I've got reading during my free period but maybe during lunch?"

"Sounds like a plan."

He watched Tommy run up the sidewalk and unlock the front door. He turned, his small body silhouetted by the warm inside lighting and waved. Derrick returned the gesture, an ache tightening his chest.

He'd always thought he and Hannah would be married and have kids by now. It had been part of their plan: get married, finish school, wait a few years before having kids so they could travel, then settle down and welcome the rug rats. How naive he'd been. To think you could map out your life to such a degree and have it actually happen. Maybe others could do it, but not him.

Once the door closed securely behind Tommy, Derrick started making his way back to the hotel. And the long night ahead. He paused when he noticed a car pulling into the driveway at Tommy's house. Under the streetlamp, he recognized Mr. Parker.

As he walked on, he thought of Hannah. Seeing her and Prescott together drove home the reality that she didn't want him. Not romantically, anyway. It was time for Derrick to back off. He'd told Dylan earlier that he should move on and he was right. Hannah had chosen Prescott over him.

Shoving his hand in the pocket of his running pants, Derrick pulled out the red gemstone. It flashed like fire under the streetlamp. Much like the way his heart heated up whenever Hannah came into view.

He had to uncover the story behind the gems and let her decide what happened next.

Someone had gone to great lengths to get him here. He needed to end the suspense. For all their sakes.

CHAPTER NINE

THE DAY OF the field trip dawned bright and sunny, a reprieve after the perpetually gloomy month so far. The thermometer had risen ten degrees, a vast improvement over the last few weeks. It was only midmorning and the sun's intense rays melted the lingering snow.

Hannah lined up the children in the hallway to check name tags and soon they walked outside to the waiting bus. Two mothers had signed up to accompany the children and were already on the bus after packing the lunch bags in a plastic tote to distribute later.

Once outside, the brightness made Hannah squint against the sun's glare and she started digging in her purse for sunglasses. She stopped short to find Derrick at the bus door, greeting the children and helping them climb inside. Despite the fact that she'd vowed last night to give Jonathan her full attention, she couldn't control the shiver of attraction whispering over her skin. Derrick's smile was just as dazzling as the sun. He'd forgone his jacket, wearing just a long-sleeved pullover and jeans, which show-cased his muscles. Muscles she should *not* be mesmerized by.

Determined not to notice anything about Derrick—right, like that was going to hap-pen—she marched over to him, pasting a smile on her face. "Thanks for helping."

He'd also donned sunglasses and she couldn't read his eyes. His lips, however, curled up into a devastating smile. "No problem. Principal Muldoon said you needed a chaperone."

Confused, she asked, "A chaperone? Are you sure? I have two moms on board."

"Yeah, you know, as part of my security-guard duty."

"I didn't know field trips fell under your job description." She frowned, not exactly com-fortable with this development. "A chaperone. For my class."

"I believe we established that already."

No. No, no, no. How was she supposed to get him out of her head if he was always around? She saw him more than her own fiancé.

"The volunteers can cover the job."

"Looks like the principal is covering all bases."

Tommy passed by in the line and stopped. "You're coming with us, Mr. Fields?"

"Sure am."

The two high-fived and Tommy moved on. Hannah shot him a curious look.

"What can I say? I've made friends."

He waited until the children had boarded the bus before taking her arm. She looked at his strong fingers wrapped around her sleeve then back to his amused gaze. But then he steered her a few steps from the bus, far enough away that the kids wouldn't overhear them.

Hannah's heart skipped a beat. "What are you doing?"

"I wanted to give you an update on Tommy," he said, voice low. She had to move closer to hear him, which ensnared her in the scent of his spicy cologne. She wanted to close her eyes and drink him in but her inner enforcer yelled, *Jonathan.*

She blinked at him. "Update?"

"C'mon, Hannah, get it together."

At his teasing words, she straightened.

"Things at Tommy's house don't sound as bad as you thought."

She cocked one hand on her hip. "How would you know?"

"Tommy and I had a heart-to-heart. He says his dad is short with him sometimes, but that's about it. I guess they're both frustrated. He and his dad aren't on the same page about responsibilities at home."

Compassion for her student swept over her, but she found herself annoyed that Derrick had been able to unearth this information and she hadn't.

"Thanks." At his brilliant smile, she asked in a terse tone, "How, exactly, did you become a chaperone?"

"Mrs. Muldoon insisted."

"Or did you insist, considering our…" She stopped, glanced around them and whispered, "…situation?"

He grinned. "Nope. She thought it would be a good thing if I tagged along and I wasn't going to say no."

That smile. It got her every time.

She shook off his hold on her arm. "Let's get going."

"After you."

She climbed onto the bus, took a quick head count, then looked for a place to sit. Tommy, in the second row, waved her to the empty front seat. "Over here, Miss Rawley. I saved you a seat."

"How sweet." She settled in as Derrick climbed aboard and the driver closed the door. Behind her she heard, "Mr. Fields. Sit here with Miss Rawley."

At Derrick's surprised look, she closed her eyes. Heaven save her from fourth-grade matchmakers. His arm brushed hers as he took a seat beside her and she steeled herself against the automatic reaction to her old boyfriend, shivers and shame. Why did she react to Derrick so easily?

Not willing to answer her own question, she scooted as far away from him as possible, which wasn't much considering the close confines. But hey, at least she tried.

Not hard enough.

Soon the bus rumbled through the parking lot before turning onto the road in front of the school. *Just breathe,* she told herself as she closed her eyes again to center herself. *We'll be at the museum in no time.*

Once under control, she dared open her eyes. Derrick leaned close and her resolve to stay unaffected failed. Man, did he smell good.

"Just so you know," he said in a low voice. "I didn't put Tommy up to the seating arrangement."

"I didn't think you did, being professional and all."

He chuckled deep in his chest. "But I won't argue the strategy."

She turned and met his gaze. "Later, we need to have a serious conversation about boundaries."

"Really? Because I recognize that expression on your face."

"Expression?"

"The dreamy one you got whenever we were tossed together at a school function."

She tugged her purse onto her lap, using it as a shield. Useless, since it was her emotions that needed protection. "Don't flatter yourself."

"Just speaking the truth."

He was. She just didn't want to go there.

The children chattered behind them and Hannah tried to focus on their conversations, which didn't work with Derrick's arm now pressing against hers.

"Remember the first time we sat together at the school rally?" He slid a tad closer. "You kept insisting you wanted to hang out with your friends, but when I walked in, lo and behold, there was an empty space next to you just waiting for me."

"One of my friends had moved."

"Right. And when kids started to fill the bleachers, we were practically plastered together."

She sent him an annoyed glance. "Your point?"

"Eventually you relaxed, and it was the first time we held hands."

Her heart squeezed at the memory. At that point she'd already been halfway in love with Derrick.

"That was a long time ago."

He shrugged. "Maybe. But you have the same exact expression on your face right now."

She smoothed her features. What was wrong with her? Where was her self-control? She wasn't a lovesick teen any longer. No, she was a mature woman who had to get her act together.

Thankfully the bus turned into the parking lot of the two-story mud-colored adobe building and she could breathe again. A banner hung over the door announcing a new Native American craft exhibit, one she hadn't seen yet. The bright red front doors gave the drab building a pop of pizzazz and invited the curious to venture inside.

Once the bus was parked, Derrick stood, holding out a hand to help her up. She hesitated, but felt dozens of inquisitive eyes on her. She graciously took his hand and rose.

"I did that to show the children how to be polite," she said as she passed him.

He chuckled in response.

Thankfully she got some much-needed space when she checked in at the main reception desk, then made sure the children had stored their outerwear in the appropriate place and still sported their name tags before she separated them into groups. A docent arrived to lead them into the interior of the building where the displays were set up. The shiny, dark brown floors echoed with footsteps, and voices bounced off the cream-colored walls, the sounds growing dimmer as the children moved deeper into the museum. The very pregnant museum director walked up to Hannah, a smile gracing her pretty face.

"Anna."

At the use of her new name, Hannah shot a panicked glance at Derrick. She had to stop doing that any time he was around.

"Hi, June."

"I was thrilled when I found out you were bringing your class here. We've missed you."

Hannah didn't miss the probing look in Derrick's eyes.

"I used to volunteer here," she explained. "Before my life got crazy with teaching and taking care of Mom."

"Please," the director went on to say. "You're being modest." The woman grinned at Derrick. "Over the summer she was a permanent fixture here."

"Really?"

His smile made her knees weak. "June, this is Derrick Fields. The principal saddled me with him today."

"Security," he explained.

June laughed. "You can never be too safe."

"See," Derrick said. "I told you."

Hannah ignored him. "When are you taking leave?" she asked the director.

"Next week. Hopefully the baby will decide to arrive soon after."

At the lovely glow on her friend's face, the dreams she'd wished for, and lost, assailed Hannah. She and Derrick had hoped to raise a family one day.

Sensing her mood, or remembering their old dreams himself, Derrick addressed the director. "Tell me more about Anna's influence here."

"She set up one of our most popular displays."

"I certainly don't work here," Hannah protested, "but June was gracious enough to let me run with an idea I mentioned to her."

"And run with it she did." June rested a hand on her swollen belly. "Honestly, she was so organized she almost didn't need my help. Anna, you should take him over to see it."

"But the class…"

"Liz has them enthralled over in the glass-blowing section."

"I'd love to see your display," Derrick prodded.

"Fine." The genuine affection in his tone touched a place in her she'd walled off for a very long time. This display had been special to her, the one-and-only time she'd ever been able to work on a museum project like she'd imagined doing since she was a kid. She'd taken Jonathan to see it when she was finished, and while he'd been supportive, he didn't understand how much the opportunity to work in a museum had meant to her. How could he when he didn't know her history? He'd praised her eye for detail, but once he'd viewed the display, conversation moved on. Sharing this with Derrick was not only bittersweet, but nerve-racking at the same time. "It's this way."

"You two enjoy." June waved them off. "I'm headed to my office to put my feet up."

Feeling a little self-conscious, Hannah removed the outerwear she'd layered over a lapis-blue sweater, black pants and boots, and led Derrick to one of the side rooms. This area consisted of wearable art and textile exhibits. She stopped at a corner hutch which had been repurposed to fit the theme of the room. The solid doors had been replaced with glass. Inside, the glass shelves shone under soft lighting, featuring the items she'd lovingly collected.

"Jewelry." Derrick sounded surprised.

"Handmade." She moved closer and surveyed the contents with fondness. "I was surrounded by such beautiful pieces growing up, so when I had the brainstorm, it just seemed a natural fit."

Derrick leaned closer, studying the bracelets of hammered metal, sterling silver necklaces and earrings adorned with natural stone such as turquoise, malachite or sandstone. Native American and vintage pieces added to the diversity of the exhibit.

"Where did you find the artists?" he asked, studying the contents.

"When Mom and I first moved here, we loved to frequent art-and-craft fairs. I would stop at booths where artisans would create these masterpieces in jewelry. June and I got talking after I'd been to a show and I mentioned how impressed I was with the local artist scene. From there, it fell into place." Hannah nodded at the hutch. "The artists were surprised and pleased that we wanted to feature them."

He straightened. "I'm sure it didn't take much to persuade them. You do have a passion for art."

"I love paintings, but I guess growing up in my dad's jewelry shop made me more aware of these pieces."

The light shone off a bracelet of moonstone and Hannah's throat clogged. Every artist had been so shocked at her interest in displaying their works. "I was honored to be able to put this collection together."

He faced her, meeting her gaze squarely.

"And it was a step toward your ambition of working in a museum."

She laughed, both sad and excited at the same time. He got her, her old dreams and hopes. "Even though our lives didn't turn out as planned, at least I got to make a small mark in the art world."

"Is Jonathan going to show these pieces at his gallery?"

Her stomach dipped. "I don't think so. His clientele goes for more high-end art."

"Did he even ask?"

"Well, no. But then, I didn't make a big deal about the display."

"He has seen it?"

"Yes. About a week after it was unveiled."

Derrick frowned.

"He was out of town at the time it launched."

He didn't say anything, but Hannah noticed his jaw flex.

Derrick glanced at the hutch, then back to her. "I'm proud of you."

Her heart madly raced. "Oh, please. It's nothing major."

"Don't belittle your vision. I can see you spent a great deal of time and thought on this exhibit by the way the pieces are situated and how the light hits the gems just so. It's very professional. I would know, seeing as I've spent a lot of time in museums all over the country."

Her chest tightened. His praise shouldn't bring tears to her eyes, but it did.

A comfortable silence blanketed them as Derrick took in the other exhibits in the room. Afterward, he stopped by her side. Took her hand in his. She held herself stiff to cover her reaction to the shivers tingling over her body at his touch.

His voice was thick when he said, "I know I've apologized, and it'll never be enough, but I'm sorry I spilled the beans about the gems to my dad. You have a real love for this world, Hannah, and I took that away from you."

She squeezed his hand, hating the remorse she read in his eyes. "It was my father's decision to get mixed up with the wrong men. If it hadn't been you, someone else could have put us in the very same circumstances. And if no one had said anything, who knows what may have happened to my dad if those crooks hadn't been caught." She placed her free hand on his cheek, the faint stubble tickling her fingertips. "I do forgive you, Derrick. Life is too short to hold regrets."

Their gazes locked. Heat flushed her cheeks as she saw his eyes grow dark. His free hand cupped the back of her neck and he tugged her so close she could detect the scent of peppermint on his breath.

"I don't deserve your forgiveness, but I'm going to take it."

He moved into her space and his lips closed over hers. With a sigh, she dropped his hand and stepped into the embrace. Memories swept over her, old and new. She lost track of time and place until the sound of loud voices from another room reminded her where she was. Pulling back, she covered her mouth with her hand, her lips warm from his touch.

"I forgot about the kids," she mumbled.

Derrick tucked a strand of her hair behind her ear. "I forget about everything when I'm with you."

She shook her head. "We can't." She waved a hand between them. "This. It isn't right. I have Jonathan to consider."

"Then consider him. Think about whether you should marry him when you can so easily kiss me."

And wasn't that the truth? He wasn't telling her anything she hadn't already agonized over herself. Jonathan was steady. Safe. Derrick stirred up emotions she'd thought she'd buried long ago. He came searching for the gemstones that had the potential to stir up chaos in their lives again. Yet she wasn't a bit sorry she'd kissed her first love.

Not willing to discuss this with him, she said, "We should get back to the students."

Derrick touched her arm before she could leave. "Thank you for showing me your exhibit. And for your forgiveness."

She nodded. "I may have forgiven you, but you can't ever do anything that'll cause my family harm again."

DERRICK NODDED, wondering if he could carry out her request.

Hannah was beautiful, with her cheeks flushed and her eyes bright. She hurried from the room, eager to get back to the children. Or eager to get away from him? Either excuse worked. Had he scared her? Made her question her commitment to Prescott? And her warning? Valid. He couldn't do anything to cause her or her mother pain again.

He took one last look at her display, his chest warm at the sight. She had a real talent for highlighting the most interesting aspects of the pieces. Guilt nudged him along as he realized once again that he'd kept her from the career she'd had her heart set on.

By the time he joined the others, the boys wrangled him into sticking with them for the remainder of the tour. Keeping the young boys' attention was tough until they came to the Kids Craft room. A table was set up for the students to hammer sheets of metal, twist leather into bracelets or fashion long strands of raffia into a basket.

Hannah had done her best to keep her back to him, which was okay. He'd pushed her; he knew it. She had to decide on her own, which direction her life would take, no matter how much he wanted to meddle. For a guy who liked to interfere in the lives of the people he loved—just ask his family—not taking control of the situation was excruciating. Maybe he could look at it as character growth.

"Over here, Mr. Fields." Tommy's voice pulled his thoughts from Hannah. "We get to use hammers!"

And who thought this was a good idea?

The older man behind the long table, whose name tag read Mason, chuckled, explaining the art of metalwork to the excited boys and girls. The hammers laid out on the table had short handles. The striking end, rather than being flat, was rounded in a ball-peen shape designed to leave deep and even impressions. A pattern was engraved in the metal. Beside the tool, small steel blocks provided a solid and compact stamping surface for the kids to pound away on.

Mason handed Derrick a hammer with a longer handle and a narrow sheet of metal, about the size to wrap around a wrist. "This'll actually form a shape."

Derrick took the hammer, looked at the textured end, but still came up short.

"Watch," Mason said. He took a narrow strip of metal and placed it on a block. Then he hammered the material until indentations formed. "The metal moves with each strike, forming a pattern."

Derrick watched, enthralled. He'd never taken the time to consider how jewelry was made. Intrigued now, he started hitting the metal, making a pattern of his own. He was so caught up in the task he didn't notice the children had gone quiet while watching him. After a while he stopped and picked up the metal. His fingertips moved over the surface and he was impressed with his first attempt at this kind of art.

Art had always been Hannah's domain.

Mason produced another rounded block on a stand. "Now we curve it."

Following suit, Derrick curved the piece and with Mason's help, rounded off the edges.

Mason announced he had created a cuff. Or a bracelet, Derrick soon learned.

Mason took hold of it and examined Derrick's work. "Not bad for a rookie."

"Thanks."

The older man winked when he handed it back. "You can give it to your honey as a gift."

He doubted the woman he wanted to be his honey would accept a gift from him.

Tommy frantically tugged on his arm. Derrick leaned over so the boy could get close to his ear. "You could give it to Miss Rawley. Up your game."

Was he that pathetic that a ten-year-old was seriously giving him romance advice?

"My mother is getting married. I think I'll give it to her."

Tommy rolled his eyes as if to say, *Sad, dude.* Derrick concurred.

Hannah's voice rose over the others. "Everyone gather up your projects and hand them off to Mrs. Lewis. She'll hold on to them until we get back to school."

One by one the students put their creations in the plastic box, then hurried off to lunch in an empty workshop room which contained long tables. Derrick slipped the cuff he'd made into his pocket, mentally debating giving it to Hannah as a gift, when his cell phone rang. When he saw it was Dylan's name on the screen, he caught Hannah's attention, pointed to the phone, then went to the lobby of the museum to talk to his brother.

"What does Mom need now?" he asked, getting right to the point.

"Nice to talk to you, too," Dylan answered with a hint of humor.

"Sorry. I'm on a field trip with fourth graders so I can't be gone long."

"Field trip?"

"Yeah. My undercover job."

"Right." Derrick could have sworn he heard a snicker on the other end. "Just checking in to find out if you have any more information."

"I read the Rawlings file. Pretty cut-and-dried. The father testified against a jewelry supplier who turned out to be a black-market fence and afterward the family went into hiding."

"Where's the dealer now?"

"Still serving time in a federal penitentiary."

"So you're not sure who, exactly, was following the family?"

"Had to be the guys who weren't sent away. Still on the payroll of the supplier, would be my guess." Derrick paused, visualizing the file. "As far as I can tell, all parties believed the feds had the gems, but they're not listed in evidence."

"Who has them?"

"I can't answer that question, but I bet Mr. Rawlings can."

"No way the guy hid them from the agents."

"Well, someone has them because they sent one to me."

Doubt tinged Dylan's voice. "You said Rawlings is in the wind."

"Doesn't mean we can't find him." With the information they had managed to piece together, Derrick could start an investigation that might uncover Hannah's father's whereabouts.

"Are you going to ask Hannah?"

Derrick thought about it for a minute. His initial answer was a firm no, but in light of what the family had gone through and his part in it, he decided being up front was a better idea. Hannah and her mother needed to know what they were up against. For now, he would continue to keep the two of them safe until he discovered who had the other gems.

"Once I come up with a game plan, I'll let them know."

"Are you going to keep the Bureau involved?"

"At this point, I'll have to. My boss wants a location on those gems."

"Good luck with that," Dylan said. "Keep me in the loop."

"I will. And Dyl?"

"Yeah?"

"Thanks for listening."

"You owe me big-time, brother."

Derrick heard something off in his brother's tone and said, "We always help each other out."

"Yes, but we don't always get wrangled into swing dance lessons by our mother so we can participate at her wedding reception."

Derrick frowned. "Swing dancing?"

"Google it."

"I'll get right on that."

"You do that," Dylan said, then ended the call.

Placing his phone back in his pocket, Derrick rejoined the children, who were finished eating. There were still a few more exhibits to view. In the final room, featuring Native American crafts and a few pieces of art, the kids started to get loud. Hannah, sensing the mood change, rounded the kids up to head back to the bus and then to school. He watched her count heads two by two, asking the children to help her keep track. Honestly, she had a way of making any situation fun.

Just before the students were ready to file out, Tommy and another boy started a scuffle. They moved out of line and bounced up against the wall, right under a framed painting. Tommy's hand accidently slapped against the frame and the piercing screech of the alarm bombarded the room. The kids covered their ears with their hands and raced out of line to huddle together. Before long, June, waddling as fast as she could given the late stage of pregnancy, hurried into the room, opened a box next to the painting and punched a code, allowing blessed quiet to calm everyone down.

Derrick strode up to the museum director at the same time as Hannah, nearly colliding on the way. He grabbed Hannah's shoulders to keep her from falling. She nodded in his direction but focused on the director.

"I'm so sorry, June. One of the students accidentally touched the frame."

June patted Hannah's arm. "It's partly my fault. I forgot to tell you about the active alarm for this piece." Her face turned red. "Pregnancy brain."

Relief swept over Hannah's features. "There's no damage, and I promise the students involved will get a stern talking-to."

June nodded as Hannah returned to the line of silent students. At the director's frown, Derrick moved closer and asked in a low tone. "Anything wrong?"

"No. I just can't believe I forgot to mention the alarm."

"Why a separate alarm on this particular piece? I didn't notice others specifically protected in any of the areas we walked through today."

She looked at him in surprise.

"Security. I notice things like that."

"Of course. Sorry, the alarm rattled me." June placed a hand over her heart. "This is a special piece, on loan from a highly regarded collector. The Native American artist only painted a few of these beautiful scenes before passing away. We were lucky enough to show it here for a few months, with the promise of strict security, so the alarm stays on."

Made sense. The artwork was part of a well-known series and would be expected to have maximum protection.

"The boys didn't mean any harm."

"And I need to have this baby before I completely forget how to do my job."

Derrick chuckled.

June sighed and ran her hand over her belly. "I wish Anna was available to fill in for me. She's so knowledgeable and has a way with the artists."

"I don't see how that's possible since she's a teacher."

"True. Don't get me wrong—Anna's wonderful with the children but I got the feeling that her heart belonged here. Or at a museum, anyway."

Derrick knew why, but asked, "She's really that talented?"

"Oh, yes. She's very knowledgeable about art and crafts featured here. Art was her minor degree in college."

She hadn't told him about her degree, but he wasn't surprised.

"It's no wonder Jonathan loves having her help with his gallery. They'll make a great team after they're married."

He didn't want to think about that. "Tell me about Anna's exhibit."

"When she set up an appointment, I knew something was up, just by the excitement in her voice. She came in, pitched her idea and I couldn't say no."

"The display is very appealing."

"Her attention to detail is amazing. The artists were so excited when she asked them to participate, but even more so when they viewed the finished exhibit. She even threw a small reception on opening day. Everyone adores her."

How could they not? She was generous with her time, caring and most of all, passionate about art. It made him fall in love with her even deeper.

"I watched her on the sidelines as the artists were having a good time and was struck by the sadness in her eyes. Here everyone else was having a grand time and I couldn't help but sense there was something missing in it for her." June shook her head. "Then I realized Jonathan wasn't there. He had a prior commitment and couldn't make it."

No, that wasn't it, Derrick thought, but he still couldn't decide what kind of jerk Prescott was for not being there for Hannah at such an important moment. In reality, Hannah had imagined a future working in the art world and this was the closest she got. And still threw a party for the artists when he had to imagine her heart was breaking over the realization that her dream had slipped through her fingers. He'd robbed her of the experience.

And now he had to make it up to her.

He cleared his throat. "Thanks for sharing that with me. Anna's pretty tight-lipped about her life here."

"I've chalked it up to her being a private person. Nothing wrong with that."

No, there wasn't. But most people had never lived through witness protection and had to give up on their dreams.

"And I'll talk to the boys about inappropriate roughhousing."

June ran a hand over her belly. "Is this what I have to look forward to if this is a boy?"

Derrick chuckled. "I'm afraid so. I know what I'm talking about. I have three brothers."

As June returned to her office, Derrick went outside to see the last of the students board the bus.

"Everything under control?" he asked as he strode to the vehicle.

Hannah looked up at him, eyes pinched. "For now. I spoke to the boys. They were upset about what happened."

"They're good kids."

A shrill ring came from the direction of Hannah's purse. With a frown, she fished out her cell phone, in the process knocking the bag off her shoulder. It fell to the ground, the contents scattering over the asphalt. Derrick sank down to the balls of his feet, picking up the bag to retrieve the belongings while she checked her phone. He lifted a small compact to toss back inside and froze.

Underneath the compact was a bright green gem that sparkled in the sunlight. His head jerked up to meet Hannah's eyes, which were wide with surprise.

"What on earth?" she muttered.

"Is there something you want to tell me?"

She shook off her shock and drew back. "What do you mean?"

He pointed to the stone. "Is this yours?"

She blinked a few times before scooping it up and standing. He slowly followed suit.

"I…ah…it must have come loose from a pair of earrings I tossed into my bag the other day."

Right. And if she thought he'd buy that explanation, she was sorely mistaken. "You expect me to believe that?"

All emotion wiped from her face, she tugged her purse against her side, turned and stepped into the bus.

Yeah, he was pretty sure the stone wasn't from an earring. More likely it was one of the gems from the collection that had gone missing.

Hannah had some serious explaining to do.

CHAPTER TEN

MORTIFIED, HANNAH SAT across from Mrs. Muldoon. The principal rested her elbows on the pristine blotter of her wide desk and peered through bifocals at the two people sitting across from her. This was the second time Hannah could recall being summoned into the principal's office. With the same person who had talked her into an ill-advised stunt back in high school.

She tried to ignore Derrick, but he made it difficult. When he leaned toward her, she caught traces of his tantalizing cologne. The close proximity of his body warmed one side of her. Derrick Matthews was one-hundred-percent unadulterated trouble.

"I know this was an accident," Mrs. Muldoon droned on. "But this isn't the first time Tommy has been part of an…incident."

"It's not as bad as it sounds," Hannah started to say, but the principal held up her hand.

"Be that as it may, I don't like hearing from

the museum director informing me our students set off an alarm."

"If it helps," Derrick intervened, "I spoke to the director before we left. The painting wasn't harmed and the museum won't need to take any further action."

Hannah jerked her head toward him. He'd spoken to June? That explained why it took him so long to emerge from the building when they were loading up the bus.

"Fine." The principal sent Hannah another long look. "This will not happen again."

"I'll make sure it doesn't," Hannah assured her, which was no guarantee. These were kids and stuff happened, even when she had them under her eagle eye. In the future, she'd have to keep better tabs on Tommy and his friends.

"There's still a half hour until the final bell rings. I suggest you return to your class, Anna." The principal turned to Derrick. "If you wouldn't mind, I'd like you to speak to the class. Remind them that their actions were unacceptable, from a security point of view."

"I will."

Hannah fumed. It was her class; she should lead the conversation, but she wasn't about to contradict the principal. Not after this dressing-down. As they rose to leave, she scowled at Derrick and sped out of the room before him.

"Hey, wait up," he called as she strode down the hallway.

"Why?" she said over her shoulder. "So you can beat me to the classroom and undermine my authority?"

Or ask about the green gemstone that fell out of my purse? Where on earth had it come from?

"Not at all." She heard his footsteps pick up speed and then he was at her side. "More like you let me be the bad guy. I'll put the fear in them and you'll still be their favorite teacher."

She snorted a laugh. "Like that'll work."

"Watch me."

They entered the room to find the students seated at their desks, more subdued than usual. Backpacks were lying on the floor at the back of the room, discarded jackets and mittens piled up nearby. The two chaperones left and Hannah took a seat at her desk, waving her hand to give Derrick permission to start. He stood at the front of the room, the blackboard with grade-four assignments written in chalk an incongruous backdrop to the handsome and confident man.

Why did she have to notice so many attractive qualities about him?

He began to pace. "Seems we have a problem."

A few heads bowed and some of the students looked anywhere but up front.

"Here's the thing about museums," he continued. "Artists trust the authorities who work there to keep their artwork safe. They know the public is going to observe their creations, but they don't expect a total disregard of their property by those visitors." He stopped. Let his words sink in. "Imagine if someone came into your house and started to fight, breaking your belongings in the process."

A girl in the front row said just above a whisper, "That's just rude."

"Exactly." He folded his hands behind his back. "What went wrong today?"

A boy with glasses slowly raised his hand. "The alarm went off."

"Because?"

"We weren't paying attention."

"Which is?" Derrick prodded.

Tommy straightened his shoulders and said, "Disrespectful?"

Derrick nodded. "Next time you go on a field trip, you'll pay better attention, right?"

He received a smattering of yeses.

"I didn't hear you."

"Yes, sir," came a louder response.

Hannah raised her hand to her mouth to cover her smile. The children had been sufficiently chastised by a man whose opinion had come to matter to them. She hoped they would remember this moment for the future, providing the principal allowed her to take the class on a field trip again.

Out of the view of the children, Derrick winked at her. Her heart nearly melted. The bell rang and over the commotion of the children digging for their coats and backpacks, she instructed, "Don't forget your science papers are due tomorrow."

Before leaving, Tommy stopped beside her desk. "I'm sorry, Miss Rawley. I didn't mean to cause trouble."

She nodded. "I know. Next time get my attention instead of taking care of a problem yourself."

"Thanks." His bright smile cheered her. "You're the best."

Shrugging on his backpack, Tommy bolted from the room. Which left only Derrick behind.

"See? I told you. He thinks you're the best."

Like she was going to admit Derrick was right. She rose and moved to gather up the permission slips to file away. "Shouldn't you be outside supervising the car line?"

"I had Glen cover for me today in light of the field trip."

"I see." Why did he have to stick around? She was already on sensory overload with him. Did she really need more conversation? Especially when she knew exactly what he wanted to talk about?

He leaned a hip against her desk and his muscles strained under his shirt as he crossed his arms over his broad chest, waiting.

Is this what it felt like to be under interrogation? She was as jumpy as a cat and he hadn't even asked any questions yet. She dropped the papers and squared her shoulders. "What?"

He slowly shook his head, lips pressed in a grimace.

Instead of saying what he wanted to hear, she went another way. "Thank you for helping today."

The grimace disappeared. "You're really going to make me ask?"

She shrugged.

With a sigh, he said, "Why was that green gemstone in your purse?"

She opened her mouth but he held up a hand to cut her off. "And don't give me the excuse it broke off an earring."

"You wouldn't believe me if I told you," she said grudgingly.

He seemed to smile. Almost. "Let's try again. Why was that green stone in your purse?"

She played with the hem of her sweater. "I don't believe it myself."

"Try me."

Debating what to say, and how, she burst out, "That's the first I've seen of it. I swear."

"No earring?"

"No. I was as shocked as you were to find it on the pavement. I didn't want to draw attention to it in front of the children."

"Okay. Where do you think it came from?"

She met his gaze, imploring him to trust her. "I have no idea."

"Wrong answer. I'd say it's another stone from your father's collection."

So would she. Even though the odds of a gem showing up in her purse were downright mind-boggling.

A slight frown marred his forehead and his jaw worked, like he was thinking hard. Finally, he asked, "Did you leave your purse unattended any time today?"

She thought back to the steps she'd taken since arriving at the museum. "I put it in June's office before we took the tour."

"We both know June left her office a few times while we were there."

What was he getting at? Did he think June had something to do with the gemstone?

"I'm going to ask you something, Hannah, and I need you to be completely honest with me."

Hannah gulped. Nothing like being on the hot seat.

"At any time during the day did you feel as though you were being watched?"

Surprise rendered her speechless for a moment. "Watched?"

"Like you explained to me the day we were at the home-improvement store."

Had anything felt off? Besides her increasing awareness for a man who wasn't her fiancé? "No. Today was normal. I know my dad was paranoid about being followed, but since Mom and I came here, I've only had the feeling a handful of times."

"Such as."

"When you came to town."

What she imagined was disappointment crossed his face, but his eyes still held a serious glint. She wondered if he was this intent when working on a case.

"Did you feel like we were being watched?" she asked in return.

"No." He dropped his arms and stuffed his fingers in the front pockets of his jeans. The blue pullover he'd worn today matched the warm color of his eyes. "I've learned never to discount anything out of the ordinary. Many times it's the small details you might think unimportant that give us a better picture of what's going on."

For the first time since glimpsing the stone

she relaxed. "Are you saying that you don't think I've imagined being watched?"

"No. And that's why another stone surfacing is so bothersome."

"Do you think it was planted?"

"That would be my guess."

"By whom?"

"That's the twenty-thousand-dollar question."

Hannah sank into her seat. He flattened his palms on the desk surface and leaned in to her. "These are not coincidences, Hannah. I received a stone. You didn't know another was in your purse. Makes me question when the others will materialize."

Her breath caught. "You're making me nervous."

"I don't mean to, but I can't wrap my head around the events. Why would someone be interested in revealing the stones when they've been missing since the trial? Why send me to you, now? I know we've voiced these questions since I arrived, but we've still come up empty."

He'd told her he was looking into the old case, which made her nervous. She considered the glint in his eye before asking, "Are Mom and I in danger?"

He paused before speaking. "I can't say for sure, but since your family willingly left WIT-

SEC, you don't have the protection you once had. Now you only have me." She glanced up at him. His eyes blazed with an intensity that scared her. She saw him as the professional he was. She had no doubt he was good at his job. Question was, would she allow him to protect her?

She closed her eyes for a moment, letting reality sink in. The gemstones that had been the catalyst to send her family from their home seventeen years ago had recently resurfaced. She needed to know why.

Even though Derrick seemed deep in thought, she asked, "What happens now?"

He reached over to tip her chin with one finger. "Do you trust me?"

She didn't hesitate. Answered honestly. "Yes."

"Then let's work together to figure this out."

Their gazes remained locked for a drawn-out moment. Promises of the past and unspoken desires for the future hung taut in the air between them before he removed his finger. Gathering her wits about her, Hannah rose and walked to the window. She stared outside as she reined in her out-of-control emotions. Did they dare work together? Could they work together? Her answer was important. Would change her life once again, as she knew it. But what choice did she have? She heard him come up behind her, but he kept his distance when what she wanted was for him to take her in his arms and promise her everything was going to be okay.

"I have contacts," he said quietly. "I can find answers, Hannah. It's what I do."

Shoring up her courage, she turned. "I can't ignore this. And I don't want to run anymore." She paused. "I'm in."

Derrick sent her a gentle smile that soothed her fears and made her blood race at the same time.

She broke the silence. "I have one request."

He went all serious at her words and her stomach twisted.

"I need to tell Jonathan what's going on. It's only right."

A flash of—was that impatience?—flared in his eyes but was quickly smothered. "How much?"

"Enough to explain why you're here and what our connection is. I never told him about WITSEC or the real reasons we left Florida. I planned to, before we got married, of course, but…" She held her hands wide.

"You'll have to keep it vague."

"Why? Do you suspect him of something?"

His stony silence said it all.

Flabbergasted, she said, "Derrick, there's no

way Jonathan has anything to do with the gems showing up."

"And you know this for sure?"

"I…well…" Her confidence faded. "No."

"Exactly. Until I can get more details, Jonathan should know only the bare minimum."

That was going to be tricky, but she understood where Derrick was coming from. "Okay."

Their gazes met and held again. With only a look, he still had the power to sweep her off her feet, if she wasn't careful. As she composed her nerves, instead of kissing him like she wanted to, she watched Derrick back up. Placing a shaky hand over her stomach, she blew out a gust of air. What was wrong with her? This wasn't the time or place.

She shoved aside her emotions and went to her desk, fuzzy about what she wanted to pack up for the night. How was it possible Derrick still had that much of an effect on her?

She rubbed her throbbing temple.

"You okay?"

"Hmm? Yes. It's been a long day."

A devastating grin curved his lips, putting her on high alert.

"That visit to the principal's office was just like old times."

"No, it wasn't," she fumed. "We're adults."

"Don't you think it's funny how we still end up in crazy situations together?"

She sent him a stink eye, not confessing the truth. Life was more interesting with Derrick in it.

Not one to let well enough alone, he went on. "I have to say, when I suggested we steal the flag from our rival high school after the baseball playoff game, I never thought you'd go along with me."

"We were excited about winning. Going to the state championships." She sent him a rueful grin. "I couldn't resist."

"Because you love an adventure."

She lifted a shoulder instead of agreeing out loud.

"Come on. Admit you have a wild streak."

"Only with you. Otherwise I'm a very dependable, upright citizen."

"Which isn't half as fun as setting off alarms."

She rolled her eyes.

He laughed, reached into his pants pocket and handed her a piece of metal. "Peace offering."

On closer inspection she realized it was a hammered wrist cuff. "Did you make this today?"

"Yep. If this special-agent gig goes sideways, I might have a future making jewelry."

She examined the piece, impressed with his workmanship. When she looked up, his rare, uncertain expression captured her heart. She couldn't be mad at him.

"Thank you, Derrick."

Pleasure beamed on his face. She didn't want to make accepting his gift a green light to resuming their old relationship so she tucked the bracelet in her purse. She had just the place for it at home. If it bothered Derrick that she didn't immediately slip his gift on her wrist, he didn't say anything, for which she was grateful. She had to speak to Jonathan before making up her mind about the future of either man in her life.

The green stone was still inside her purse. She removed it and handed it to Derrick. "I think you should hold onto this for now."

He nodded, taking the stone from her outstretched palm.

"I should get home," she said, reaching out to grab her coat from the peg on the wall behind her. "Once I get more intel on this case, I'll fill you in."

She stopped with only one arm in her coat sleeve. "Are you sure we can work together and not get involved? Not kiss again?"

"Kissing? I can't make any promises…"

When she made a face he laughed, reminding her of the old days when he told her that kissing her was his favorite pastime.

"Hannah, I'm good at what I do. We can work together professionally and I'll only kiss you when you ask me to."

"Me? Ask you?"

"Hey. Gentleman here." Derrick moved closer to take hold of her coat and help her with the other sleeve. His breath tickled her neck and she pressed her lips together. While she wasn't sure working as a team was a good idea, she was willing to give it a try. Turning, she pulled her hair from the collar just as Lynny rushed into the room, her coat draped over her arm and a frantic expression on her face.

"Derrick, thank goodness."

"Lynny, what's wrong?" Hannah asked, concerned by her friend's obvious anxiety.

"It's Roger. He was gathering the basketball equipment in the utility closet and somehow tripped over a ball. He thinks he might have broken his arm. I'm going to drive him to the ER now, but he needs someone to cover practice."

"I can fill in," Derrick assured her. "I've been staying after school to give pointers so I'm like a part of the team."

"That's what Roger said." She shook out her coat. "I need to get back to him."

"Call me later," Hannah said, following her friend to the hallway. "Or if you need anything."

"Will do," Lynny replied over her shoulder as she jogged back to the gym.

"I hope Roger will be okay," Hannah said.

"Lynny will take good care of him."

Hannah raised a brow at him. "Basketball coach?"

"Just in case this FBI gig—"

"—goes sideways," she finished for him.

He winked at her, making her toes curl up in her boots, then took off, leaving her to stand alone in the dim hallway, wondering how on earth she ever thought she could withstand Derrick's charm.

THE FOLLOWING AFTERNOON, Derrick had just placed a cupcake with thick red frosting and a green gumdrop on top of Hannah's desk when his cell phone rang. He pulled it from his pocket, biting back a retort when he read the caller ID.

"Daisies for a winter wedding. What do you think?" his mother asked.

"You're the florist, Mom. Plus, you have a

perfectly capable groom who can answer these questions for you."

"Yes, but after the hard time you boys gave him, he's enjoying my phone conversations with you."

Maybe being on Team James wasn't all it was cracked up to be.

"Since the ceremony will be held close to Valentine's Day, I'm going with a red color scheme, but roses are so expected. A pop of white flowers might do the trick."

"Sounds good, Mom."

"You seem distracted."

"I'm trying to have a vacation here."

She chuckled. "One last question."

Derrick dropped his head back and stared at the ceiling. "Shoot."

"What do you think about us dressing up in medieval clothing?"

"Like I'll fall off the side of the earth and never return."

"Just checking to make sure you were paying attention."

"Go with daises, Mom. They're your favorite," he said as Hannah strolled into the room.

"You remembered," she whispered in a choked voice.

"Gotta go."

He hit the end button and angled his body to hide the treat on her desk.

"Flowers?"

"Mom wants daisies for the wedding."

"Simple and cheerful."

He nodded. "You liked daisies if I recall."

"I did."

"Does Prescott send them to you?"

She frowned. "That's none of your business."

"Sorry. I was out of line."

"You were." She paused. Wrinkled her nose. "He sends me carnations. I'm sorry, but not a fan."

He chuckled at her expression.

"So, why are you here?" she asked as she moved around him to get to her desk.

All the parents in car line had picked up their kids. He had an hour before the middle-school boys intramural basketball game, a short window of opportunity to visit with Hannah until he had to be back and coach the team. She'd changed from a proper dress into a green sweater that highlighted her hazel eyes, jeans and boots, to work the snack bar during the interschool game.

"What did you do?" she asked with an accusatory tone, hands resting on her hips.

"I left you a treat." He moved away, swinging

his arm toward the desk. She met his amused gaze, then moved forward to pick up the cupcake.

"You aren't very subtle," she said, inspecting it.

"I'd never be accused of that trait."

"But I get your motive here. Red and green, just like the gemstones." She popped the gumdrop in her mouth.

Stifling a groan, he leaned against her desk. "I got home too late last night to make any calls, but I want you to know we'll figure out what's going on. Together." Actually, he was a bit uncertain about including his boss because he understood that Hannah might have reservations. But while her family lacked faith in the government's ability to keep them safe, he needed access to case files he couldn't get on his own. For now he'd keep the identity of his sources to himself.

"I thought a lot about that last night." She swiped her finger through the frosting and took a taste. She licked her lips to remove the stray icing. "Mmm."

When Derrick had placed the cupcake on her desk, he never thought watching her taste it would conjure up ideas of kissing her again. He cleared his throat. "And what did you come up with?"

"Though I'm happy to stay far removed from

any government agencies, I agree it's time to look into this matter." She set the cupcake down, her expression grim. "I hope you don't mind, but I told Mom what's going on."

"As you should. She needs to know what's transpired so far."

"She was pretty quiet about the matter. Makes me wonder if she was thinking about my father."

"I imagine she still misses him."

Her throat moved as she swallowed. "We both do."

Throwing caution to the wind, he wrapped his arm around her shoulder and tugged her close. To his surprise she didn't resist; instead she relaxed against him. A comforting silence settled over the room, calming in the midst of the emotional turmoil over their relationship, or lack of one. If he had his way, they'd stay this close forever, but she soon pulled back.

She'd fashioned her hair into a braid, but pesky auburn curls escaped and framed her beautiful face. He met her gaze, loving the deep hazel of her eyes, her soft skin and the freckles spotting her nose. He'd so missed being this close to her and his heart ached with the uncertain future ahead of them.

A smile curved her lips. "Ready for tonight?"

"As I'll ever be. Roger could easily coach

tonight, since his fall caused a bad sprain and not a break, but I think he's looking forward to sitting back and letting me take over. His wrist is taped up nice and tight so he has an excuse."

"The boys like you."

He shrugged. "You know, I like my job at the Bureau. It's exciting and the cases are challenging. But I can see why you enjoy teaching. There's a sense of…accomplishment when you can give advice or point a student in the right direction."

"Sounds like your dad talking."

A wave of sadness washed over him. "I hadn't thought about it that way."

"Your dad knew just what to do to connect with you and your brothers. Woodworking with you, boating with Dylan, science exhibits with Deke and cars with Dante. That wasn't just luck. He cultivated deep relationships with all four of you by finding out what your passions were, then he took the time to pour his insight and values in you." She reached out to brush his jaw with her soft fingertips. "He was a wise man."

He blinked hard. The electricity of her touch was marred by the truth. "And I ruined it by being mad at him. I never got a chance to apologize for being a jerk."

Hannah moved closer, enveloping him in her

vanilla snare. "Derrick, I have no doubt he understood. He did what he thought was right, just like you coming here to see Mom and me."

"You haven't made it easy."

"No, but after the other gemstone showed up yesterday, I'll admit, I'm glad you're here."

Her confession pleased him. Gave him hope. "Glad enough for us to start over?"

A shadow crossed her face. She dropped her hand. "I still have to talk to Jonathan. I won't make any promises until then."

He respected her answer, even admired her for it. Just because he was impatient didn't mean he should keep her from doing the right thing. "Hey, a guy can wish."

He got the chuckle he'd been going for, then Hannah sobered. "I'm going to talk to him after the game." She pulled the cuff of her sleeve back to check her watch. "In fact, he should be here any minute."

"He's coming here tonight?"

"Yes. He's been busier with the gallery exhibits than he expected so we keep missing each other, but I need to explain about this gemstone mystery before it goes further."

"Smart."

Her face brightened. "Yes, I am."

"You're making this difficult." When she scowled at him, he said, "I'm sorry. It's just…

Hannah, I never thought I'd see you again. To be honest, I'd given up hope. Was ready to move on. And now, you're right here, within reach and I can't help myself."

She placed a hand on his arm. "I get it. Derrick. For years I dreamed about reuniting with you. But as time went by, I had to be realistic. You weren't going to be in my life. And once I'd made peace with the idea, I met Jonathan." She bit her lower lip before going on. "I admire him. He's been there for me and my mom."

"But do you love him?"

Her eyes welled. "Yes. Not the way I felt about you, but in a different, more adult way. I can rely on him and after the trials my family has been through, that's important to me."

"And I show up, a reminder of the past, with news of a gemstone that set events in motion seventeen years ago." How had he ever thought getting Hannah back would be so easy? "I understand why you're torn."

"I sometimes think it's because there was no closure. To anything. Not having the choice to leave or stay. Not being able to say goodbye. With Jonathan I feel like I have choices."

He was standing so close to her, yet they still felt hundreds of miles apart. It hurt right down to the marrow of his soul.

"I would never pressure you to make any decision." Even if she chose to walk away from him.

"I know. That's what makes this even more confusing."

At least he wasn't the only puzzled person here.

With a weary sigh, Hannah gathered up her purse and tote bag. "We should get to the gym."

He pushed from the desk, his heart just as broken and lonely as the years he'd spent away from Hannah. "Right. The game." Keeping busy to get over losing her had been his mantra for longer than he could remember. Looked like that wasn't going to change any time soon.

They left the room, Hannah switching off the lights, and stepped into the hallway just as Jonathan rounded the corner. He stopped short and frowned. Hannah hurried toward him.

"You made it."

He glanced over her shoulder, shooting a *What are you doing here?* look at Derrick.

"I'll see you two later," Derrick said, then passed by, even as every fiber in his body shouted at him to stand his ground. He didn't want to make things uncomfortable for Hannah. She'd said she'd talk to Jonathan and he had to trust her decision.

Once in the gym, he strode to the group of boys waiting for him. They moved to the side, went over the plays and once they'd high-fived, he walked over to his place at the bleachers while the boys took warm-up shots. Sneakers squeaked on the highly polished floor and family and friends filled the bleachers, chatting and getting ready for the excitement to start. The buttery scent of freshly popped popcorn filled the air.

Derrick looked over to find Roger and Lynny sitting behind him. "Sure you don't want to take over?" he asked as he set his clipboard down.

Roger tilted his head toward Lynny. "I don't think she'd let me even if wanted to say yes."

"You're more than capable, Derrick," Lynny informed him in her no-nonsense tone. "If I couldn't keep Roger home, at least I know he won't overdo it tonight."

The men exchanged amused glances. Yeah, Roger was lapping up the attention. Couldn't say he blamed the guy.

After checking his playbook one final time, Derrick watched the boys' progress, catching sight of Hannah and Prescott as they walked into the gym. He couldn't make out her expression as she hurried to the snack bar, but he didn't miss the thundercloud on Prescott's face as he aimed directly for Derrick. Steeling himself, he met the other man head-on.

"Prescott."

"Fields. A word?"

Derrick nodded and led Prescott to a relatively quiet corner of the gym. Folks still filed in minutes before the game and boys streaked by as they took practice shots at the hoop.

Prescott's voice rose over the din. "Anna wants to talk to me after the game. Any idea what that's about?"

"You'd have to ask her."

"Really, because it seems like the two of you have been in cahoots ever since you showed up."

Cahoots?

"I'm sure once you and Anna have a conversation, this will make sense."

Prescott folded his arms over his chest. He barely wrinkled his fashionable wool blazer. "What makes sense is you leaving her alone. We're engaged."

The strike hit him right in his heart. "I'm aware."

"Then act like it."

A nagging sense of guilt crept over him. He'd kissed this man's fiancée. He knew he'd be murderous if someone was kissing Hannah behind his back. He had to give her time to work this out, even if the results were not in his favor.

"Do you trust Anna?" he asked.

Prescott frowned. "Certainly, I do."

"Then give her some credit. Hear her out and then decide if you want to come after me."

Prescott's eyebrows rose. "Come after you?"

"Yeah. It's pretty clear you're drawing a line in the sand."

For a moment Prescott looked unsure, then squared his shoulders. "I'd appreciate you giving us some room."

"I can only agree for so long." Derrick spotted the referees walking onto the floor. "I need to get ready for the game."

Prescott seemed confused. "With Anna?"

Derrick clenched his fists. "She's not a game to me."

"Me neither," Prescott declared. The two stared at each other, not giving in an inch. "Seems we're at an impasse."

"Then may the best man win."

Prescott turned on his heel and made his way around to the far side of the gym. Derrick returned to the bench.

"That looked awkward," Roger remarked.

"Yeah, but we laid our cards on the table."

"More like made it clear you both want the girl?" Lynny asked. She slipped her hand into the curve of Roger's arm and smiled at him. "I don't envy my friend."

"Any suggestions?" Derrick asked.

Lynny sobered. "Win."

Leaving him to wonder, was she referring to the basketball game or his future with Hannah?

CHAPTER ELEVEN

"ONCE MY FATHER TESTIFIED, we were okay for a while," Hannah said a few hours later as she and Jonathan sat at her kitchen table, mugs of freshly brewed coffee at their elbows. The light over the sink cast a warm reflection over them. "Until he was convinced someone was following us. That's when we left WITSEC and moved around."

"And you and your mother ended up here."

"Yes. My dad is…" Hannah held up her hands. "Well, I'm not sure where he is."

"Explains why you take such good care of your mother."

She allowed a small smile. Taking care of things had become her specialty.

"But if you're out of the program, you don't have to hide any longer. Why the secret?"

"Old habits?"

Jonathan had followed her home after the game, intently listening to as much of her backstory as she'd deemed safe to confide in him. At first, Hannah wasn't sure how he'd react, but then realized her fears were unfounded. He'd been overwhelmingly understanding, which shouldn't have been a surprise since he was in her corner, even when he hadn't known many facts. She waited for the other shoe to drop—because in her experience, the other shoe always dropped—but her anxiety soon eased at his gentle expression.

"That's quite a story." His brow wrinkled as he hooked his finger in the mug handle.

"We aren't in the protection program any longer, which is problematic now that the past is suddenly making an appearance."

"In what way? You haven't explained that part."

"Someone sent Derrick our address. That's why he's here."

"Because your pasts are tied together?"

"Yes." She mustered up the resolve to keep going. "We haven't seen each other in seventeen years. Out of the blue he gets the location of where we live after I'd made sure to keep it under the radar. That's definitely fishy."

"What does he think is going to happen?"

"That's just it," she told him truthfully. "We don't know."

"So he's going to stay here until what, something does happen? Seems like a long shot."

Not if you'd seen the gemstone. Which she couldn't tell him about. Not yet, anyway.

"This is not only upsetting your life, but Derrick's as well?"

She nodded.

"I suppose that explains why he's so determined to play your knight in shining armor."

Was he? Hannah hadn't perceived it that way. He was just being Derrick, protective, and a little bit maddening when he smiled at her like she was the only woman in the world. He'd watched out for her, even when they were kids. These days he had a way of making her feel secure, even while he made her blood race.

Jonathan broke the silence. "What happens now?"

"Derrick…knows people. He's trying to find out why someone sent him in our direction."

Jonathan frowned. "Because you left the program? What does it matter now?"

Hannah pictured the green stone in her mind. Apparently, it mattered a great deal to someone.

"I'm not sure how that factors in. I can't ask my dad why he thought we were being watched or what he thought might happen, so we're in the dark." And if she was currently in any kind of danger, she couldn't warn him. The thought broke her heart as much as it scared her.

Jonathan nodded, then lifted his mug to

drink the remainder of his coffee. When he grimaced, Hannah knew the brew had grown cold.

"Refill?"

"No, thanks. Not that I plan on getting any sleep tonight while I mull through this information, but any additional caffeine won't help."

"I don't want you to worry."

"Like that won't happen?"

"Exactly why I didn't want to burden you with the story of my past." She looked down at the diamond ring. "But you should know."

He leaned over and took her left hand in his. His thumb traced the diamond solitaire on her ring finger.

She eased her hand from his. "Everything is so…topsy-turvy right now," she said as she slipped the beautiful solitaire from her finger. "Why would you want to be saddled with the drama in my life? Your gallery's reputation is gaining traction, especially with Bernard signing on. Clients love your artists, including Layla. What if events from my past ruin your hard work?"

He tried to stall her action by placing his hand over hers, but she removed the ring and held it out to him.

He stared at it, then met her gaze. "This is a lot to take in, but it doesn't change my feelings. I knew you had some baggage and that one day you'd tell me. Even if it was after we walked down the aisle, I was still ready to marry you."

Her eyes burned with unshed tears. "I can't commit to a date. Not as things stand."

His deep brown gaze met hers. She didn't detect any acrimony there. "What do you say you hold on to the ring for the time being. I know I've been pushing the wedding plans along lately, but I want us to be together, Anna."

Anna. That untruth was enough to push him away forever.

"As husband and wife," he continued. "Take all the time you need."

Husband and wife. Had it only been a few weeks ago that the idea had filled her with joy? Now, confusion muddled her brain. She closed her fist around the ring. Was it possible to be in love with two men at the same time? She tucked the ring in her jeans pocket.

"Think this over and I'll see you at Bernard's showing Friday night. You're still helping, right?"

How could she refuse?

He continued. "You've already lined up critics you know personally and I have a full guest list who have RSVP'd that they're attending."

Which was why she needed to be at Bernard's opening night. She'd met a few reporters when she'd unveiled her own exhibit at the arts-and-crafts museum, which had created additional connections for Jonathan. He hadn't asked her to approach the reviewers, not outright anyway, but suggested she join forces with him to throw an opening-night party for Bernard and invite her new contacts. Honestly, she didn't know if she had the energy to smile and make small talk all evening. Before she could say anything, Jonathan stood.

"I should head home," he said, carrying his mug to the sink. "The gallery opens late tomorrow morning, but Michelle and I have an early breakfast appointment."

"An appointment with another new artist?"

"No, her ideas to promote the gallery. I have to say, she understands my vision and is eager for us to capitalize on it." He glanced her way. Must have read her hesitation. "You aren't thinking of backing out, are you? Not on my big night."

His big night? She'd been part of the process of wooing Bernard from the beginning, along with the critics. And Michelle? When had they suddenly become an us? Okay, feeling just the tiniest bit jealous was like the pot calling the kettle black, but still, his attitude rankled. She'd helped Jonathan and all she seemed to get was a pat on the back while he took the credit. Was this how it would be after they got married? He seemed more concerned about her not showing up to do her part at the gallery, than putting off the wedding.

On the heels of that thought came another. How on earth could she be upset about Jonathan and Michelle when she had so many unresolved issues to deal with? Derrick being one of them. Sure, Michelle made no secret of the fact that she'd like to be an exclusive fixture in Jonathan's world while Derrick made no bones about the fact that he still wanted them to be together. Good grief, what about what she wanted? She was so busy worrying about everyone else that she'd lost sight of herself.

"I'll call you during your lunch break tomorrow to go over the final details," he said, leaning down to brush his lips over hers. When she didn't throw herself into the kiss, he pulled back, his eyebrows arched.

"Not one of our more enthusiastic kisses."

"I'm so tired," she said, wondering when making everyone else happy had become her full-time job.

He chuckled and threw his arm over her shoulder as they walked to the front door. "Go lay your pretty head down. This can't be as bad as it seems."

If only.

He pulled on his heavy jacket and opened

the door. The frigid air barreled inside, causing chills to break out over her skin. She tucked the hems of her sleeves around her hands and crossed her arms over her chest to seal in her body warmth. With the outdoor lights on, she watched Jonathan make his way to his fancy sedan, noticing the heavy fog hovering in the damp night.

"Be careful," she called out.

He sent her a reassuring wave and drove away.

Hannah stared out the door into the still darkness. What-ifs plagued her mind. What if her father had never gotten involved with the shady supplier? What if he'd never testified? Or left her and her mother behind? What if Derrick had never discovered her address? Would she and Jonathan go blithely off into the future as if nothing had ever happened and her past hadn't existed?

"You're letting the heat escape."

Hannah jumped at her mother's voice. So lost in her thoughts, she hadn't considered the impact the cold winter air would have on her mom. "Sorry."

"Don't be. I can't imagine the conversation with Jonathan was easy."

After throwing the dead bolt, Hannah began turning off the living room lights. "He still wants to get married."

"And you?"

"I don't know, Mom. I want the gemstones to be gone. I want life to go back to normal."

"We haven't lived a normal life in a very long time," her mother answered, amusement in her tone. "I'm not sure there is such a thing."

"If there is, that's what I wish for."

Her mother stopped Hannah as she brushed past and pulled her under the hall ceiling light. "You look exhausted."

"I need a month-long vacation. A spa trip would be my first choice. A monastery where no one talks to me, a close second."

"I don't know about the latter, but you could use a break." Her mother cupped her cheek. "For everything you do."

Hannah shrugged.

"When this is over, we'll see about getting you some much-deserved time off."

Nice thought, but there was no telling what would happen next, who would show up on their doorstep or if another gemstone would appear in the most unexpected place. She needed to be on her toes.

"Until then I'm going to bed." She bussed her mother's cheek and reeled back. "You feel warm."

"You were right. I'm fighting a cold."

"You're doing too much, Mom."

"I won't stop living," she retorted, steam in her words. "I did that during the treatments. Now I want to be out and about, making up for lost time."

"Please slow down."

The stubborn woman shook her head.

"Then let's both head to bed."

She turned toward her bedroom doorway.

"You should have told Jonathan you couldn't make it Friday night," her mother said, following on her heels.

Hannah stopped short and turned, her eyebrows raised in a silent question.

"Yes, I caught the tail end of the conversation." Her mother frowned. "He has an assistant to take care of gallery events."

"I'm the one who organized this art show opening."

"She can't finish it? The only reason I'm asking is because it feels like you're hesitating and don't want to go."

Hannah resumed walking to her bedroom. "I have to be there. That's what engaged couples do."

"Are you still engaged?"

Once in her room, Hannah dug the ring from her pocket. Laid it on her bedside table and slumped down on the bed. "I think so."

"Meaning?" her mother asked as she leaned against the doorjamb.

"I suggested we take a break but he insisted I hold on to the ring." Hannah flung herself back onto the mattress. "I didn't have the heart to say no."

"You never say no to him. He doesn't expect otherwise."

Hannah felt the mattress sink as her mother took a seat beside her.

"He means well."

"Maybe, but does he make your heart pound? Your blood rush?"

Hannah lifted her head. "You and Lynny have been watching too many chick flicks."

"Just answer the question."

She fell back and threw an arm over her eyes. "I guess."

"Well that's not the least bit romantic."

"What's romantic about telling a lie to the man I'm supposed to marry?"

"You have a point."

Hannah levered her elbows on the bed and raised herself up a bit. "I wouldn't marry me if I found out the real story."

Lying down again, she crossed her arms over her middle, fighting the tears filling her eyes.

"What about Derrick?"

"What about him? He has a life, Mom. A career." Her voice went wobbly. "He's probably just trying to make up for the past by helping us now."

"You don't believe that."

Her voice got smaller. "I don't know what to believe anymore."

"Oh, sweetie."

Needing a shoulder to cry on, Hannah let herself be tugged up into her mother's comforting embrace, her tears flowing freely.

"You've been so strong for everyone else. No wonder you're worn out."

"You know I'd do everything over again in order for you to stay well," she whispered.

"And I appreciate it." She held up her hands when Hannah wanted to speak. "And I promise to take care of myself and get rid of this cold, but it's not your job to be strong for everyone. To plan parties and solve cases and…" She paused. Hannah pulled back to see sorrow lining her mother's face. "It's times like these that I miss your father, never mind his poor judgement."

This was the first time in ages Hannah had heard her mother refer to her father's leaving. When she'd gotten sick, Hannah had decided not to make her mother feel worse, so she never mentioned her father. Could that have been a mistake?

Her mother firmly took Hannah's shoulders and held her at arm's length. "You and I are strong. Don't ever forget that."

Hannah laughed. "You forgot the part where we don't need a man to make us whole."

"We don't. But sometimes being held in a pair of strong arms is just plain nice."

EARLY THURSDAY MORNING Derrick went for a run before school. The winter temperatures had plummeted again, but at least he didn't have to dodge crusty snow piles along his route. He hadn't slept well the night before, pictures of Hannah and Jonathan having the long, overdue conversation running through his head. The guy was much too nice to let Hannah down when he learned about her past, and he'd made it clear he was prepared to fight for her. Well, he was prepared to fight for her, too.

He still had a little over two weeks before his mother's wedding. Could he miss her big day if he had to? She'd understand, but wouldn't like it and would probably spend the rest of her life telling him so. A chance he'd have to take.

Or, he could invite Hannah to go with him. It was a long shot, but maybe Hannah would want to see his family. Her mother could come, too, and it would be like a reunion of the two families. Except half of Hannah's was missing, so that probably wasn't a wise suggestion.

He rounded a bend before heading back to the hotel, a distant thought nagging at him. The gemstones. It all circled back to Hannah's father. He'd claimed at the trial he didn't know what had happened to them, but as far as Derrick could tell, her dad had the missing information needed to make sense of the reappearance of the gemstones. The man was in the wind. Seemed like a good time to find him. The clock was ticking down on his leave and Derrick needed to make some strides in the case soon, for Hannah's sake.

After running five miles he was ready to get back to work. He left a message for Dylan and dressed in his security shirt and jeans, prepared for the routine of his workday. He greeted students, carried on a conversation with Tommy, where he learned that the boy's father had come to Tommy's basketball game, which they won, and confabbed with Glen about the state of the new security system.

At four that afternoon, he was in the gym, standing with Roger while they watched the younger boys run drills.

His phone rang. Reading Dylan's number, he excused himself and moved into the main hallway away from the noise.

"Hey. I was hoping to hear from you today."

"Sorry I didn't check in sooner. New case." Dylan spoke to someone, then returned to the conversation. "What's up?"

"Sounds like you have your hands full."

"I do, but you know I want to help."

"I need to find Hannah's father."

"Makes sense."

"Glad you agree." He paused a moment, considering how to execute his plan. "How about hiring the soon-to-be newest member of our family to find him?"

"Huh?"

"Serena's boyfriend, Logan. From the way Mom talks, I expect them to be married soon."

"Good idea. We can get a family discount."

Derrick chuckled. "You have Logan's contact information?"

Dylan did.

"I'll text you the aliases that Hannah's dad used in hiding. I'm hoping he went back to his real name, thinking no one would look for him that way."

"Are you going to tell Hannah?"

"Not until I know more. I don't want to get her hopes up."

In the background, someone yelled Dylan's name. "I gotta run."

"I'll be in touch."

"Oh, and heads up. Mom is serious about us dancing at her wedding."

"I forgot about that."

"For your own safety, get on it. She's making her wedding the event of the century."

From her many phone calls to keep Derrick in the loop, he knew what he and his brothers were up against.

"Later, brother."

After Dylan hung up, Derrick Googled swing dancing. He found a tutorial and watched the light-footed tutor moving back and forth on his feet, explaining the rock step followed by the triple step.

"You have got to be kidding me," he muttered.

A light, amused voice reached him before Hannah strolled into his peripheral vision. She was dressed in a pale pink sweater with gray pants and dark shoes. Her hair was free today, curling over her shoulders. She carried a stack of folders in her arms. "Let me guess. Your mother made another request?"

He lowered the phone with a groan. "She's insisting we learn how to swing dance for her wedding."

Her interest turned to raucous laughter. "You? Dance?" She chuckled even more. "Priceless."

"Hey!"

"Derrick, you can do many things. It's maddening the way you can swoop in and fix any problem, but dancing? I have to say, not your forte."

"We've danced together."

"Exactly. That's how I know you're terrible." She sent him a dazzling smile. "I'm actually a very good dancer."

"Prove it." Derrick took the files from her hands and led her into the gym, placing the pile on a nearby bleacher. He'd noticed right away that the engagement ring was missing. He couldn't deny the rush of hope that washed over him. What had happened when she spoke to Prescott last night?

"Here?" she asked, looking around the gym.

He let his questions go for now. He had Hannah to himself and didn't want to share, not even to find out what happened with Prescott. "If I step on your toes there's lots of room to move away."

She glanced at the boys on the far end of the court throwing free shots at the hoop and shrugged. "Why not?"

"That's the spirit."

She took the phone from his hand and replayed the video he'd been watching. When the tutorial ended, she handed the cell back to him. "Piece of cake."

"I'm glad you think so. I need to get this right so my brothers don't give me a hard time."

"Competitive much?"

He grinned. "You know us well."

"If I remember correctly, you can manage to slow dance."

"You remember?"

She shook her head at him and ignored his question. "Basic position. My hand on your shoulder, yours on my waist. Free hands clasped together, held away from the body."

When he moved closer, her vanilla scent, along with her warmth, breached his senses.

She moved into his embrace and before long they were gently easing back and forth. "I could get used to this," he breathed into her ear. He actually felt her shiver before she hopped back.

Tone crisp, she instructed, "Let's move on." Snapping her fingers, she shifted gracefully, backstepping on her left foot, then stepping once on the right, swinging her hips in the process. "Even you can do this," she teased.

Right. He went to her side and in a few moments followed her rhythmic lead. The boys hollered at each other as they passed and dunked at the coach's command, a backdrop to the dance lesson.

"Now that you have the basic step mastered, I'm going to take three steps to the left." She demonstrated by gliding across the floor.

He followed, his feet tangling. Her merry laugh should have irked him but for once he was having fun, even though it was at his own expense.

"Slow down," she said when he nearly ran over her. "This isn't a race."

He stopped, made a show of shaking out his arms and legs before trying the routine again.

"Better," she encouraged.

He concentrated and before long captured the basic steps. "Next?"

"Don't get cocky on me." She took position in front of him. "For learning purposes I'm going to lead."

He sent her a slow smile, hitting his intended mark when she flushed.

"We're going to put it all together now," she explained, her voice shaky. Was she as unsettled by this closeness as he was? "We move opposite. My left foot goes back, your right foot comes forward."

He looked down at their shoes. "Got it."

"Let's practice this a few times." She grasped his hands and he almost forgot what he was supposed to do, her touch had such a strong impact on him.

They rocked, laughing when he stumbled into her. She lightly pushed on his chest, recentering them both. This was the first time since he'd arrived in town that the worry slipped from her face. Her hazel eyes were shiny and bright; her smile didn't fade. This was how she should always look, as if she didn't have a care in the world.

"Now that we've gotten the timing, we triple step together. In the same direction."

She showed him the move and after a few times back and forth, she stopped to tuck a stray curl behind her ear. His fingers itched to touch her lustrous hair. "Now, let's do it together."

She took his hands again. For a long second they stared at each other. Memories bombarded him and he wondered if she was thinking about the great times they'd once shared. The hopes only a young couple in love could dare to dream. Their connection was so strong, stronger even than before they were separated. Was it truly possible after all this time? She finally broke eye contact and shook her head. "Okay. Rock step, triple step, triple step, rock step."

He blew out a breath as the magical moment between them dissipated. "That's a lot of steps."

"You're a pretty capable guy. I'm sure you'll catch on."

"Thanks for the compliment."

Rolling her eyes, she led him in the steps once again. He could get used to this. Working with Hannah was easy, as if they were both on the same wavelength.

"Pay attention," she chided as his mind wandered. "The steps are small and close together."

"I can do close together."

Her head snapped up, her eyes warm and inviting.

"Hey, add the side bump," a voice came from behind him, shattering the moment. Derrick swung around to find that the boys had quit practicing and had taken seats in the bleachers to watch the show. Roger stood near the bench, holding a clipboard and nodding in their direction, a huge grin on his face.

"You know how to swing dance?" Derrick asked.

"Sure, who doesn't?"

"Apparently me," he muttered under his breath.

"C'mon, Mr. Fields. You got this."

Great. Tommy and some of the boys from Hannah's class now had a front-row seat to witness his failure if he didn't get serious.

Not wanting to look totally incompetent in front of them, he held out his hands to Hannah. "Again?"

She took her position. "Step toward me."

He did and their hips bumped before she stepped back.

"Cool," announced one of the boys.

"Very," Derrick said only loud enough for her to hear. Her cheeks colored.

"This time," she said, "when our hips meet, spin to the side."

He did, only he went the wrong way and ended up staggering to the side, taking her with him. He kept them from tumbling as the spectators burst out in raucous laughter.

"C'mon, Mr. Fields. You can do better than that."

"Pipe down, peanut gallery."

He heard raspberries blown behind him.

"You said this was easy," he accused.

"For some of us." Hannah grimaced as he stepped on her foot. "Hopefully the band will play a slow tune so you don't maim your partner."

"Practice makes perfect. How about you be my permanent partner?"

"Derrick…" she warned.

"Dance partner?"

"Don't push it."

"When have you known me to leave well enough alone?"

"Never."

"Exactly."

They moved in sync as if they'd been dancing forever. In his mind that's exactly how he'd thought of them, together forever.

"Imagine if this was our life?" he couldn't resist adding. "Enjoying new experiences. Trying out new adventures."

A shadow eclipsed the joy on her face. "You know that's not possible."

"I noticed you're not wearing Prescott's ring."

"No, but we're still together." She released her hands from his and stopped dancing. "In fact, we're featuring a new artist at the gallery tomorrow tonight."

Dang. He shouldn't have pushed. His brothers always warned him about going too far, but he never listened.

Roger and the boys moved on now that the show had ended. Once Hannah left, he'd be alone. Again.

"Thanks for the lesson." Trying for light, he sent her a smile he hoped covered his disappointment at her leaving. "Now I don't have to go to a studio."

"Either way, you'll make your mother proud."

"I hope. This wedding thing is getting out of control."

"That's what happens. Wedding planning takes on a life of its own."

"Well, I'll be there to walk her down the aisle and then my duty is done."

Hannah smoothed the hem of her sweater. "Did you get them a gift?"

He stared at her.

"A gift," she repeated.

"I forgot about that." He frowned. "I have no idea what to buy."

"You still have time."

He stuffed his hands in his pockets. "Any suggestions?"

"You can't be that clueless."

"No, but what do you get a couple who have been on their own for years?"

"Be creative." She gathered up the files.

"Before you leave, I have one more request." She hitched her chin in his direction.

"Would you mind shopping with me?"

"Derrick…"

He held up his hands in surrender. "I have no ulterior motive. I honestly have no idea where to start."

"I also remember you used to hate to shop."

"Still do."

He thought she might tell him to figure it out on his own, but instead said, "Are you free this weekend?"

"I'm free any day you ask."

"Saturday. We can take the entire day to find the perfect gift."

"I really appreciate it. You know my mom means a lot to me and I want to get it right."

Her expression softened. "Then I'm happy to help." She turned to walk away.

"Hannah?"

She stopped. Pivoted on her heel.

Once again their eyes met and held. What-ifs danced in his head as he viewed the woman he loved. No matter what happened, he would always love her. She was the one. Always had been. Always would be.

She pressed her lips together and he read the confusion on her expressive face.

"I'll pick you up Saturday morning."

She nodded, then continued on her way.

It would be so easy to swoop in and prove he was the right guy for her, but deep down he knew she had to decide that for herself. If they ended up together, their happiness would only be sustained by mutual love. And so far, she hadn't mentioned the L word. For now he would do what he did best.

Wait for Hannah.

CHAPTER TWELVE

AN HOUR BEFORE school started on Friday morning, Derrick and Roger hauled a half-dozen long tables from the storage closet to set up in the gymnasium. The boxes of books lining the wall for the annual book fair had been delivered the previous day after basketball practice. Once they'd placed the tables around the large room, they started opening the cartons. Teachers would be arriving soon to organize books by age groups before the parent volunteers came after the first bell to work the sale.

"That was quite a show you and Anna put on yesterday," Roger remarked as he hefted a box onto a table.

Thankfully Roger hadn't witnessed Hannah shutting him down when he'd asked about their relationship. He was lucky enough to have Saturday with her and he'd take it as a win, if Hannah didn't change her mind and bail on him last-minute.

"The dancing?" Derrick chuckled instead of revealing his fears. "I need to get ready for a wedding." He paused. Pictured his mother's triumphant face and his brothers' matching grimaces. "The more I think about it, I should get hazard pay."

"I hear you. Those events require endless patience and a permanent smile."

Derrick shot him a questioning glance.

"I have three older sisters. All married."

"Three brothers. Mostly on the way to the altar, but this is my mother's big day."

Roger lifted another box. "Wow. My folks are still married after almost fifty years together."

Derrick took the letter opener he'd borrowed from the main office to slit the box tape. "Mom's a widow and wants this wedding to be perfect."

"Is that even possible?"

"Don't ask me." Derrick shivered in mock horror. "I've stayed away from serious entanglements."

Roger waited a beat, then asked, "Until Anna?"

Derrick stilled. Ignored the twitch over his left eye. "Because of." He tore open another box, his heart seizing like it did when he thought about what they'd had and lost.

"Lynny said you were high school sweethearts."

"Yeah. Planned on getting married."

"What happened, if you don't mind me asking."

He rolled a shoulder to give the impression the past wasn't that important. "Her family moved and we lost touch."

A look of surprise crossed Roger's face. "Even though you were going to tie the knot?"

"It's complicated."

Roger unpacked a stack of books from the box to place on the table. "Usually is."

As much as he wanted to talk about it, Derrick wouldn't reveal the story that was Hannah's to tell. He owed her that much. "You and Lynny? Anything new going on there?"

"I asked her out to dinner this weekend."

"Took you long enough."

He shrugged, but Derrick didn't miss the pleasure reflected in the other man's eyes. "I like her, but she's so confident and sure of what she wants. I don't know, maybe being the youngest in a family of girls made me cautious around women who have a serious-relationship gleam in their eyes."

Derrick chuckled. "Have you known Lynny long?"

"Two years. We've been in the friend zone, which had worked for me, until lately. When she stopped dropping hints about getting together, I missed them and realized I was being hardheaded not to have acted sooner. I'm actually looking forward to dinner. She's fun. More than any other woman I've ever dated."

"A guy could do worse than be involved with a woman like Lynny. It seems like once she's on your side, she's a great friend."

"She is. I can't tell you all the ways she's helped her fellow teachers. Especially Anna. She needed a friend and Lynny was there for her."

Because Hannah had been alone. Even though he was thankful for Lynny, the never-ending guilt raised its ugly head.

They emptied more boxes as teachers started to arrive and pushed up their sleeves to sort books and place them on the appropriate tables.

"Maybe you'll be putting a ring on her finger before long," Derrick commented to Roger as they emptied the last of the boxes.

"I'm not in a rush," Roger said as the two carried the empty boxes to the corner of the gym. "Not to be indelicate, but I noticed Anna isn't wearing her engagement ring."

As much as it had thrilled Derrick, he knew the decision had taken a toll on Hannah. "She and Prescott have to work some things out."

"Like her obvious interest in you? And your mutual interest in her?"

Derrick stacked the boxes. "It's that apparent?"

"A dead man could feel the heat between you two."

He wanted her attention, like he craved air itself, but she had to decide her own future. She'd made it more than clear that she hated the fact that choices had been taken away from her in the past. He wouldn't push and make her resent him all over again.

"What are you going to do about it?" Roger asked.

Voices echoed off the high ceiling as Derrick considered the question. "After all she's been through, Anna should take the lead on whatever happens between us."

"Yeah, her mother getting sick was terrible."

Along with a list of events that Derrick couldn't get into. "But that doesn't mean I'm not throwing my hat into the ring."

Roger slapped him on the back. "I like your thinking."

"Oh, no," a light and airy voice sounded behind them. Derrick turned to find Lynny headed in their direction, a frown wrinkling her brow. "Male bonding. Never good for the single ladies."

"You make it sound like we're discussing the merits of permanent bachelorhood," Roger said, but Derrick didn't miss the smile he couldn't withhold. Despite Roger's insistence on not being that serious about Lynny, the moment she walked in the room, he only had eyes for her. Much the way he was with Hannah.

As Derrick stacked the last box, he realized he needed some fresh air to get these ideas out of his head. "You can leave me out of this conversation."

Lynny laughed. "Like you're one to talk."

"I've never debated the benefits of being a bachelor."

"And we both know why."

Just as Lynny spoke, Hannah strode into the gym. Today she wore a green sweater and gray pants, her hair pulled up with strands escaping around her face, just the way he loved to see her. Her cheeks were red from the cold morning air and her eyes shining like the sun had come out from behind cloud cover to brighten the day.

Lynny waved and Hannah looked over and nodded, speaking to another teacher before heading their way.

"You know you have a limited window of opportunity," Lynny said in a low voice as she sidled next to Derrick.

"For what?"

"Sweeping Anna away from Jonathan."

"Maybe she doesn't want to be swept away."

Lynny sent him a *get real* look and grabbed

Roger's arm. Together they went off to another section of the gym.

Hannah stopped beside him and placed her hands on her hips. "Lynny motioned me over and then she left."

"It's that matchmaker thing she's got going on."

"She needs to worry about her own love life." Hannah shook her head. "Which I must say looks like it's taken a turn for the better."

"Yeah, Roger's interested. Just give them time." He met her gaze and held it. "Like us?"

She let out a sigh. "Just because I took off Jonathan's ring doesn't mean I don't want to marry him."

Derrick ran a hand over the back of his neck. The volume level in the gym rose as more people arrived. "I guess I'm confused. If you love him, what's the problem?"

"You," she said, turning on her boot heel to head to a table with a grade-four sign. She picked the top book from a stack and stood it up so the students could view the colorful cover.

"It's not like I haven't made my intentions known," he said as he joined her.

"Yes." She held a book in her hand, gripping it like it was a lifeline before she glanced his way. "But once your reason for being here is over you'll be gone."

"I don't have to stay away."

"Your job is back east."

"I can transfer." He'd given it a lot of thought. If Hannah wanted them to try again, he'd gladly pull up stakes and move here.

She replaced the book and picked up another to showcase. "Right now all I can think about is finding out why the gemstone came into your possession after so many years. Once that chapter is closed, I'll be able to move forward."

"Will you? I know you have feelings for Prescott. I get that. He was there for you when I wasn't. But I'm here now." His heart picked up a beat as he spoke the words burning in him. "I've lived half my life without you, Hannah, like part of me has been missing. I want to be whole and I think you do, too."

Her face went soft and her eyes welled. "Not fair."

"It's the truth."

She ran a finger over the spine of a book, refusing to look his way.

"I remember the hours we spent in the library," he said, hoping memories would make her see what he thought was unmistakable: that they belonged together. "You were always reading something about art. Your face would light up when you came to a part that caught your fancy and you'd have to tell me about it."

A slight smile curved her lips. "You always humored me."

"Because I didn't care where we were or what we were doing as long as we did it together. You felt that way, too."

Her voice was barely audible when she said, "I remember."

"Would it be so hard to give us a second chance?"

She straightened a row of books and finally looked straight at him. "Did you know I pressed the corsage you gave me on prom night into one of my favorite books?"

"I remember giving you flowers, but more than that, I remember that was the night I gave you my promise ring."

She nodded, her voice thick when she spoke. "When we left our home so suddenly, all those memories, everything I treasured from growing up were gone. Just gone. No getting them back. Not for any of us."

His stomach sank. "The ring?"

"Just another memory."

Regret swamped him. The other people in the room ceased to exist as he focused solely on Hannah. "I can't change what happened. I'd do anything if I could, but we both know that's impossible. But you have to know I never stopped loving you. Not ever."

When she didn't respond, he gathered up the courage to keep going. "Since I've been here, I've fallen even more in love with the woman you've become, Hannah. The attention you show your students, how you make sure your mom is happy and has the best health care, you even have time to help struggling artists make a name for themselves. How could I not want a future with such a wonderful woman?"

She tilted up her chin. "You said you'd give me time to untangle my emotions. To decide where we go from here."

Guilt pressed on him. He'd gone back on his word, again. But when it came to Hannah, he couldn't help but push the issue because the clock was steadily ticking. Couldn't she see what a gift this was? To find each other again? How often did that happen to people? How could he not remind her of what they'd shared? Of what could be and how precious it was? He'd been surprised by his restraint at her request for more time, but as the days passed and he saw her slipping away, he was losing patience. And that rashness may have lost her in the process.

"You're right," he said, backing down. "I'm sorry."

"Don't be sorry—just listen to me."

"Like Prescott does?"

Her eyes darkened. "Stop bringing him into the conversation."

"I can't help it. He's part of this."

Her sadness quickly turned to annoyance. "I need more time."

Derrick nodded. If she was truly done with him, the void in his heart would never be filled again.

THAT NIGHT HANNAH STOOD before the mirror in her bedroom. She'd dressed for an evening at the gallery: a simple black dress with tall black boots. She'd styled her hair to curl over her shoulders and added dangly earrings to finish what she hoped was a sophisticated look. Critics would be there and Hannah wanted to present a professional air.

As she reached for the bangle bracelets, she couldn't resist adding the one Derrick had made for her at the museum. Then her gaze landed on the ornate jewelry box he'd made and presented to her on her sixteenth birthday. One of the only things she'd been able to grab the night the Marshals had come to whisk them away. She gently ran her fingers over the wooden lid. Derrick had carved a design of flowers in bloom. She picked it up and walked to the bed, taking a seat as she eased it open.

Inside were the pieces of costume jewelry

she'd collected as a kid, ticket stubs and a strip of pictures taken in a photo booth with Derrick, both of them making funny faces. She couldn't contain a smile. How young they looked. As though nothing bad could ever touch them and their future was secure.

Picking through the mishmash of trinkets, she found notes from Derrick buried underneath. *What she was doing?* It had been so long since she'd left Florida, yet the pain in Hannah's heart still felt fresh.

Nestled in the corner of the satin-lined box was a gold ring. Hannah picked it up and placed the box beside her. In the bedside lamp light, the small stone sparkled. She swallowed around the lump in her throat as tears blurred her vision.

Why hadn't she told Derrick she still had his ring? Was she really so frightened by her feelings for him? Afraid of what she might say or do if she unlocked the floodgates of her emotions?

She slipped it on her finger, surprised the beloved ring still fit. It had been ages since she'd looked at the symbol of the love she and Derrick had once shared.

He was the same man, yet so different. When he was a teen, he'd been cocky and headstrong. Now, his tenderness with the children, particularly Tommy, the solicitous care and respect he showed her mother, the protectiveness he revealed in his attempts to safeguard her, all these things were making her fall harder for him than ever.

Was it possible to share her life with him again? To take a chance?

She had a decision to make and time was running out. Guilt crawled over her. She'd been right to tell Jonathan she couldn't wear his engagement ring. At least until Derrick's time here was over. But Derrick had said he'd move here to be near her, so she was back to square one, not wanting to make the choice that would hurt one of the men in her life.

Coughing sounded down the hallway. Dabbing her fingers under her eyes to get rid of the tears and not mess up her makeup, Hannah placed the ring in the special hideaway, but not before her mother caught her action from the doorway.

"Your cough is getting worse," Hannah said as she rose to carry the box back to its place on the dresser.

Her mother's voice was hoarse when she said, "I guess if I admit I have done too much lately, you won't let me live it down."

"Oh, Mom. You know I'm just concerned."

Her mother smiled. Pulled her robe over her chest. "I may have to call the doctor on Monday."

"I could stay home with you tonight. Jonathan will understand."

Her mother waved a hand. "Carol is coming over. I'll be fine."

"You're sure?"

"I'm not going to let you use me as an excuse not to go to the exhibit."

"Is it that obvious?"

"Why else would you be poring over old memories? The ones involving Derrick."

The ache that wouldn't abate in her chest grew stronger. The answer was right there, but she refused to voice it. "Mom, what would you do if you were in my shoes?"

"Oh, my." Her mother wrinkled her brow. "That's a question."

"Seriously. I'm afraid to make the wrong decision."

Her mother took a tissue from her robe pocket and wiped her nose. "Sometimes just making any decision is a step in the right direction."

"But in the end, someone gets hurt."

"Unfortunately, that is the case."

Hannah looked down at her finger. No matter what she decided, she would break a heart. Her own even? Would the decent thing be to walk away from both men, giving neither an answer? Giving them freedom to move on and find women worthy of their love? Stringing them along wasn't admirable and she was coming to despise her actions daily.

"It's rather telling that you put Jonathan's ring away and you're admiring Derrick's right now."

Hannah smiled. "Just for old time's sake. I don't plan on wearing it out of this house."

"There was a time you wouldn't have removed it for any reason."

"Until I had multiple reasons to take it off."

"Still, you wore it for a long time."

She had. Until hope had flickered out and she tucked childhood dreams away.

Silence blanketed the room before her mother spoke again. "I know you have a true affection for Jonathan, but what does your heart say?"

Derrick, a voice whispered deep inside her.

She met her mother's gaze and received a knowing smile in return.

"Am I that far gone?" Hannah asked.

"To those who know you."

She placed a hand over her heart, hoping to ease the flip-flopping in her chest. "I've kept Derrick at a distance, even though I've wanted to throw caution to the wind and tell him I never stopped loving him."

"But?"

"I made a commitment." Hannah glanced at her reflection and frowned. "I've changed and grown since I first loved Derrick, then met Jonathan. Are my feelings for Derrick echoes from the past or because of the man he is today? I accepted Jonathan's proposal, knowing Derrick was my first love, but now?"

"You made your decision with the information you had at the time. Derrick didn't know where you were, therefore he couldn't find you."

"Doesn't change the fact that I made a promise to Jonathan."

"You're seeing Jonathan tonight, Derrick tomorrow. Listen to your heart, Hannah. It won't steer you wrong."

Hannah would have quipped that the organ hadn't been working up to par lately, but didn't want to squelch her mother's advice. She was right. Hannah had to decide.

Her mother walked into the room. "You took on a heavy load when we separated from your father and carried it quite effortlessly," she said, her voice husky from coughing.

"You're kidding, right? Mom, you lost more than me."

"We both lost a great deal. But instead of wallowing, you shouldered the responsibility, took care of me and still managed to have a fulfilling career and relationship."

"I feel like I'm slipping on the job." Hannah frowned as her mother moved into the light. "You're pale, Mom."

Her mother took a step back and ducked her head as another coughing jag took over. Once her breathing had calmed, she turned back. Hannah couldn't miss the moisture in her eyes and the way her chest raggedly rose and fell.

"That's it—I'm staying home."

"Absolutely not." Her mother coughed again, then took a deep breath. "I'm just going to rest on the couch. There's nothing you can do."

"Mom—"

"I'll be one-hundred-percent happier knowing you are out having a good time."

"How can I have a good time when I'm worried about you?"

"You're sweet, but I insist you go."

Hannah knew her mother well enough to realize there was no point arguing any further. "Promise you'll keep your cell phone nearby so you can call me if you feel worse."

"I promise."

Hannah could only take her at her word.

She ran a finger over the box holding Derrick's ring. There was only so much procrastinating she could do so she picked up her clutch and walked with her mother into the living room. She made a cup of tea and had her mother nestled on the couch when Carol arrived.

"Mom sounds worse, so please let me know if you think I should come home early."

Carol patted her arm. "Gave you a hard time, did she?"

Hannah chuckled. "You know her."

"I do. Now be on your way and I promise to contact you if she gets worse."

After another round of goodbyes, Hannah left for the gallery.

A sappy love song drifted from the radio as she drove through the dark, dank night. "You've got to be kidding me," she said and turned the dial. Silence was better than reminders of love. Until the silence made the thoughts in her head run in a relentless loop, so she switched to a twenty-four-hour talk station.

The temperature wasn't as cold as it had been for the last few weeks, but Hannah made sure to button up her coat before walking the few blocks to the gallery. Couples strolled by, arm in arm, a constant reminder of the decisions that lay ahead of her. She should have coaxed Lynny into coming tonight. At least her friend would have kept her from wallowing in her misery.

Bright lights spilled from the gallery windows. From her vantage point, Hannah could see a crowd. Pushing past her worries, she mustered up a smile and stepped inside.

Immediately she was greeted by critics and longtime gallery clients she'd come to know. She removed her coat and made her way to the back of the room to leave it with an attendant. Squaring her shoulders, she set out to mingle, on the lookout for Jonathan. He was conspicuously missing, which seemed odd, but she attributed it to him meeting with a client in his office as he often did on a busy night.

As she made a circuit of the room, she bumped into Bernard, the artist of the night, who wrapped her in a hearty hug.

"My favorite person on earth," he gushed, his eyes sparking with excitement.

"What a turnout," she said as they parted, pleased to see the prickly artist having a good time.

"I don't know why I didn't listen to you sooner. The Prescott Gallery is the perfect place to showcase my sculptures."

"I really don't want to say it…"

"Go on." He said with a flourish of his hand, "Get it over and done with."

"I told you so."

"Yes, you did and I'm forever grateful." He pulled her closer and lowered his mouth toward her ear. "The critic from *Culture Today* is here. I can't decide if I'm more nervous or pleased that he's going to mention my work in the magazine."

Hannah couldn't have been any more thrilled. "Pleased, of course."

"I knew I could count on you to rally around my work."

"Who wouldn't?" His talent with glass and metal was singular and quickly gaining popularity.

He frowned, jutting his chin in the direction behind Hannah. She turned to see Jonathan and the always chic Michelle coming from his office. Michelle wore a smug smile which grew wider when Hannah met her gaze.

"That's a woman to watch out for," Bernard warned before moving on to the next fan.

With a sinking feeling swirling in her stomach, Hannah waited for Jonathan to notice her. When he did, his eyes flickered away and back again, and his smile slipped. He walked over to her, giving her a kiss on the cheek.

"I was getting worried," he said in greeting.

"Mom caught a cold so I took a little extra time to make sure she was settled for the night."

"You are much too generous, looking out for everyone but you."

She shrugged, assuming his words were a compliment, but not sure from his unusually reserved tone.

Michelle came up beside him and offered a smile that didn't quite reach her eyes.

"We weren't sure if you were going to show up tonight," she said.

"I was just explain—"

"It's okay," Jonathan interrupted. "You're here now."

"And I spoke to some of the reviewers already. They're quite taken with the exhibit."

A genuine smile curved Jonathan's lips.

"Speaking of which," she said, "here's our very own *Nevada Now* reporter."

Hannah suspected Jonathan had forgotten the young woman's name so she quickly put out her hand to shake. "Nice to see you, Marie."

"Same here. Thanks for the invite."

"No problem. We look forward to reading your article about the opening."

They chatted for a few moments before Marie moved on. Hannah lifted her hands to make a gesture and Michelle's eyes went wide. She'd zeroed in on Hannah's bare ring finger. Hannah's stomach dropped and she waited for the inevitable.

"Jonathan, why isn't your fiancée wearing your engagement ring?"

CHAPTER THIRTEEN

AT THE AWKWARD PAUSE, Hannah lowered her left hand. Honestly, she hadn't considered the ramifications of arriving at the gallery tonight without her engagement ring. She fought the urge to hide her hand behind her back, but the move wouldn't accomplish anything since Michelle had already noticed. She squeezed her hand into a fist and tried to come up with an excuse.

"I…ah…"

Jonathan's eyes blazed. "Michelle. A word."

Realizing that she'd not only embarrassed Hannah, but also her boss, Michelle blanched. Under the bright lights, she was caught wide-eyed and nervous. For the first time since Hannah had known her, Michelle looked uncertain.

Before steering Michelle away, Jonathan glanced at her. "I'll be right back."

She nodded. In a way, wasn't this partly her fault? She was the one taking the time to decide where she and Jonathan stood, but she hadn't pictured what her indecision would mean to him. She was messing up everyone's life lately.

Bernard shuffled over to her.

"What's going on?"

"Nothing to worry about." She painted a smile on her face and glanced around the room. "I'm going to get a drink. Want anything?"

He held up his glass. "I could use a refill. Sparkling water."

"You got it."

Hannah wove through the guests to reach the refreshment area the caterer had set up. She deposited Bernard's glass on a nearby tray and ordered two waters. As the bartender went to work, she rested her elbow on the portable bar and watched the crowd enjoy themselves.

"Quite a turnout," a tall man with dark hair said as he came up to her.

"Prescott Gallery only represents the best."

"I can see that."

Hannah glanced away, not up to chatting with a stranger, but the man didn't move.

"Are you new to the gallery?" she asked.

"Yes. I just arrived in town a short while ago." He smiled, but his gaze was rather unsettling, like he was searching for something. "Trying to get the lay of the land. Meet new people, that sort of thing. I was interested in the exhibit tonight so I decided to stop in."

An uneasiness settled over her. "Well, you picked a good place to start. The people involved in the local art scene are wonderful."

He held out his hand. "Mike."

She reached out to return the gesture, but a sudden shiver stopped her. Unsure of what to do, she was saved by the bartender, who handed over the two drinks she'd ordered. Tucking her clutch under her arm, she accepted the glasses. "Nice to meet you," she said. "I have to deliver these."

"Sure," he said, but she didn't miss the flash of impatience in his cold eyes. "We'll talk again."

Who was this guy? The odd feeling of being watched, the one that had returned during the last few weeks, had her looking over her shoulder. She caught the man following her movement and the uneasiness shot up tenfold. When she faced forward, she nearly collided with Bernard.

"Here you go." She noticed her hand shaking as she passed him his glass.

"Are you okay? You look like you've seen a ghost."

Not a ghost. Maybe worse? She couldn't be sure, but the fact that the gems were still fair game had her suspecting the stranger might be up to no good. Or she was imagining things. But didn't Derrick tell her to trust her instincts?

"I'm fine. It's been a long day."

Bernard leaned over to kiss her cheek. "I appreciate you coming out tonight."

She managed a smile until the artist found another guest to chat with. When she looked back toward the bar, the stranger was gone.

How she wished Derrick was here. He'd know just what to do. He'd been trained for situations like this. Should she call him? Leave? Her mind was so busy coming up with options, she jumped when Jonathan appeared beside her.

"I didn't mean to startle you," he said.

She placed a hand over her racing heart. "Sorry, I was...daydreaming."

"About us, I hope."

Instead of answering, she peered around him. "Michelle?"

"She realized she overstepped. It won't happen again."

"It wasn't her fault. She was right to ask. I took off the ring."

"Which I hope you'll put back on once Derrick leaves."

A shadow passed over Jonathan's face. She reached out to place her hand on his arm. "You've always had faith in us."

He shrugged. "Why not? We both want the same things."

Did they?

A few weeks ago she would have agreed. But her life had been upended once again and she had to be smart about her decisions. She'd run on fumes for so long, she hadn't taken the time to truly examine what *she* wanted, but with her mother's cancer scare over and Derrick showing up, there was no excuse not to.

"We have plenty of time to plan our future," he said, no doubt in his tone. "This is just a small setback."

"Thank you. For being so patient."

He lifted her hand to kiss her palm. She waited for the tingly shivers that accompanied a loved one's romantic actions. Nothing. Guilt swamped her all over again.

"It's a good thing I have the gallery to focus on until then."

She blinked. Why did he do that? Manage to make what they were going through take second place to the gallery. She'd be annoyed if she hadn't put them in this situation. Until she voiced a firm commitment to the man, of course he'd put his gallery first.

"What do you think of the exhibit?" he asked.

Thankful for the change of topic, she said, "It's quite stunning. I forgot how unique Bernard's pieces are."

"I've had a real interest in sales. Plus, there

are new faces here tonight. You're right—the reputation of the gallery is growing."

"About that. I met a man who said he was new to the area. I was wondering if you knew him." Searching for the tall man she'd spoken to, she located him on the other side of the room, alone, but watchful. "That guy over there."

Jonathan followed her direction. "Oh, yes. Mike, I believe. He's a serious buyer. Told me he wanted to complete his collection."

"Did he mention what that entailed?"

"He wasn't specific. You know how collectors can be, protective of their acquisitions."

That bad feeling from earlier made her stomach swirl again. Time to listen to her intuition. "You know what? I think I should head home."

"So soon?" His look of disappointment almost had her changing her mind.

"I'm worried about Mom. She's not shaking this cold."

"I understand. Let me get your coat."

She grabbed his arm before he left. "Would you mind walking me to my car."

He tilted his head. "Is something wrong?"

"Just a weird feeling I've had all night."

"Of course. I'll be right back."

As he went to get their coats, Hannah returned her glass to a serving tray. She glanced around but couldn't find the stranger in question. The tingle running down her spine had her wondering if she was overreacting.

"Anna."

It took a moment for Hannah to realize someone was speaking to her. She met Michelle's questioning gaze.

"Sorry," she mumbled. She needed to get her nerves under control. The stranger could be exactly who he said he was, a collector looking for another piece, not some shadowy guy looking for the missing gems.

"No, I'm the one who should apologize," Michelle said. "Jonathan pointed out that the status of your relationship is off-limits. I guess I was surprised not to see you wearing the ring."

"There's a lot going on right now and Jonathan has been so wonderful to give me the space I need."

"So why end the engagement?"

"It's not ended. I'm..."

She nodded to a few people passing by and stepped out of the way, not wanting anyone to overhear.

"You're having second thoughts," Michelle said.

"No," Hannah blurted.

Michelle's eagle eye didn't miss a thing. "It's that handsome friend of yours who showed up in town, isn't it?"

"I think you've misunderstood."

"No, I don't think I have." The usual haughty look disappeared and one of concern replaced it. "I've made no secret of the fact that I don't like you and Jonathan together, but he's happy. And I'll admit, I've tried to interfere, but he's been very committed to you. I don't know what's going on, but I'm asking that you don't hurt him."

"I don't want to hurt him," Hannah replied in a subdued tone.

"Then don't. He's a good man."

"On that we can agree."

Michelle sent her another steely glance, then turned on her fashionable heel and disappeared into the crowd. Jonathan strode up as soon as she walked away.

"Ready?"

More than, but she said, "Yes, thanks."

As Jonathan helped her with her coat, she noticed the stranger in her peripheral vision. He was chatting with a couple, discussing one of the sculptures. She took her phone from her clutch.

"I should get a picture of Bernard's work to show Mom," she said, snapping a shot with the stranger in it. She quickly dropped her phone back in her clutch and headed for the door.

The temperature had dropped considerably

and the wind had picked up since Hannah had arrived. As they braved the cold night together, she shoved her hands in her pockets to find her gloves. They walked in silence, nodding at passersby. At the end of the block, one of the lamplights flickered on and off.

"I suppose someone from the city will have to come out and fix that."

Is that where they were now, engaging in random conversation? "I suppose."

After a car drove by, Jonathan took her elbow and they crossed the street to the public parking lot. They stood by her car as she searched for her keys.

"This is more than not wearing the engagement ring," Jonathan said, the air clouding before his mouth as he spoke.

She shivered, her reaction from more than just the frigid night.

"Whatever is going on is serious, isn't it?"

She nodded.

In a solemn tone he said, "Please figure it out so you can come back to me."

He placed a kiss on her head, then opened her door and assisted her inside. She started the ignition, wishing she could reassure him, but didn't know what to say. She waved, then pulled away. When she glanced in the rearview mirror, he still stood in the same place, making her question every decision she'd ever made.

How could he be so accepting? So calm? She hadn't told him a thing, yet he trusted her. At this moment in time she didn't think she deserved him. She truly didn't want to hurt him, either, but couldn't deny her heart's desire.

LOADED WITH TWO cups of coffee in his gloved hands, Derrick shuffled to keep warm while standing out in the biting cold. He was meeting Hannah in the downtown area of Carson City, full of trendy shops and boutiques, to look for a wedding present for his mother. She'd requested they meet here instead of him picking her up at home, which he couldn't decide was a good or bad omen. But he had coffee prepared just the way she liked it and warned himself to be patient. He had her company for the day—what more could he ask for?

She joined him a few minutes later, bundled up in a pale blue jacket, a scarf around her neck and a hat keeping her wild curls in place. His heart banged against his chest. She grew more dear to him every day.

She smiled when he held out his hand with the offering. "You read my mind," she said, taking a quick sip. Her eyes closed as she savored the hot drink, then she braced her shoulders.

"I know I said I'd spend the day with you, but I want to head back home around noon. Mom has been fighting a nasty cold and when I left this morning she was coughing pretty badly."

"Hey, we could have rescheduled."

"I would have, but she insisted I meet you. Her friend Carol is going to be with her until I get back."

"I appreciate this. You could have stayed home."

"I could have." She paused, her eyes growing troubled. She seemed to shake it off and said, "Where to?"

"I was hoping you'd guide me."

"You didn't come up with any ideas?"

"I thought maybe we could stroll around. I have a feeling this is one of those, I'll know it when I see it, times."

"Sounds good."

They moved down the sidewalk, shoulders brushing as they dodged other Saturday morning shoppers. He'd pause before a window and Hannah would point out a potential gift, but so far nothing interested him. When they reached a bakery, he dragged her inside for a pastry, loving that she insisted she shouldn't indulge, but eating the treat with gusto. They resumed the search, unsuccessful until Hannah pulled him into a boutique featuring interesting gift ideas for weddings, baby showers and retirement parties.

Removing her gloves and unwinding her scarf, she stopped at a table. "How about a frame for your mom's wedding portrait?"

"It's an idea," he countered, stuffing his gloves in his jacket pocket as he roamed around the sales floor in the wedding section.

"Here's a lovely wall clock. You could have it personalized."

He shook his head.

"His and hers matching robes?"

He grimaced. "This is weird. I haven't thought about weddings since we were kids and planned to elope."

"How on earth did we think that was a good idea?"

"We were young with no responsibilities."

"Times have changed."

"They have." He picked up a champagne glass and twirled it in the light. "After spending time with you lately, I can't help but wonder about the direction of our lives if we'd stayed together. Would I have joined the FBI Art Crime Team? Would you have become museum docent or curator instead of a teacher?"

"It's hard to say. And pointless, really."

He sent her a sharp glance.

"I don't mean to be insensitive, Derrick, but

wondering won't change anything. Our lives turned out the way they did and I think we both adapted pretty well."

"Pragmatic, I see." He set down the glass. "We're surrounded by these gifts and I guess it made me speculate."

Hannah rounded the table to sidle up beside him, a mischievous grin on her lips. "Have I told you I like the man you are now?"

His breath stalled in his throat. "No."

"You're exactly where you're supposed to be, protecting people like me…" She grinned. "… and works of art. I admire you."

"Wow. I don't know what to say."

She playfully tapped his arm. "Now that is totally unlike you."

He chuckled. "I guess it is. You have a way of making me want a better life."

"We've only been back in each other's lives for a short time."

"That's all the time it's taken."

She shook her head and moved to another table.

"I know you wanted to work in a museum, but Hannah, the way you are with kids? It's a gift."

"Thanks. It was kind of unexpected at first, but I love the job."

"It shows."

She peered at him through lowered lids, with

that teasing look that always made his heart race. "We're just a mutual admiration society, aren't we?"

"Catching up for lost years, I'd say."

Hannah looked away, but not before he caught the pleasure on her face.

"Here's a pretty wedding album. If you don't like the frame idea, this would certainly showcase your mother's memories of the day."

He walked over, quickly enveloped in her sweet scent. He stood a little too close, wanting this moment with her to last forever, but knowing they were on the clock. The album cover was quite pretty, something his mother would go for. "I like it."

"Finally. You are the fussiest shopper ever."

"Well, I never thought I'd be buying a wedding gift for my mother."

Hannah picked up the album and held it to her chest. "Is she happy?"

He glanced at her, at the freckles dotting her pert nose and smooth skin, the hazel eyes he dreamed about, the total package that was Hannah. The events of the past were just that, the past. Since being reunited with her, Derrick had fallen in love with her on a whole new level.

"I could ask you the same thing."

"But we aren't talking about me."

He grinned at her comeback, then said, "Yes, I believe she is."

"Then she'll love anything you give her. And having you at the wedding? That's icing on the cake."

"I wish you could come with me. My Mom would love to see you."

Her smile faded. "I don't think so, Derrick."

Yeah, he figured as much.

She put the album back in place and he followed Hannah to another display. "What about you?"

"Me?" She frowned.

"When you walk down the aisle. Won't you want your dad there?"

She stiffened. "That's impossible."

"Is it?"

"What are you up to?"

His brother hadn't gotten back to him with any updates, but now seemed the perfect time to fill Hannah in on his request. "I've looked into finding him."

She gasped. "Derrick, why?"

"For many reasons, one being we need answers and your father must have them."

"And you didn't think to inform me? I don't want the government involved."

"Not the government, a friend. And I didn't

say anything because I don't want you to be disappointed if we're unsuccessful."

The anger that had tightened her features eased. "You said you'd keep me in the loop."

"I did. And I'm sorry for going forward. I'm still learning not to do things solo. Poor excuse, but I'm working on it."

"Honestly, I would like to know about Dad. Especially with Mom being sick."

"I haven't heard anything yet, but you'll be the first to know."

She pressed her lips together for a beat, then she sighed. "Dad learned how to hide from the best. The Marshals started us on the journey, but running from imagined crooks did the rest."

He wrapped an arm around her shoulder. "My guy is pretty good."

Her expression lightened. "Like you'd expect anything less."

He gave her a squeeze meant to reassure, and also just plain out of pleasure, then backed away. To his surprise, she reached out for his hand.

"Thank you."

"For?"

"Looking out for us. Helping figure out this whole gemstone thing."

"Hannah, you've done a great job on your own."

"But it's nice to share all this with someone."

"Jonathan?"

She bit her lower lip.

He held up his hand. "I said I wouldn't press."

"Then don't." She laughed and pointed at the album. "So, is this the gift?"

Derrick plucked it from the table. "It is."

"Good. Now let's go get another coffee for the drive home."

He carried the item to the counter and made his purchase. Before long he and Hannah were back outside. The wind had picked up and dark clouds rolled across the gray sky. They'd walked a block when her steps slowed.

"What's wrong?"

She nodded down the street, in the direction of the Prescott Gallery located a few blocks away. He held his breath, waiting to hear her tell him she liked it here in Nevada with Prescott, but she crossed her arms over her chest and frowned.

"I told you I was going to the exhibit last night."

"Yes."

"Something odd happened."

He led her to a secluded spot under a store awning.

"Odd in what way?"

"There was a man there." Her shoulders rose

as she took a breath. "He said he was new to the area and had just found the gallery."

"But?"

She turned her face to him. "I thought about how you said that the warnings inside me are telling me something is off. Well, something was way off."

"Like he didn't belong?"

"Yes. Everyone I spoke to last night was excited and happy to be there. He was, I don't know, scowling? Impatient? I chalked it up to overreacting about the gems but now that I see the gallery in the light of day that weird feeling is still there. I should have told you sooner."

"It's okay. You told me now."

"There's more." She took her phone from her pocket and pulled up a picture.

"Is that the guy?"

"Yes. I had this sudden impulse to snap a picture."

"Great job. Send it to me."

She hit buttons on her phone. "What will you do?"

"It may be something or it may not, but I'll check into it." He glanced down the street. "Is the gallery open?"

She looked at her watch. "Not yet. On the weekends Jonathan opens around noon and keeps later hours at night."

"I'll talk to him then. See what kind of security protocols are in the gallery."

She stuffed her phone in her jacket pocket. "Am I overreacting? Because of the gems?"

"I'd be surprised if you weren't suspicious. We haven't found the other two stones and with the way they've been randomly showing up, it's good to keep your guard up."

She blew out a shaky breath. "Okay. Good. Now that we have that decided, coffee?"

"One last thing before we go."

She looked at him and their gazes met. He saw her soften and his insides trembled. Her red nose made him smile and as always, he was lost to her. Taking a chance, he leaned over the short distance and captured her lips with his. She rested her hands against his chest, returning the fiery kiss with a heat of her own. He poured all his dreams and desires into the gesture, hoping she could feel his love for her deep down in her heart.

"What was that for?" she asked, her voice husky, when he pulled away.

"I'm proud of you," he said. "Any man would be honored to have you as his partner."

Her cheeks flushed, from the compliment, the cold wind or both, he wasn't sure. But he'd spoken from the heart and that's what mattered.

"You're a pretty good catch yourself," she said,

this time initiating another quick kiss. "I only expected this to be a shopping trip," she said.

"Spending time with you is always an adventure."

Her eyes twinkled. "Like hiking in the mountains?"

"Or canoeing on the lake."

She tapped a finger against her chin. "Sounds like we need to pull out a calendar and plan some dates."

He went still. Had she decided on a future with him? "Does that mean what I think it does?"

"That I've figured things out?" Her cell phone rang. She fished in her pocket. "Hold that thought."

Hold that thought? Why would the universe choose that moment for a phone call?

"Mom?" She glanced up at him, her eyes going wide. "Carol, slow down. What's wrong?"

At her expression, his muscles went taut.

"Okay, we'll meet you there." She hung up. "Mom couldn't breathe so Carol called an ambulance."

"Let's go."

She grabbed his arm. "What if—"

"No thinking the worst. She'll be fine." He hoped his words were true. Hannah and her mother had been through enough turmoil. They didn't need more piled on them.

As they hurried to their cars, Hannah took his hand. He'd stay close, no matter how long.

"I'll meet you there."

"Sure you can drive?"

"Yes, but you'll be right behind me?"

"The entire way."

For once, he thought as he raced to the hospital, Hannah wouldn't be in this alone. She'd have his arms to hold her, his shoulders to lean on and his heart to love her through whatever came next.

CHAPTER FOURTEEN

HANNAH CHARGED INTO the hospital, her heart pounding in her ears. She barely remembered the drive over, her mind a whirlwind. How could she have let her mother's condition get so serious?

She rushed to the information desk, her voice barely able to squeeze around the lump in her throat. After asking for her mother's status, she was pointed to the emergency room. She took off briskly down the hallway, trying to keep from a flat-out run. The memory of weeks spent here after the surgery bombarded her. She passed hospital personnel, dressed in scrubs or official white lab coats and her stomach sank.

She followed the signs and once she reached the emergency waiting room, Lynny and Carol rushed to her side.

"What happened?"

Carol's eyes were red rimmed. "When I stopped over for breakfast this morning, your mother suddenly got the chills. I sat her on the couch and the coughing started, coming so hard she couldn't catch her breath. Then suddenly she just stopped, as if she couldn't breathe at all. That's when I called 911." She sniffled. "I'm so sorry, Anna."

"No, you did the right thing."

"I should have known better than to wait. She was hot to the touch and with her lung issues…"

Her mother had worked so hard to overcome the cancer; what would this new condition do to her?

Hannah felt a hand on her shoulder and twirled around. Derrick. She fell into his arms and breathed deeply, regaining her composure. How easy it was to accept his comfort, like he'd always been there for her and this time was no different. After a brief minute of indulging in his strength, Hannah pushed away from his warmth, tucked her hair behind her ears and faced her friends. "Where is she?"

"Room three."

Squaring her shoulders, Hannah let the woman manning the ER desk know who she was and asked if they would let her back to see her mother. The older woman smiled gently and took her to the room. Pressing a hand on her stomach, she slowed her rapidly beating heart and stepped behind the drawn curtain.

At the sight of her mother, she let out a gasp.

Sophia's face was deathly pale. She was hooked up to an intravenous feed and an oxygen mask covered her nose and mouth. Her eyes were closed, but Hannah could see the slight rise and fall of her chest. She ventured closer, taking her mother's hand in hers. Sophia's eyelids fluttered and slowly opened.

"Han—" she labored to say.

"Don't talk, Mom. You're going to be fine."

Her forehead wrinkled. "I…was…fine."

Stubborn to the end. "I don't think so. You scared Carol enough that she called for an ambulance."

"Someone…needs to…keep us…on our…toes."

Hannah let out a half laugh, half sob. "What am I going to do with you?"

Her mother started to cough. Hannah stood helpless, watching her mother until she stilled again.

"Mom?"

Her mother waved a hand. Telling Hannah she was okay?

The scratch of curtain hooks against a metal rod sounded and a nurse, dressed in pink scrubs, briskly strode into the room carrying another fluid bag to hang on the IV stand.

"Are you Anna?"

"Yes."

"I'm Diane. She's been asking about you since she arrived."

"Is she going to be okay?"

Diane hung the additional bag on the stand. "The doctor started her on intravenous antibiotics and we gave her something to soothe the cough."

"I don't think it's working."

"Just give it time. We only administered it a half hour ago."

Hannah nodded. Right. As the nurse rolled the workstation on wheels beside the bed to document her mother's chart, Hannah stood back, trying to keep the tears from escaping. For all her insisting to Derrick that she could take care of anything thrown her way, she needed to be strong once again for the woman lying in the hospital bed.

The nurse finished up and rolled the station against the wall. "I'll let the doctor know you're here. I'm sure you have questions."

She did, but her brain wasn't up to maximum speed this very minute.

The nurse brought a chair closer to the bed and sat Hannah down, patting her shoulder before leaving.

Quiet settled over the room as Hannah stared at her mother's dear face. "I can't lose you," she whispered. With trembling hands she tidied the blanket and made sure to tuck in the edges, the fear digging deeper when she noticed her mom's bluish fingernails. For a long moment she closed her eyes. Whispered comforting words to the only person in her family she had left.

Moments later a doctor came in. Hannah wiped her eyes and sent him the best smile she could muster. "What's wrong with my mother?"

"Pneumonia," he said succinctly. His grayish hair was cut short and he wore gray scrubs, Dr. Blackstone stitched onto the front of his white lab coat.

"We thought it was a bad cold," Hannah explained, wishing for the hundredth time that her mother had listened to her advice to slow down her activities and attend to her health.

"Unfortunately, it's worse than the common cold."

At the sound of rustling from the bed, Hannah looked over to find her mother alert. She placed a hand on Sophia's shoulder, hoping to give her the support she needed. Or was it Hannah herself who needed the support?

"So…no painting…the town…red?"

Hannah tried not to panic at her mother's phlegmy voice. The coughing that immediately followed her question didn't sound any better.

Once she was breathing regularly again, Dr. Blackstone listened to her chest with his stethoscope. "We have some work to do to get rid of the fluid in your lungs."

"Spoil…sport."

The doctor grinned as he pulled over the workstation and typed on the keyboard. "I'm afraid so." He glanced at Hannah. "Can I take a wild guess that your mother hasn't slowed down since she became ill?"

"No." Hannah sent a stern look her mother's way. "Despite my badgering her."

"I don't take…instruction well."

The doctor glanced at Sophia, his expression serious. "Now you're here and we'll make sure you rest."

"No fun."

The doctor chuckled, then addressed Hannah. "We've started her on antibiotics and look for a complete recovery." He paused as he read the computer screen. "I see here your mother recently finished cancer treatment for a lung tumor."

"Yes. Will this newest issue create a problem?"

He tapped a few keys and then focused on Hannah. "I've ordered a chest X-ray to see what we're dealing with. I'll also put in a call to her oncologist."

"Thank you."

"We're going to move your mother to a room shortly. Why don't you go get some coffee or something to eat and we'll let you know when she's admitted and settled."

"I'd like to stay."

"It's best if you let the staff get her ready to transport to a room. Trust me, we'll take good care of her."

"Go…tell Carol."

"Okay." Hannah squeezed her mother's hand. "I'll see you soon."

"I'll…be…here."

"I love you."

"Back…at ya."

Fresh tears flooded her eyes at her mother's use of their favorite tagline. The comforting words had Hannah blinking the moisture away. No losing her composure in front of her mother. The woman was a survivor and Hannah wouldn't let Sophia worry over her tears. The nurse returned and she and the doctor spoke in low voices. Hannah went to the waiting room, her muscles so taut with fear she could barely walk.

Derrick jumped up and hurried to her side, wrapping his arm around her waist.

"Everything will be okay," he whispered in her ear.

She wanted to believe that promise, but until her mother left the hospital, she wasn't relying on false hope.

She pushed away, more steady now, to explain the diagnosis. When she'd finished relating the news, she reached over to pull Carol into a tight hug. "Thanks for getting Mom here."

"Of course."

She hugged Lynny next, who then held her at arm's length. "You look terrible."

Hannah sputtered a laugh, appreciating her friend's attempt at humor to lighten the mood. "Thanks for your unnecessary candor."

"I called Roger. He's going to spread the word to the teachers so they can keep your mom in their thoughts."

The tears stung again. She didn't have words for these precious friends who had adopted them like family.

Lynny hesitated, flicked her glance to Derrick and back, then said, "And heads up, Jonathan reached out to me since he couldn't get ahold of you. I had to tell him what's going on."

"It's okay," Hannah told her friend. Lynny had done the right thing. Hannah would fill Jonathan in later.

"Why don't we get you some coffee," Carol suggested with a nod at Lynny.

"Want to come to the cafeteria?" Lynny asked.

"If you don't mind, I'm going to stay here. They're going to let me know when they move Mom to a room."

The two women hugged her again and set off to another area of the hospital.

Derrick led her to a grouping of chairs and a couch, away from other visitors in the room. She sank into the soft couch and let out a ragged breath.

"Bad?" Derrick asked as he lowered himself onto the cushion next to her.

"Serious, but the doctor didn't act like it was an emergency. They've gotten some medicine into her. Will do some tests."

"How are her spirits?"

"Incredible." Her laugh sounded shaky to her ears. "Joking around as usual. How can she do that?"

"Probably for you."

She frowned at him. "Me?"

"To keep you calm."

She stared across the room, focusing on the entrance to the emergency area. "It's not working."

"Hannah, look at me."

She met his gaze, holding on to her control by a thread. When she and her mother had received the cancer diagnosis, Hannah had kept it together. During treatment, she had been a rock. Why now, with friends here to help shoulder this newest setback, was she falling apart? Could it be that she simply didn't want her mother to have to go through one test after another or schedule multiple doctor visits like before? Or did she finally recognize that it was okay to let her guard down and be vulnerable because these wonderful people, including Derrick, had her back?

"We're in this together."

His gaze was steady, the deep blue eyes she'd never forgotten reassuring. She still loved Derrick, the young man she remembered, the solid, dependable man he'd become. Nothing would change that fact.

"Derrick, I—"

"We have your back," he said, thinking she was going to argue with him, not express her feelings. She swallowed hard.

"There's nowhere I'd rather be, nothing more important than you, so get used to having me around."

She sent him a wobbly smile. How had she gotten so lucky to have him back in her life? She needed to stop questioning the reasons for his sudden appearance and simply rejoice in his presence.

She held out her hand. His gaze never breaking from hers, he twined their fingers together. As much as she was worried, she knew she had a support system. She wasn't as alone as she'd made herself believe.

A few people came in through the sliding doors, bringing with them a cold breeze. Outside, the clouds had grown heavier, blocking the sun from fully shining. She inhaled the crisp air, a welcome contrast to the hospital smells.

"I'm not sure how long they'll keep her here," Hannah said after they'd been sitting quietly for a long time.

He tugged her closer and she snuggled into his side. "Like I said, not going anywhere."

She savored his arm around her, this calm in the storm, when a thought occurred to her. She leaned away to view his face. "What about your mother's wedding?" she couldn't help asking. Derrick couldn't stay here indefinitely, could he?

"We'll play it by ear."

Her chest went tight. He wasn't going to leave her.

"How about we all make the trip?" he suggested. "The three of us, if your mother is up to it."

He wanted her to come to his family event.

How odd to be asked after years of refusing to make any lasting relationships. Maybe that's why the gesture touched her so deeply.

Overcome by emotion, she twisted toward him to rest her forehead against his. She inhaled his tangy cologne. Felt his breath on her lips. She wanted to kiss him, to let the touch of his lips make her forget what was going on in this place, but she forced herself to relish only his very solid presence.

A discreet cough sounded nearby. Startled by the sight of Jonathan, she pushed away from Derrick. Her fiancé—were they exes because she'd taken the ring off?—stuffed his hands in his coat pockets, clearly surprised to find her in another man's arms. She leaped up. Derrick rose slowly beside her.

"I've been trying to get ahold of you, Anna. When you didn't answer, I became worried. I was finally able to contact Lynny. She told me your mother had been brought here."

"Yes. That cold I told you about? It turned to pneumonia."

"She'll be okay?"

"As long as nothing goes wrong, I believe so."

He shot a glance at Derrick, then back. The awkward tension between the three of them grew. Jonathan finally nodded at them both. "I should probably leave. Please give my regards to your mother."

"I will." He turned to walk away. Hannah hurried after him. "Jonathan. Wait."

He stopped. Slowly faced her. "I see how it is, Anna."

She blinked away fresh tears. "I'm sorry."

He merely nodded again, his face emotionless, and walked away.

She sensed Derrick come up behind her. She looked over her shoulder and when he moved closer, she reached out to him.

"Talk about terrible timing," she said.

Derrick tugged her into his arms. "Sorry he had to see us like that."

"I suppose it was for the best." But the guilt left a horrible taste in her mouth. She'd decided she was going to tell Jonathan that she couldn't marry him. Return the ring, apologize and hope he wouldn't be hurt. Now he had every reason to think the worst of her.

Before Derrick could say anything, the older woman from behind the desk headed in their direction.

"Your mother is being moved to room 330. Give the team about thirty minutes to get her settled."

Hannah thanked the woman. With time to

kill, she and Derrick took their seats on the couch. "It's going to be a long day."

"It's a good thing I'm a patient man," he said, sending her a gentle smile.

She scooted closer, hooked her arm through his and rested her head on his shoulder, still amazed that they were indeed in this together. Both she and her mother couldn't ask for a better gift than to have Derrick in their lives.

Everything would be fine now, she convinced herself. For her mother. Between her and Derrick. Despite their uncertain future, she refused to entertain any other possibility.

It was late when Derrick returned to his hotel room. Carol and Lynny had gone home after Sophia was made comfortable in her room. Hannah refused to budge, so he hung out until Sophia insisted they both leave in order to get a good night's sleep. After she drifted off, he'd persuaded Hannah to drive home and rest. He imagined it was going to be a long night for all of them, but she needed some downtime to recharge her batteries.

Tossing his keys on the dresser, he pulled his phone from his jeans pocket. He hadn't checked his phone for hours. Messages and multiple missed-call alerts dotted the screen. He tapped one, seeing that Dylan had been trying to reach him. He found his brother's number and soon had him on the line.

"Dude, I've been trying to reach you all day."

"Sorry." He ran a hand over the back of his neck. "Hannah's mother is in the hospital. Pneumonia. I've been with them."

"Sorry, man. Will she be okay?"

"Looks like it." He went to the tiny bathroom and filled a glass with water. "The medicine was already working when I left."

"How's Hannah?"

He mentally visualized her face, pale yet stunningly lovely, shoulders squared as a determined glint flashed in her eyes. She was exhausted, but would have stayed by her mother's bedside all night if need be. "Coping. She actually let me fuss over her. Since I've been here she's made sure to hammer home the fact that she can take care of every problem by herself. Truthfully, I think she was glad for the backup."

"And you?" Dylan asked.

His chest pinched in the vicinity of his heart. He took a sip of water. "Thankful to be here for her."

"You always did like being in everyone's business."

He dropped onto the bed. "I'm learning to

let go." He lay back and stared at the ceiling. "What's so important?"

"We got a lead on Hannah's father."

Derrick shot up. "So soon?"

"You were right—he went back to his real name."

Wow. He'd never expected the hunt to be this easy. "Has anyone made contact?"

"No. Logan wanted instructions on how he should proceed."

Derrick rose and began to pace the length of the room. "Text me the info you have. There's another issue developing and I think it's time to bring the Bureau in."

"What kind of new development?"

"Hannah met a guy the other night at a local art gallery. In light of the missing gems, she was unnerved by his attention on her and managed to snap his picture. I'm going to send it to my superior and have him check into this guy's identity. If he has any connection to the gemstones, I want our bases covered. No point in giving away Mr. Rawlings's location yet."

"Okay. Sending the info now. Let me know where we go from here."

"I will. Thanks, Dylan."

"Hey, what are brothers for?"

"I always thought to mess with, but I appreciate all you've done." He paused a moment.

"Listen, if things don't look up here, I might miss Mom's wedding. You up to walking her down the aisle if I can't make it?"

Dylan let out a slow whistle. "You're a brave man, risking her wrath."

"In this case she'd understand."

"Want me to give her a heads up?"

"Better you than me."

Dylan chuckled. "Keep me updated."

"Will do."

After signing off, Derrick debated contacting his superior, Ron Collins. Hannah had asked him not to get the government involved, but this case was getting messy and had too many moving parts for him not to gather reinforcements. He battled with his decision for a full twenty minutes before going with his gut.

Ron wasn't happy about the late night call, but once he heard the story, he told Derrick he'd do a search on the guy in the morning. Derrick hung up, not exactly relieved, but at least feeling like he was doing everything he could to keep Hannah safe. He took a long, hot shower and got ready for bed.

He'd just turned on the television when his phone rang. He read the caller ID and grimaced. His mother. Didn't take Dylan long to run with the news.

"I have a bone to pick with you, young man."

"Threats? Nice way to start the conversation, Mom."

"Why didn't you tell me you'd found Hannah?"

"I see Dylan filled you in."

"My goodness, Derrick, you must be over the moon."

"I'll rest easier when Mrs. Rawlings gets a clean bill of health."

"Tell me everything."

For the next thirty minutes Derrick told his mother how he'd gotten a lead to Hannah. That it was rough going, but their relationship seemed to be headed in the right direction. If time, and Sophia's health, were amenable, he hoped to bring Hannah to the wedding.

"That's quite a tale. Witness protection? Hiding out? It's like a movie."

"It is. Will you be all right with me missing the wedding if Sophia isn't better?"

"There are still two weeks until the day, so hopefully Sophia's health will be back on track. If she's up to it, bring her along, as well."

"Thanks, Mom." Grateful to know his mother was happy, healthy and in love, Derrick swallowed around the lump in his throat. "Have I told you lately that you're the best?"

"No. But I never mind hearing those words."

He chuckled. "It's been a long day."

"It has. I'll talk to you again soon."

"Count on it."

He hung up and tried to get into some cop show playing on the screen, but he kept losing focus. His mind was ten steps ahead. He kept wondering what his boss would find, how it would affect Hannah and her mother. He had yet to inform Hannah he'd gotten the Bureau involved, but he justified the solo step, especially with Hannah's worry over her mother's newest health crisis. He didn't want to burden her with his decision.

At least that's what he told himself.

With the green stone safely stowed away in his luggage, he pulled the red gemstone from his pocket, the constant reminder of what had been and what could be. Absently, he ran it between his fingers as he stared out of the window over a sleeping city. He hoped Hannah wouldn't be upset with him. Hoped the new bond they'd forged was strong enough that she'd understand he wanted to protect her. Hoped his love for her was enough to weather another storm.

But deep down he worried he'd made the same mistake with her again.

CHAPTER FIFTEEN

MUCH TO HER CHAGRIN, Hannah slept until eight the following morning. She'd intended to rise early and be at the hospital first thing, but after a sleepless night her body took over and demanded the rest it craved. She rolled out of bed, fuzzy headed and achy, shaking off her funk in order to get moving.

She headed to her mother's room to pack her a bag. The doctor wasn't sure how long her mother would be hospitalized, so Hannah wanted to bring her some comforts from home. Her worn robe. Slippers. Toothbrush.

After making a pile on the bed, she rifled through the closet to find an overnight bag. Once located, Hannah tossed it on the bed, then opened the bag to place the items inside. As she did so, her hand brushed against something at the bottom. She felt around, then her fingers clutched a solid object. She pulled it out. A jewelers' box, very much like the kind her father had stocked at their store before they fled Florida. Curious, she pried open the lid. Could it be a small token her father had saved before they left? Or a gift her mother had been hiding? Her mind whirled, then came to a walloping halt as she viewed two gemstones, one blue, the other topaz, nestled in the satin lining.

The last of the missing stones.

How on earth…? She stared at them, her mind blank. Then the questions bombarded her. Why did her mother have the gems? Did she know they were in the bag? She had to. But if so, why hadn't she mentioned them, especially when the first two had shown up? Now, more than ever, she needed to get to the hospital.

She closed the lid and finished packing, then she quickly showered and dressed in a cream-colored blouse, black pants and boots. Grabbing the bag and her purse, she took off to find out some answers.

Soon, she hurried into her mother's hospital room. Sophia was eating breakfast, a good sign that she was doing better. The oxygen mask had been replaced by a nasal cannula. Her skin tone had improved and her eyes were clear. She smiled as Hannah placed the bag on the nearby chair and rummaged inside.

"You brought some things from home? Oh, Hannah, how sweet."

"It's the least I could do."

"Did you get any sleep?"

"A little." Hannah stood and got right to the point, holding out the jewelers box. "I found this in the bag."

Her mother's smile slipped. Hannah opened the box. The gems flashed under the fluorescent lighting. "Can you explain?"

"Oh dear."

Hannah reined in her impatience. "That's not an answer."

"Sit," her mother commanded. Hannah moved the bag to the floor and scooted the chair closer to the bed. She handed the box to her mother, who gingerly took it and stared at the contents. An aide came into the room to take away the breakfast tray, giving her mother a moment to gather her thoughts. Her mom's anguished expression meant this was going to be a hard truth for them to face.

Her mother finally met her gaze. "I never meant for you to find the box."

"Then you shouldn't have left it in the bag."

"I've moved it around to different hiding places ever since we left Florida."

"Why not tell me?"

Sophia ran the tip of her finger over the stones. "Because I thought we might need them for leverage." She looked up. "Your father was involved with some awful men."

"You knew?"

Sophia shook her head. "Not until the extortion started. Your father had no idea what to do. He got in deeper and things escalated."

"You never told me."

"I didn't want you to worry then, you were just a kid. Over time, you took on the role as protector. It was a way for you to cope and I didn't want to take that from you."

Hannah frowned. "I still don't understand."

Sophia set the box aside. "Before your father spoke to the authorities, he told me the man he worked with, the supposed jewelry supplier he testified against, had learned about these gems and wanted them. Jerome locked them in his office safe, but I knew the men wouldn't let that stop them from getting what they wanted. I took them and hid them, just in case your father decided to hand the stones over. If he did, he would never be free from their demands and I didn't want us to live that way. I believed the police and others would protect us." A defensive look crossed her face. "I made sure Derrick's father stepped in. I trusted him, so I convinced your father to confide in him."

Hannah's mouth fell open. "I thought Derrick was the one who got his father involved."

"In a way. Mr. Matthews was already going to talk to your father, I reached out to him first. Together, we came up with a plan. Once I told your father, he was more than happy for a way out. We just never realized what the cost would be."

"Hiding and then being separated." Hannah thought about her mother's story. Frowned. All these years she'd blamed Derrick for the Marshals showing up that night. "Dad didn't know you had the gemstones?"

"No one did. Like I said, I hid them before all the chaos started. The authorities thought they were in evidence, along with the other jewelry they confiscated before the trial. It wasn't until they were doing an inventory in the case that it came to light they were missing. Thankfully, your father's testimony was more than enough to put that horrible man behind bars. The gemstones weren't necessary." She shivered. "Besides, your father rightfully owned the gems. I just didn't tell anyone I had them in my possession."

"And Dad never knew?"

"No. I decided to take matters into my own hands, like he had done for years. I had to protect my family."

Hannah sat back, digesting this new information. Humiliation, followed by a bone-deep hurt, buffeted her. Her mother could have filled her in at any time, but chose not to. Even after Derrick had shown up and awakened painful memories.

"It was time," her mother was saying, firmly closing the lid of the jewelry box.

At the determination in her mother's eyes, Hannah pushed aside her pain and grew wary. "Mom, what did you do?"

Her mother glanced at the door. "I looked out for you."

Hannah twisted around to find Derrick standing just inside the room, shock etched on his face. Her stomach flip-flopped at the sight of him. He looked handsome, dressed in a blue sweater, worn jeans and boots, his heavy jacket resting in the crook of his arm. His hair was mussed, from the wind perhaps, and his spicy scent drifted her way.

He asked her mother, "You sent me the stone?"

Hannah froze.

"Guilty as charged," Sophia answered.

Derrick brushed past her to get to Sophia. "But why?"

Sophia shook her head slowly. "I was dying. I needed to make sure Hannah would be safe."

Reeling from emotions that were racing from one extreme to the other, Hannah said, "But you didn't die, Mom."

"Yes, well I didn't know I'd make a full recovery at the time." She gazed at Derrick, then her daughter. "I'd held on to those gems for a purpose. I couldn't think of anyone in the world who would do more in their power to keep you safe than Derrick."

Derrick's phone rang. He pulled it from his jeans pocket, swiped the screen and the sound stopped, as if he let the call go to voice mail.

"How did you know where to find me?" he asked.

"I have a few computer skills."

"What? How?" Hannah asked, trying to recall her mother spending hours at the home computer and coming up short.

"You don't think I sat around doing nothing while you were working," she huffed. "I found ways to keep myself busy."

Hannah sank down into the chair. The things she didn't know about her mother were mind-boggling.

"And the green stone in Hannah's purse?" Derrick asked.

Her mom smiled. "I planted it. I had to find a way to keep you two together." She scowled at Hannah. "I'd worked hard to get Derrick here and you wanted him to leave. I had to take drastic action."

Hannah glanced up at Derrick. His shock had changed to annoyance, if the narrowed eyes were any indication. She knew how he felt.

Derrick's voice was tight when he said, "But

here's the problem. I believe someone, besides me, knows you're here."

Her mother crossed her arms over her chest. "I didn't factor that in."

Hannah counted to ten. Voices came and went in the hallway. "Then the precautions you and Dad employed to shield us might come to nothing."

Now her mother looked worried.

Hannah heard a buzzing come from Derrick's pocket. He ignored it as he focused on her mother. "Is there anything else you haven't told us?"

Sophia seemed to sink deeper into the bed as the situation hit home. "No. I honestly don't know where Jerome is. I wanted to use the gemstones for good, that's why I sent one to you, Derrick. It was misguided, but I had good intentions."

Derrick ran a hand over the back of his neck, a gesture Hannah noticed he did when stressed. And how had she become so in tune with him in the few weeks he'd lived here? Was it a leftover reflex from when they were young? Perhaps. But in the time she'd spent with him lately, she'd come to appreciate new, wonderful things about Derrick, first and foremost his strength and dedication. She hadn't felt this safe since before the Marshals secreted them away.

As much as she'd fought against it, she couldn't deny that knowing Derrick had her back had revived an inane boldness she thought she'd lost years ago. They'd made a good team while he was here. What would happen when he left?

"You know you could have called me, right?" Derrick's gaze flicked from her mom to Hannah and back. "I would have come no matter the circumstances."

"I know you would have," Sophia said. "But Hannah would have fought it."

"I—" Hannah wanted to argue, but couldn't. Hadn't she given him a hard time about being here since he'd arrived? It wasn't until they'd reconnected that she'd let down her guard. Started enjoying their time together. "You're right. I would have vetoed contacting Derrick. Or anyone we used to know."

Her mother reached out for her hand. "You were so angry. Not only at Derrick, but at the world. Over time, I realized the only way for you to move on was to confront Derrick. Forgive him for the past. See that you two belong together and begin a brand-new relationship." She wrinkled her nose. "I suppose I overplayed my hand."

"Mom, you didn't have to be so sneaky about it."

"Again, if I'd told you, you would never have

given Derrick a chance. And as much as I like Jonathan, I never felt he was the right man for you. Yes, he's been a constant companion and was considerate to us during the cancer treatment, but he always puts his gallery first."

So, her mother had noticed that too? Hannah told herself she didn't mind Jonathan's passion for the gallery, it was his livelihood, but lately she'd been concerned at coming in second best. Especially when Lynny felt the need to point the fact out to her. Since Derrick had arrived, she hadn't exactly put Jonathan first either, so she couldn't be too mad at him.

"It's just that Jonathan never looks at you the way Derrick does, like you're the most important person to him." Sophia smoothed the blanket over her lap. Her eyes grew misty. "I'm sorry I lied to you, Hannah, but I wouldn't do it any differently. The results are exactly as I'd hoped them to be." She blinked, allowing a tear to escape and roll down her cheek. "You and Derrick have another chance at love. Life is precious, Hannah. We certainly learned that during the cancer scare. I don't want you to waste any more time clinging to anger when you can forgive and share a bright future with your true love."

Hannah stood and stepped past Derrick, who held his emotions in check so well, she couldn't read his face. His blue eyes were dark and veiled, his lips in a grim line. Her mother had gone to great lengths to get them back together again. How were they going to process this?

"It's all too much, Mom." She walked to Derrick's side. Wanted to take his hand, but resisted. It took all her self-control not to touch him. "Too, too much."

No one spoke for a long moment.

The doctor entered the room, his manner brisk as he made his way around Hannah to approach her mother's bed.

"You're looking much better this morning, Mrs. Rawley," he said and unwrapped the stethoscope from around his neck.

Her mother was uncharacteristically silent.

"I went over your recent vitals and labs." He placed the bell over Sophia's chest and listened. Nodded as if pleased and said, "The medicine is working well, so we'll be discharging you tomorrow."

"Thank you," Sophia said, her demeanor stiff.

"I'll have some prescriptions for you to fill when you leave, but I expect a full recovery. Your chest X-ray was clean, but I'd suggest a follow-up with your oncologist."

The buzzing sound came for Derrick's pocket

again. Hannah frowned at him, but he continued to ignore the phone.

The doctor turned to Hannah. "Any questions?"

"No. My questions have been answered."

Was it her imagination or did her mother wince?

"Wonderful. Mrs. Rawley, make sure to rest in order to ensure a complete recovery."

"I've learned my lesson."

In more ways than one, Hannah thought.

"You have a good day," he said as he left the room.

A nurse came in and began typing on the keyboard under the computer screen mounted on the wall. "I'll get your vitals in a minute," she informed Sophia.

"Take your time."

The pressure that had been building in Hannah's chest was ready to burst. Before she did or said anything she might regret, she announced to the room, "I'm going to the cafeteria."

The nurse nodded, unaware of the tension hanging over them.

She grabbed her purse and walked to the corridor, riding on a wave of emotions. There was so much to wade through, she didn't know where to start.

"Hannah, hold up."

At Derrick's deep voice, she slowed down. He came to her side and they continued to the elevators. She stabbed the call button.

"This was a surprise," he finally said.

"You think?"

He placed a hand on her arm. She took a deep breath before meeting his concerned gaze. They stood still for a minute before he sighed and guided her to the large window overlooking the parking lot.

"Are you okay?"

"I have no idea." She wrapped her arms over her chest.

"We should probably talk about this."

In a matter of a few weeks her life had been upturned again, just when she thought she had found a semblance of peace. How wrong she was.

"—before your mother goes home," Derrick was saying before she tuned back in to the conversation.

Derrick took her hand. She wanted to lean on him. Let his strength seep into her. But she'd learned long ago to stand on her own two feet. Now was not the time to let her defenses down.

"I know this is a lot to take in."

A bitter laugh escaped her.

"Why don't we go somewhere a little more private. I have—"

His phone buzzed again.

"Aren't you going to answer that?"

"Whoever it is can wait."

She wanted a few minutes to herself before the well-meaning conversations started. Derrick never knew when to back off. Hadn't he been pushing her for more in their relationship since he blew into town? She needed space to figure out her messy love life and her mother's revelation, without being pressured. She ran a shaky hand over her temple. "Please, just take it."

Derrick hesitated, then pulled the phone from his pocket. As he paced the length of the elevator bank, Hannah stared out the wide window at the picture-perfect day. The sun was shining, a welcome treat after weeks of gloom and snow. The white-capped mountaintops glistened in the distance. From here she could see cars zipping down the interstate. People came and went below, going about their lives.

How she wished for the same. Instead, her life was like a tangled maze. Every time she made headway and things seemed to settle down, she rounded a corner to a new disaster, like learning her mother had the gemstones all along. She closed her eyes against a wave of tears. Was this how her life would always be? One surprise after another?

"Do you have a location?" she heard Derrick ask. "ETA?"

Hannah turned her head his way. Guilt flashed in his eyes. Oh no, he didn't... Her stomach clenched.

"Keep me informed." He ended the conversation, refusing to meet her eyes.

"Important?"

He finally looked her way, not appearing the least bit sorry. "Yes."

With a sinking heart, she said, "Please tell me you didn't speak to the authorities."

"I had to," Derrick said, no remorse in his voice.

The ache that had abated ramped up once more. "I asked you not to."

"And I wouldn't have if that stranger hadn't approached you at the gallery. I needed to make sure you were safe and in order to do that, I needed access to the Bureau."

The pain tearing through her chest made it difficult to breathe. She dropped her arms from the protective stance and headed to the elevator.

"Please, hear me out," Derrick said behind her.

She swung around, hurt now morphing to anger. "Why would I?"

"Because your instincts were right. That guy was following you."

She stopped. "What?"

"I sent the picture you gave me to my superior. He searched our system and discovered a connection between him and the man your father helped put in prison."

She brushed her hair behind one ear, confusion making her unsteady on her feet. "How did he know I was in Dark Clay?"

"I don't know yet. That was my boss. When I didn't answer my phone, he got the local field office involved. They found a location on the suspect and are en route to question him."

She swept her hand toward the elevator doors. "Then you should get going."

"I don't want to leave you."

"This is why you came to Nevada," she reminded him, anger lacing her tone. "To do your job."

"It was more than that. Hannah, you know I came here because I never stopped looking for you. Never stopped loving you."

He was right. He'd been up-front and honest about his reasons for the trip. But no matter how well-intentioned he was, she couldn't appreciate that now. She was juggling so many problems that her head pounded.

She glanced at him, his resolve to take care of every single detail imprinted on his face. Was it possible for Derrick to change? She had asked him not to get the authorities involved. Could she give her heart to a man who wouldn't listen when she expressed her wishes? The way her father had kept secrets from her mother—destroying their family because he thought he knew best?

No, she was capable of being in control. Had been for many years.

Derrick watched her carefully, his eyes pleading with her to see his side. She stuck out her chin and said, "And once again, you did the one thing sure to push me away."

His face went pale. "You can't mean that."

"Oh, I do. I'm finished with half-truths and trusting people who keep secrets from me."

She couldn't stay here any longer. Not until she got a handle on the hurt and anger. Spying the door to the staircase, she headed that way.

"Where are you going?"

"I don't know," she said over her shoulder, "but one thing is certain, I don't want you to follow me."

With more force than necessary, she shoved open the door to the stairway and hurried down, her footsteps echoing off the concrete walls as she made her escape.

HIS WORST NIGHTMARE had come true. Hannah hadn't accepted his reasons for contacting the Bureau. Given everything she'd been through, he got it. Still, he'd hoped that she'd look at the current situation and understand his motives came from love, not an intent to deceive her.

He ran a hand over his chest. The ache he'd lived with for years returned with a vengeance.

As much as he wanted to race after her, she needed space. This morning had been a series of revelations she should process in her own time. He was barely keeping up with it all himself.

It took everything in him to walk past the stairway door and head to Sophia's room. She was staring out the window, but turned her head and leaned forward when he entered.

Her eyes were filled with distress. "Where's Hannah?"

"She needs some time alone."

Sophia sank onto the mattress. "She's never going to forgive me."

"Or me." He shoved his hands in his pockets. Tried to breathe around the tight band squeezing his chest. "When I found her, I thought we'd fall back into each other's arms. Plan a future together." He tried to grin, but his lips wouldn't comply. "I expected some hesitation, confusion even, but Hannah's so stubborn."

"You forgot about that trait?"

"Seems I forgot a lot." He shook his head. "I never meant to hurt her."

Sophia clasped her hands together. "On the contrary. I haven't seen her this happy in years."

"I blew that all away." He proceeded to explain what was going on and why he'd called in the Bureau.

"We're quite a team," Sophia said with a hitch in her voice. "Loving my daughter hasn't kept us from wounding her."

Derrick ran a finger over the red stone in his pocket. He grasped it and pulled it out, handing it to Sophia. "This is yours."

"Won't your superiors want it?"

"Since the gemstones weren't an integral part of the trial and they are legally yours, you should take it."

She reached out to wrap his fingers around the stone. "I want you to keep it."

"As a reminder of the second-biggest mistake I've made?"

Sophia bit her lower lip. "For years she's been the one taking care of us. Handling every situation head-on with an inner strength she doesn't realize she possesses. I know you meant well…"

He recalled Hannah's face, crushed by the hurt he'd unintentionally inflicted on her. "But she probably won't give me a third chance?"

Sophia straightened the covers, her silence answering his question. He'd blown it big-time and he doubted there was any going back. Still didn't make him regret calling in reinforcements. Honestly, it wasn't like he could have done this on his own. Would Hannah eventually understand his dilemma?

He placed the stone on the rolling table. "You should keep it. I'll also get the green stone to you."

"If I can't convince you…"

Derrick shook his head.

Sophia sighed and picked up the stone.

"I need a clean slate with Hannah."

"I understand."

A buzzing interrupted the conversation. Derrick looked at his phone screen and took the call. It was the local field office special agent informing him they had the suspect in custody. "I'll be right there." He hung up. "I need to go."

"Is this about our case?"

He smiled at her wording. "We're finally going to get answers."

"Good." At Sophia's sad smile, he swallowed around the knot that had formed in his throat when Hannah stormed away. "I can't thank you enough for all you've done."

He would have disagreed, but Sophia continued.

"Hannah asked you not to say anything about the gemstones all those years ago, but partly because you did, your father got involved and helped us in a very difficult situation. She can't see it, but your actions forced us to tell the truth instead of being pressured by some very unpleasant men. And yes, she doesn't like how events have repeated, but again, you've managed to make us safe. She'll come around."

Derrick wasn't so sure. Hannah usually said what she meant and what she said was that she didn't want Derrick to follow her. But for how long? How could he make amends? He would be leaving soon; his mother's wedding was in two weeks. Then he had to report back to work in DC. If she couldn't see things like her mother did, what chance did they ever have of restoring their relationship?

With his heart torn to pieces, he left the hospital and wove through the parking lot to the rental car. As he slipped on his sunglasses, he vowed to finish the job he'd come here to do: keep Hannah safe. Then he'd apologize for his high-handedness. Promise to be a better listener. Hope she would take his words at face value.

But as things stood right now, he'd be lucky if she ever spoke to him again.

CHAPTER SIXTEEN

A WEEK AND A HALF after her mother was discharged from the hospital, Hannah worked up the nerve to walk into the Prescott Gallery. It was empty. Contemporary music flowed from the hidden speakers. A fresh bouquet of colorful flowers scented the room. Squaring her shoulders, she moved toward the back office to complete her mission.

The past few days hadn't been easy. She and her mom had sat down for an overdue conversation. You would have thought living together for years under strained circumstances would have kept them from secrets, yet it hadn't. But after explanations, tears and, finally, hugs, they were able to overcome their differences. Hannah had to let the hurt of her mother not trusting her go. She loved her mother and despite everything, wanted to keep their relationship intact.

Hannah had also worked up the courage to tell Lynny who she really was and why she and her mother had been in hiding. Instead of being mad at the deception, Lynny told her it was the best story ever and wanted to write a book about it. Happy to still have her best friend on her side, Hannah agreed to give her pointers. Until Lynny decided it would have to be a romance novel and Derrick would be cast as the hero. In that case, Hannah would pass.

Derrick. That was another story.

Jonathan emerged from his office, leafing through some papers. He stopped short when he saw her. His lips pulled into a tight line. Anger? Probably. She deserved it.

"Hello," she said uncertainly, moving closer. She wiped her damp palms on her jeans and suddenly grew warm under her heavy sweater.

He nodded but didn't voice a greeting.

Okay, this was going to be harder than she'd thought.

Ready to take care of the business at hand, she reached into her jeans pocket and pulled out the diamond engagement ring Jonathan had told her to hold on to until she was ready to move forward with their plans. This time instead of refusing, he took the ring from her fingers and placed it in his jacket pocket without trying to talk her into keeping it.

He cleared his throat and asked, "I guess you'll be moving on with Derrick now?"

"No. He left. I'm staying here."

Astonishment flashed over his features. "I must say, I'm surprised. He certainly worked overtime to convince you that the two of you belong together."

He had, until she'd had enough. Each day she'd put off any conversation with him, unable to accept what he'd done. With her pride holding him at arm's length, she hadn't given him a reason to stick around. And in the exact opposite fashion than when he arrived, Derrick accepted her silence and gave her plenty of room to decide the direction of their relationship. Like Nevada to Florida room.

"I'll admit, I wasn't thrilled when he was around," Jonathan said. "But on reflection, he did bring an inner light out of you, Anna. Something I was never able to do."

She looked down at her boots. "Hannah."

"Excuse me?"

This time she met his bewildered gaze. "My real name is Hannah."

His shoulders slumped as if he was finally resigned to the endless hurdles between them. "Well. I see there are even more layers to you that I don't know about."

Uncomfortable, she shoved her hands in her pockets. "I'm afraid so."

Jonathan sent her a strained smile. "Then it's a shame you let Derrick walk away."

"Come again?"

"It was very plain to everyone around you that he made you whole. Happy. I would have thought after all you'd been through that you would have fought for him."

Why didn't she fight for him? The answer was simple. He'd betrayed her once again. But in the past days, as she'd replayed everything he'd done in her mind, she realized that his actions had been to protect her. Both times. She really couldn't fault him for that.

Too little too late.

"I'm sorry it didn't work out with us," she said, truly meaning it. "Can you forgive me?"

"So am I. And with time, perhaps."

An awkward silence descended. She wanted to say more, but was it fair to Jonathan? Nothing he said would change her mind about breaking the engagement. And she'd certainly hurt him. A decent person would leave now and let him get on with his life. That's what she intended to do.

He must have sensed her withdrawal. Nodding in the direction of the door, he said, "Go live your best life, Hannah."

She pressed her lips together, regret and gratitude vying for first place. "You, too."

Stepping outside, she pulled her scarf closer to her ears. In time Jonathan would forgive her.

Can you say the same about Derrick? Could she? She'd forgiven her mother, hadn't she? Was it harder to make peace with Derrick because he'd wounded her heart? The heart she had so much wanted to give to him? She stood alone as people hustled by, busy with their daily routines. Moving forward while she felt suspended in time.

Jonathan was right; she had been different with Derrick. Because she loved him. The hurt was fading now and the stark truth was that she'd let him walk out of her world. By thinking her pain was deeper than his, she'd pushed him away when all he wanted to do was love her.

Her heart sank. What had she done?

AN HOUR LATER Hannah unlocked the front door and stepped into the house she shared with her mother. Sophia hurried out from the kitchen. "You're home."

"Yes. I told Lynny everything after school. Then I drove to the gallery to see Jonathan."

Her mother cringed. "And?"

"Lynny thinks the entire story is bookworthy." She unwound her scarf and tossed it, along with her jacket, on the couch. "Jonathan was quite the gentleman about the end of our relationship."

Her mother placed an arm around Hannah.

"What a day. How about you come into the kitchen. I have a surprise for you."

Without much enthusiasm, Hannah let her mother drag her into the other room. When she recognized the person waiting there, she thought she might faint.

It took long seconds for her voice to work. "Dad?" she croaked. Not waiting for an answer, she ran across the room to hug her father. "How?"

"Derrick sent a PI to find me," he explained. "I was informed by the Bureau that it was safe to be reunited."

Derrick had done this? He had mentioned he'd been looking for her father, but not that he'd found him. She wanted to be mad at him for risking her dad's safety, but was too happy to muster up the appropriate fury.

"When did you get here?"

"An hour ago," he said, wrapping his arm around Sophia's waist as if she never wanted to be separated again. "We have so much catching up to do."

After a quick hug for his wife, her father walked over and kissed Hannah on the forehead. "Thank you." He stopped to visibly compose himself. "Your mother told me how well you've taken care of her, especially through her health scare." He shook his head. "I can't believe I thought it was ever a good idea for me to part ways."

"You were right from the beginning, Dad. People were looking for us."

He nodded, wiping his eyes. "I thought by moving away I'd take the spotlight off you and your mother. I'm sorry it didn't turn out that way. Or that things didn't end happily with Derrick."

Not that it mattered now. Hannah had flat-out refused to see him. But even in her stubbornness she couldn't deny that she missed him as much as she needed air to breathe. He'd been the only man she'd ever loved, would ever love, and in the height of anger, she let him leave.

Except that anger didn't soothe her when she was lonely, didn't reassure her with a comforting touch or searching glance when she had doubts. Derrick could have done all that if she'd let him in and now he was gone.

Her mother's voice interrupted her miserable thoughts. "Derrick explained what he'd done before he left."

"What do you mean?" Hannah asked.

"Even though I was the one who set things in motion with the gemstones, Derrick found a way to unite us." Sophia walked to Hannah. "The man your father testified against wanted revenge. He had our complete family history. Knew you and Derrick had dated in high school, so he had people keep watch on Derrick for years, hoping he might be the one to lead him to our family. Derrick's superior at the FBI discovered a connection between the man you talked to at the gallery and someone who worked at the Bureau who was leaking information. When Derrick left to find you because of the gem I sent, the man was alerted and followed Derrick here."

From the beginning, Derrick had been as puzzled by events as she was. Yet he stuck it out, ready to insert himself in a dangerous situation to make sure Hannah was safe. To make up for the past. And how did she repay him? By turning her back on him.

"So that feeling of being followed wasn't in my head?"

"No." Her mother turned to smile at her dad. "Your father taught you well. When it counted, you knew to listen to your instincts."

Relief washed over her. Derrick had believed her when she'd expressed her concern. He'd been on her side and she'd let him go. Even though he wasn't responsible, knowing Derrick, he was probably blaming himself for bringing danger to her after she'd successfully remained in hiding for years. Her heart softened at the idea of the strong, honorable man kicking himself.

Her mother walked to the counter, picked up an envelope and carried it back to Hannah.

"What's this?" she asked as she took them.

Her mother pointed to the one on top. "Go ahead. Open it."

With shaky fingers, Hannah slit the seam and lifted the flap. She pulled out the paper inside. When she read it, she gasped. "It's a plane ticket to Florida."

"Derrick hoped you'd use it to arrive just in time for his mother's wedding."

The ceremony was in a few days. She read the information again and her heart squeezed tight. "But…?"

Her mother cupped her cheek. "Don't worry about us. You need to see how this ends, Hannah. Not only for your sake, but Derrick's, too."

She voiced her deepest fear. "What if it's too late?"

Her mother nodded to the second piece of paper.

She opened the sheet of paper. Her heart began to race when she spied Derrick's script covering the page.

You have every right to be mad at me. I deserve it. But know this, Hannah, it's always been you. Always will be you. I'd do everything over again to keep you safe. If you can find it in your heart to forgive me, I promise to make you happy each and every day. If not, I hope you have an amazing life because you are an amazing woman.

She read the words with wonder. He still wanted her, even though she'd slammed the door on their relationship.

"He was hoping you'd change your mind," her mother said.

Hannah's breath froze in her chest. His words not only revealed the enduring depth of his love, but made her face the honest truth. She loved Derrick. He was the only man for her. And dear as he was, he was still giving her a way out. She could ignore his request to join him and he'd still love her. Or she could put aside her anger and forgive him. Plan a future of their own.

She looked up at the expectant faces watching her. "But you just got here, Dad. How can I leave?"

"I remember how crazy Derrick was about you. The fact that he still feels the same way is a gift. Don't regret not accepting what he has to offer.

"Besides," her father continued. "Now that we don't have to worry about any unwelcome visitors coming after us, we have plenty of time to reconnect. We'll be here when you get back."

Her mother walked over to her father and hooked her arm through his. "Or maybe we'll see you in Florida after the wedding. When we go home."

Home. Derrick. One and the same. Whether in Nevada, Florida or DC. She pulled her family into a group hug. After a few tears, she leaned back and said, "Thanks. I love you, Mom."

"Back at ya."

Wiping her eyes, Hannah went to her bedroom. She had so much to do: pack, call the school to tell them she was taking time off, fill Lynny in on her plans. She only hoped her silence hadn't gone on too long and Derrick had decided she wasn't worth the trouble.

DERRICK STOOD AT the back of the church, loosening the tight collar of his new dress shirt. Just an hour until the ceremony. It would have been easier to get through today if Hannah had taken him up on his offer and come to Florida for his mother's wedding. Her silence spoke volumes, so he shoved his emotions aside, hoping no one would notice that his heart had split into a million pieces.

"Psst."

Shaking off the depressing direction of his thoughts, he looked to the side of the vestibule. His mother's face was partially obstructed by a door. She waved her hand, beckoning to him.

"Is there a problem?" he asked when he joined his mom in the side room.

"No. Just checking to make sure you're okay."

"Mom, don't worry about me. Today is about you and James."

"Mothers worry about their children," she gently scolded. "No matter what else is happening."

"I'm fine."

She patted his cheek. "And you're a good liar, but I'll let it slide."

Yeah, he was getting good at deflecting. Not that his family believed him when he insisted he was okay, but they didn't call him on it and he appreciated their efforts.

His mother picked up a bouquet of daisies. "I'm truly sorry things didn't work out with Hannah."

No one was sorrier than he was, but he'd done what he'd done and now had to live with the consequences. Hannah was right; he hadn't listened. He'd decided what was best, instead of giving her a chance to weigh in on the decision. Because of that he'd lost her.

"I'm glad we were together as a family last night." His mother turned to him, her eyes misty. "The next time we get together, I'll be a married woman."

The previous night the Matthews clan had met at the beach gazebo to celebrate. It was bittersweet to see his family so happy. He'd been surprised to learn that Eloise and Dante had eloped. Kady and Dylan were moving closer to their wedding date, and Serena and Logan announced their engagement, which meant a fall, mountain wedding. Grace and Deke were still enjoying their relationship, but Derrick expected another engagement soon. And every minute, he was still missing Hannah. He supposed that would never change.

Envy burned a hole in his chest. Everyone was moving on except him. At the bonfire back in January, when he'd told Dylan that he was ready to consider a life without Hannah, he'd never believed he'd see her again. And now, having been with her and discovering the amazing, capable and beautiful woman she'd become, there was no way he'd be able to have a serious relationship with any other woman. When he told Hannah she was the only one for him he'd meant it.

Speaking of family, he was so glad that Hannah's situation had changed for the better. Derrick wished he could have witnessed her reunion with her dad, to see the expression on her face when they met up again.

He also missed the school. Missed Tommy and the other students, the friends he'd made there, even the class guinea pig.

He heard his mother's voice and glanced in her direction.

"You're not listening to me."

He ran a hand over the back of his neck. "Sorry."

She straightened his dress-jacket lapel. Pinned on his boutonniere. "I do wish you'd come back with better news."

But he hadn't and he didn't want her sympathy or sorrow. Hers or anyone else's. He'd gotten himself into this predicament because he couldn't leave well enough alone. His brothers had told him he overstepped, but he thought he knew better. Lesson learned. He would revisit it all during his very lonely future.

"I think I'll go check on the guys. Make sure they're ready to roll."

"Good idea. I'll meet you in the vestibule very soon."

He nodded and made a quick escape.

As he entered the main part of the church, he

stopped dead in his tracks. A stunning woman wearing a pale green dress, her riotous auburn curls piled on the top of her head, stood before him in the center aisle. His heart nearly burst with joy.

"Hannah. You came."

She shrugged. "You told me to meet you at the altar."

He slowly moved to stand in front of her, spotting a gleam in her eyes. "That's not exactly what I said. I asked you to join me at the wedding."

"That's not what I heard."

He hesitated, and at her encouraging smile, as bright as the sun itself, he looped his arms around her waist. With a giggle, she leaned in to kiss him. Their lips met and in the kiss he realized that she had forgiven him. That they had a chance for their own happily-ever-after. She tasted of sunny days and heated nights and children and family and love. Lots and lots of love.

He pulled back, couldn't wait to get their future started. "Now what?"

"Well…" She tapped a finger on her lips. "We had plans to get married seventeen years ago. It's a little late, but we are in a church…"

He couldn't hold back a grin. "My mother is going to love this."

"Not as much as I love you," she said, her

luminous eyes serious. "I'm sorry it took me so long to come around."

"No," he rushed to say. "I deserved it."

"You did." She palmed his cheek with her hand. "I guess after years of looking over my shoulder, it was hard for me to trust you. But you know what? The Derrick I fell in love with in high school and the Derrick who has turned into a caring, determined man both have one thing in common. My best interests."

"That's true. You know I would die to protect you."

"I get that now."

"But I also learned a very important point. I can't solve every problem by myself."

Hannah nodded in agreement, amusement twinkling in her hazel eyes. "That's why I believe you need a certain woman to keep you from making the same mistakes over and over. I'd be honored to be that woman."

"I accept." He tugged her close again. "It looks like we're both willing to work on our... issues."

"Together," she said, wrapping her arms around his neck.

He grinned. "Does that mean we're finally getting married?"

"Not today, because every woman wants her special day with her groom, including your mother. But soon." She kissed him again and again, pulled back and told him with surety ringing in her voice, "We're definitely getting married very soon."

* * * * *

*For more great romances
in this series from
award-winning author Tara Randel,
visit www.Harlequin.com today!*

#319 TO SAVE A CHILD
Texas Rebels • by Linda Warren

When a baby and the beautiful Grace Bennet wind up unexpectedly in Cole Chisholm's life, the by-the-book cop might just have to break his own rules to protect them...and let Grace into his heart.

#320 SECOND CHANCE FOR THE SINGLE DAD
by Carol Ross

Rhys McGrath is no dancer, but he'll learn in time for the father-daughter dance at his niece's cotillion. He's smitten by beautiful dance instructor Camile—and he's dying to know if she feels the same!

#321 RANCHER TO THE RESCUE
by Patricia Forsythe

Zannah Worth hates change. So her new business partner, Brady Gallagher, has a tough time swaying her opinion with his flashy ideas for the family ranch. He makes her feel too much—frustration, anxiety...and something like love?

#322 CAUGHT BY THE SHERIFF
Turtleback Beach • by Rula Sinara

After her sister goes missing, Faye Donovan flees with her niece to Turtleback Beach. But when Sheriff Carlos Ryker offers a shoulder to lean on, Faye faces a choice—keep lying, or trust him with all of their lives...

ReaderService.com has a new look!

We have refreshed our website and
we want to share our new look with you.
Head over to ReaderService.com
and check it out!

On ReaderService.com, you can:

- Try 2 free books from any series
- Access risk-free special offers
- View your account history & manage payments
- Browse the latest Bonus Bucks catalog

RS19